Hit it and Quit it

Kelly Reynolds

Contents

Author's Note

Welcome to Rose City, Oregon! Clarke and Soren's story marks the first installment in the Rose City Roasters series, a small-town baseball romance series about big girls and boys with balls . . . baseballs.

Please be advised that this book is an **open-door** romance, meaning there is **on-page, explicit** sexual content (between consenting adults), including oral sex, vaginal sex, light spanking, choking, and shower play.

There is also recreational use of alcohol, discussions about fatphobia, homophobia, and ableism, generational trauma, pregnancy, and brief mention of the death of a grandparent. Mature readers only.

Happy baseball (pants) season.

Roasters Lineup

#12   Roman Garcia   1B
#16   Wesley Nuñez   CF
#2   Johnathan Tucker   2B
#4   Soren Sinclair   3B
#18   Matty Miller   SS
#9   Peter Diaz   LF
#6   Bennett King   C
#16   Nathaniel Wu   RF
#0   Jared Pink   P

Clarke

Two Months to Opening Day

*W**ho does a girl have to fuck to get some waffles?*

I cringed from behind my Waffle House menu and made a mental note to put a dollar in Mama's swear jar first thing in the morning. Hell's bells, she was going to be madder than a wet hen.

Make that two dollars.

I couldn't help myself. All it took was a few shots of tequila (and then a few more) to bring out the filthy-mouthed, carb-loving bitch—three dollars—inside of me. The one I kept buried beneath layers of Stella McCartney dresses and sensible peach lipstick because any other shade would "send the wrong message," according to my mama.

Mama wasn't here tonight though—thank heavens—and as every one of my sorority sisters knew, when drunk Clarke came to play, the debutante went away. Drunk Clarke wore sequined rompers and glossy red lipstick. Drop Dead Red, to be precise. Drunk Clarke rode on the back of strangers' Vespa scooters through downtown Charleston.

Drunk Clarke ate carbs. Lots of carbs.

Which was exactly what had brought me to Waffle House tonight. At 3 a.m. On the night of my botched bachelorette party.

"Hi, honey."

I lowered my menu to find a woman about my mother's age with a pen and notepad in hand. I didn't know what surprised me more, her cheerful disposition at such a late hour—or early hour, depending on how you looked at it—or her violet bob. *Mama would never.* "Can I start you off with some coffee or hot chocolate?"

"How about an upside-down, quad-shot caramel macchiato?"

She smiled. "Sorry, we're fresh out of those."

"That's alright." I stopped to read her name tag. "Trixie."

Surprisingly, I had never met a Trixie before now. Beatrice, yes. Patricia, yes. I had even shared a room with a French-Canadian girl named Beatrix during my year abroad in Paris, but no Trixie until now. Nicknames weren't a commonality amongst . . . the people I'd grown up with. And that was what they were. People, not friends.

"Do you know what you want?"

"Well, Trixie," I said, setting aside my plastic menu, "that's a funny story. Because for a long time, I *thought* I knew what I wanted. And wouldn't you know it? Tonight, I found out that what I *thought* I wanted—what everybody *told me* I wanted—was, get this, something I never wanted at all. In fact, come to think of it, you might be the first person to ever ask me what I want."

"Man problems?" Trixie asked without missing a beat.

I heaved an exasperated sigh and nodded. "Life problems."

I had every intention of apologizing to Trixie for my outburst . . . and the lone trucker in the corner booth who was clearly calculating how long it would take him to make it to the door in the event that the girl covered in Givenchy and glitter went full-blown psycho.

I would happily apologize and explain and placate—my mother had trained me well in all three—but not before I got something thick and creamy in my stomach.

That didn't sound right . . .

"I'd like some waffles, please."

"I think we can make that happen." Trixie winked. "Any kind in particular?"

"What's *your* favorite?"

"Well, that all depends." She cocked a hip and brushed her purple bangs to the side. When I grew up, I wanted a modicum of Trixie's confidence. "If you're feeling like something sweet, I recommend the caramel pecan."

I felt the corner of my lips kick up. Trixie's drawl was thicker than mine—six years of dialect coaching had tapped most of it out of me. Only in the South did you hear *carra-mel* and *pee-KAN* in the same sentence.

"Then again," she continued. "We have a lovely egg, bacon, and cheese breakfast sandwich served between two waffles."

"Which one comes with hashbrowns?"

"Both of them."

"Both it is." I handed her my menu.

"Alrighty then. I'll go put that in for you, darling."

"Thank you."

I leaned forward, resting my head on the table that was no doubt covered in sticky syrup and who knew what else. The thought barely phased me. Not when my brain was busy replaying the events of this evening in 4k resolution and surround sound.

This was not how tonight was supposed to go.

This was not how my *life* was supposed to go.

The bell above the front door chimed, and I looked up, naively hoping that someone—anyone—had come after me. Erica, maybe? My sorority sister and former roommate. I'd held her hair back on several occasions over the years and was the maid of honor at her wedding, so I didn't think I was asking for the impossible. Or maybe Jesse, whom I'd met during the Junior Miss pageantry circuit over a decade ago. We'd lost touch, but that didn't stop her from calling to ask for a personal loan last year after her divorce.

That's what friends are for, right?

Much to my unsurprise, it was not one of my bridesmaids entering the Waffle House, but instead, a grizzled man in tattered clothing that looked like they hadn't seen a wash in weeks.

"Hiya, Jeff. Coffee?" Trixie called over her shoulder, coffee pot already in hand.

"Thanks, Trix."

The man set his oversized backpack down beside the counter and began fishing through his pockets for change.

Geez, Louise. Here I was, inner monologuing about my failed engagement and lack of friends in a four-hundred-dollar outfit, and meanwhile Jeff was literally counting coins to pay for his coffee.

What an asshole.

Me, not Jeff. I was the asshole.

I swiped a wayward curl away from my eyes. It was hard to tell what had deflated more, my hair or my ego. Reality was a bitter pill to swallow, and as any of my ex-boyfriends would unabashedly share—all two of them—I had never been much good at swallowing.

The harsh reality was this: never in my twenty-seven years had I struggled.

Not really, at least. Not in the ways that most people struggled.

From my prestigious, private school education to summers spent abroad and extracurriculars, like sailing and show jumping, it was safe to say that my upbringing wasn't that of the typical American teenager. However, I was ashamed to say that it took far too long for me to one, realize that, and two, recognize how uncomfortable that made me feel. To know that some girls were selling door-to-door magazines to fund their scholarship dreams, while I read magazines by our backyard pool was enlightening, to say the least. Call it naivete or ignorance, but that was all I'd known.

The purse, however, came with strings. And unfortunately, those strings had been used to puppet me for years.

Even now, as a fully grown, twenty-seven-year-old woman, I was living in a townhome south of Broad Street my parents had bought for me and Walden. I was driving a gas-guzzling Range Rover they had given me, regardless of the fact that I wasn't comfortable driving an SUV. I was marrying a man they might as well have picked out of a catalog called *Sons of Charleston's Most Affluent Families Monthly.*

And I had let it all happen. I had let them dictate my life.

Well, not anymore.

My phone vibrated across the table, sending a wave of shivers down my spine. Walden had called nearly thirty times in the span of an hour before I'd blocked and deleted his number. But that didn't mean anything. He could have just as easily borrowed a phone to use. Maybe from the woman he'd been fucking in *our* bed. Then again, better him than my parents. To say I was dreading that call would be an understatement.

I flipped my cell over, heaving a sigh of relief when I saw my sister's name instead.

"Clarke, where are you?" Viv shouted through the phone before I could even get out a greeting.

"Oh, you know." I paused just as Trixie set down the tray of dishes on my table. The sugary sweet aroma had my toes curling better than any orgasm I'd had—or pretended to have—with Walden during our five-year relationship. "Eating waffles."

"Are you kidding me? Waffles?"

"And hashbrowns," I said around a mouthful of carb-loaded goodness. "Mm, so good."

"I just got off the phone with Mama."

"She's up late."

"Oh, please. You're too smart to play dumb," she chastised. I could almost hear her eyes roll back in her skull, all the way in Asheville. "First you disappear from your bachelorette party."

"Which you didn't come to, by the way." I shoveled another forkful of potatoes into my mouth.

"You *know* I couldn't."

Egging my big sister on was too easy even when she wasn't six-and-a-half months pregnant. When you added in the extra hormones, though . . .

"Then you break off your engagement with *Where's Waldo—*"

"Walden. And how do you know that?"

"He called Daddy, who told Mama, who—"

"Called you," I finished for her. I should've known he'd go sniveling to my parents to tattle on me. Just another perfect example of his priorities. "Good news sure travels fast. Look, V, I'll talk to them tomorrow. Just as soon as I figure out what I'm going to say."

"Forget them. Talk to me." Her voice evened. "Are you okay?"

I answered her honestly. "Physically? Yes. I'm not sure about the rest just yet."

"Are you somewhere safe? Do you need me to come pick you up?"

"V, stop." My fork clattered onto the plate. "It's the middle of the night, not to mention a four-hour drive back to Charleston. I'm not the first idiot whose fiancé cheated on her, okay? I'll be fine. Besides, I thought you were on bed rest."

"Don't remind me," she grumbled. "I'll lie in the back seat and make Ellie drive."

Viv and her wife, Ellie, were what one might call wilderness women. On their first date, they went axe throwing. On their second, they took a week-long camping trip in the Catskills. By the time they reached their fourth anniversary together, they'd visited every national park in America. There wasn't a doubt in my mind that her mandated bed rest was driving her nuttier than this pecan waffle.

"Save yourselves the trip. I don't plan on staying long anyway."

"What do you mean?"

"I need to get out of here," I told her. "I need . . . a change."

If there was anybody who would understand, it would be Viv. It was no secret that she and our folks didn't exactly get on. Sure, they made pleasantries during Christmas—for the sake of appearances—and Mama was over the moon at the prospect of having her first grandbaby—though I doubted she ever predicted that her tattooed, lesbian daughter would be the first to marry and procreate—but the buck stopped there.

Unlike me, Viv had cut ties with Charleston—and the purse strings that came with it—at eighteen and never looked back. I'd always envied her for her strength. Quietly, of course, but still.

"That's not going to be easy," she said.

"I know."

"You're going to need some money. And not *their* money."

"I know." I suddenly lost my appetite. "I've got some saved from my internship. Not a lot, but enough to get out of here."

I had been interning with South Carolina Symphony's social media team for nearly a year, but the money I made barely covered my daily commute. I didn't have any savings. I had never needed to save. Not as Dr. Walden Winters's bride-to-be and certainly not as Pat Myers's daughter. I had always been taken care of. So much so that without knowing it, my name and identity had been completely erased.

It was a startling thought. To realize that as a woman living in the twenty-first century, much of my worth was still determined by my proximity to men. Well, fuck that.

I'll mail Mama the swear jar funds tomorrow.

On second thought, no. I'd need every penny for my fresh start.

"Where are you going to go?" Viv asked. That was the real question. One that I didn't have an answer for just yet. "You know you're more than welcome to come stay with us."

I smiled. "I think this is something I need to do on my own . . . for once. But I appreciate the offer."

We said our goodbyes, and I assured her I'd call her first thing in the morning. Hopefully by then, I'd have some sort of plan. Hell, I'd settle for a vague idea. How was it that somebody who knew so many people could have so few friends to turn to?

I'd told Viv that I needed a change, but really, *I* needed to change. It was time the world met Clarke. Not some man's daughter or some other man's wife. Just Clarke, whoever that was.

It was about time I figured that out. A fresh to-do list would be a good place to start. Maybe Trixie could lend me a pen and paper.

Mind made up, I scooched out of the booth, twisting my mouth when my shapely thighs clung to the vinyl seat. Just one more reason to get out of Charleston—humidity. When I finally detached myself and righted my romper, I approached the counter.

"Excuse me, Trixie."

"Yes, darling?"

"Could I bother you for some pen and paper?"

"Sure thing, honey."

While she rifled through her apron pockets, I turned to the man seated at the counter. "Jeff, is it?" I asked softly, so as not to startle him. He turned toward me, coffee cup still clutched in his hands.

"Yes, miss."

"My name's Clarke." I extended my hand. He eyed it wearily before taking it in his. "Would you mind joining me for breakfast? My treat."

Soren

Six Weeks to Opening Day

"We need to talk."

There was a phrase nobody ever liked to hear. I wished I could say that this was the first time I'd been on the receiving end of those four simple but deadly words.

Like a 102-mph fast ball straight to the gut.

There wasn't a sentence today that packed nearly as much of a punch. Then again, what did I know? I'd flunked eleventh grade English. Twice. The fact was, I only knew of one other phrase likely to make a grown man cower in fear. And that one did it in three words.

"Ooo, Sin's in trouble."

I gritted my teeth and turned toward Jared Pink—first-round draft pick and world-class loudmouth. One of these days, Pink's mouth was going to get him in trouble. And just my luck, he'd been assigned the locker next to mine.

I wordlessly gathered the last of my equipment together before heading toward our coach's office, where the door was already open for me.

"Have a seat, Sinclair." The imposing figure from behind the desk gestured to the empty chair across from him.

Brooks Bailey-Ward. The Third.

That was three generations of baseball royalty.

Ward was a two-time World Series winning catcher. His father, the second Brooks Bailey-Ward, was awarded a Golden

Glove during his tenure with the Cubs. And his grandfather, the original BBW, had played alongside the two Willies—Mays and McCovey—in San Francisco.

There wasn't a baseball fan alive who didn't know the name Bailey-Ward.

I let the strap of my equipment bag slide off my shoulder before (gently) letting it fall to the floor. The last thing I needed was a fine for scuffing the boss man's reclaimed-faux-whatever-the-fuck flooring. I took a seat, coughing to cover up the audible creak of my bad knee.

Damn, I need to get back into yoga.

I did my best not to recoil when my arm settled against the cool leather, sending a wave of shivers up my spine. There was nothing faux or reclaimed about this chair. Trust the guy who handled baseballs for a living to know real leather when he saw—er, felt it.

"I love what you've done with the place," I told him. Truthfully, there was no way for me to know what the coach's office had looked like before Brooks Bailey-Ward III made his mark on it. This was only our second time meeting in person. I'd gotten off the bus to Oregon two weeks ago, and I'd spent most of the time since then holed up in a buddy's loft in SE Portland, dodging the paparazzi as best I could while gorging myself on ramen noodles.

"The floor's refinished wood from Wrigley Field."

"Of course it is," I mumbled under my breath.

"Let's cut to the chase, Sinclair." He leaned forward and threaded his fingers together. The inch or so of ink creeping beyond his Rose City Roasters hoodie surprised me; his steel, stoic demeanor did not. "You're one hell of a player."

"Um, thank you?" I stuttered. Every previous coach and teammate would say I wasn't typically one without words. But considering the way I'd been unceremoniously pulled out of the locker room, I'd been mentally preparing for one hell of an ass-handing. And not the good kind.

"Seriously, it's a wonder you were available, let alone for the price we got you for. Thirty-one home runs last season, seventy RBIs. Not to mention your .360 career batting average." My knee—the good one—twitched as he rattled off my stats. "And you're what, thirty-three?"

"Thirty-four." I smirked. "Getting up there." I had to joke. It was either that or cry if I thought too long about the fact that most of my new teammates were still in diapers during Y2K.

"You've still got time."

What the fuck is going on here?

There was no way the head coach of the Rose City Roasters, the latest edition to Major League Baseball's American League West, had taken time out of his busy day just to sing my praises.

"And yet . . ."

There it is.

". . . nine teams in twelve years. And only two games in the big league." His eyes darkened before shifting to my knee, the one that was bouncing full-on, as if controlled by an evil entity. "Care to explain?"

"I have a hard time sitting still."

The pinch of his lips told me he was neither convinced nor amused. "Not your leg, Sinclair. Your record."

I shrugged. What was there to explain? My stats spoke for themselves. I was a fan-fucking-tastic player. Plus, judging by his demeanor, he already had the answer. Ward didn't strike me as someone who entered a fight unless he already knew he'd win.

He dropped a folder on his desk before turning it around to face me. Scrawled across the top in thick black ink was my name. The name I loathed but pretended to love. *Sin.*

And just like that, I was seventeen again. Back in Principal Kim's office, my mother on one side of me, my grandmother on the other, both seething over whatever nuisance I'd caused that week. For two years, I'd gotten to know that office well. I'd counted every ceiling tile in Principal Kim's office (thirty-two), cataloged the knickknacks that decorated the room (from the handmade paperweight crafted by her goddaughter to the collection of miniature chairs—*what the fuck?*—adorning the bookcase), and learned every office aide's name, astrological sign, and cup size (Lara Schmidt, the Gemini with 38 Ds, took my virginity after Junior Prom).

Much like my high school permanent record, the folder on Ward's desk was thick. And though I often turned to my two older sisters when it came to dating advice—because who else did a guy raised by all women turn to?—I didn't need them to tell me that bigger was not always better.

"Let's start with these," Ward said as he flipped open the folder, exposing the good, bad, and ugliest moments from my past. As I'd said already, I was a fan-fucking-tastic player.

On *and* off the field.

At least, that was what they'd written about me.

I thumbed through the contents of Ward's folder of pictures, articles, and a few not-so-flattering dick pics from my early twenties. I'd upped my dick pic game in the last few years after a few helpful tips from teammates, and yes, my sisters, but naturally, *those* were not the photos circulating the internet. This was what I had to show for my decade-long career. As it turned out, the only stat anybody cared about was my cock size.

"This," he said, drawing my attention to a newspaper clipping dated two days ago, "is not a good look for the team. And I'd bet my left nut it's *one* of the reasons why you're still playing at AAA level."

"What about the right nut?"

"The left one's bigger," he said without missing a beat. Call me crazy, but in another time and place, one where Ward didn't control my livelihood, we could've been friends.

I looked at the paper in his hands, wincing when I noticed last week's headline.

POP PRINCESS TAINTED BY "SIN."

What an original play on words.

I'd thought things with Monica might be different. Boy, had I been wrong. Again. The ill timing of our breakup couldn't have been worse.

"Don't believe everything you read," I told him. He tossed the paper back onto his desk.

"Look," Ward said, scrubbing a hand across his well-trimmed beard. "I don't care what you do in your personal life. I don't care if you've got a different partner on standby in every state. The point is, I don't want to hear about it. And I sure as shit don't want to read about it. It doesn't look good for the franchise. Especially in our very first year."

"I don't know what you want me to do about it." I was being honest. I'd had thousands of interactions with the press over the years, been coached by media specialists, and even rehearsed lines with my agent (and the agent before that.)

"You can start by keeping your dick in your pants and off of page six."

Way to sugarcoat it.

Not that I could eat sugar anyway, but still.

Ward cleared his throat before adding, "I think your best bet is to focus on nothing else right now. Put all that energy toward your game."

Easier said than done. In Milwaukee, it had been a knee injury—my first one—that took me out mid-season. In Detroit, it had been a bar fight with some disgruntled fans. My teammate in Tampa had had it out for me from the moment he'd found out about a previous fling with his wife. And Atlanta . . . Atlanta was a can of worms I wasn't ready to unpack just yet.

My string of bad luck had followed me clean across the country and back again for over a decade.

I knew this was it. Rose City was my last shot.

I shifted uncomfortably in my seat as Ward studied me. What was it about my presence that had him so deep in thought? You know, aside from my 6'4" bulky frame hunched over a chair more expensive than my grandmother's farmhouse. Or the five o'clock shadow and darkened circles under my eyes to match. The latter was a souvenir from my recent breakup with Monica.

"Look, Mr. Ward." My voice faltered. I swallowed and tried again. "Sir. I'll do whatever you need me to, say whatever you need me to. Please give me a chance—"

"Relax, Sinclair." He folded his hands together in front of him, perfectly at ease, a stark contrast to the panic coursing through my veins. "Something you should know about me is that I don't give up easily. And despite your checkered past, I can tell you don't either."

The breath I'd been holding whooshed out of me.

His lips tilted to one side, perhaps the closest thing to a smile for Brooks Bailey-Ward III. "You've been staying in Portland?"

"Yes, sir."

Rose City was about a forty-minute drive north of Portland, perched alongside the Columbia River, just beyond the Lewis and Clark Bridge. From what I knew, most of the guys were commuting. After all, there was a whole lot more to do in Portland than in Rose City.

"Have you found a place in town yet?"

I rubbed a hand over the back of my neck. "Haven't really been looking."

Understanding dawned on him. With my record, the chances of sticking around one place were slim. I'd figured renting in Portland would be the safest bet, rather than looking for a more long-term option.

"Why don't you stick around Rose City? I know a place on the edge of town."

"What about the—"

"Trust me, the press won't be looking for you there," he said, answering my question before I'd asked.

"I'll need my stuff."

He nodded. "I'll have my assistant take care of the arrangements and have a driver pick you up in the morning."

Good enough for me. My mom had raised me not to run away from my problems, but she also taught me never to let my pride or ego get in the way. Something had to give, and by the sound of it, Brooks Bailey-Ward III was willing to give it to me. At the very least, I needed to get some goddamn sleep without worrying about paparazzi masquerading as UberEats delivery drivers. It had happened twice this week alone.

He stood from his chair—throne, more like—and rounded his desk. I took the hint when he held his hand out toward the door.

"While you're at it," he said gruffly, stopping me when I was halfway out the door, "take a few days off from training. Let the dust—and the media vultures—settle before you come back on Monday for team pictures."

I blinked. That was four days from now. "But couldn't I—"

His grim expression was all the answer I needed.

"Okay."

"I've set up a meeting for you with the social media team next week. They might have some ideas for rehashing your image."

"Fine," I managed through my teeth. Because fuck social media. "Anything else?"

"Would Smell as Sweet."

That had me scratching my brain. Was he talking in code?

"Huh?"

"The bakery in town," he explained. "Would Smell as Sweet. You should check them out. I recommend the empanadas."

I nodded. Because how else was I supposed to respond to a restaurant recommendation from my boss?

"You can go."

My streak of bad luck continued when I exited his office, only to bump into Pink once again. This time by the vending machines.

"How'd it go?" He wagged his eyebrows. "You in trouble, Sin?"

"Don't call me that."

I narrowed my eyes and gave him a look. One that I hoped said he ought to shut up if he knew what was best for him.

"Say please," he taunted while grinning like an idiot.

"Pink."

Ward's voice echoed through the locker room, commanding attention from my straggling teammates. His physical presence was even more intimidating. Anybody who thought his signature black-frame glasses might soften his features had clearly never come face-to-face with Brooks Bailey-Ward III.

Everything stopped as he crossed the locker room, conversation and stretching of any kind momentarily forgotten. Even our shortstop, Owen Miller, who was halfway through pulling up his boxer briefs, froze. Dick on display for public perusal.

None of us cared about Miller's dick, though. No, we were here for the ass-handing of one Jared Pink. Though, judging by the paling of his face, he might have to change his name to Jared White.

Ward approached Pink until they were toe to toe. Pink might have had a few inches on our GM, but Ward had at least fifty or so pounds on the rookie pitcher. Not to mention a lifetime of experience and accolades.

"Don't call him that," he growled.

"S-sorry?" Pink stuttered. I couldn't blame the kid for his surprise. Ward's defense shocked the hell out of me, too.

"I said, don't call him that." Ward's eyes shifted to mine, just for a second. Long enough to let me know that for the first time in a long time, I had somebody in my corner. Somebody rooting for me. When he turned his attention back to Pink, he added, "Please."

It wasn't a request.

Clarke

*I*t's cold enough to freeze the udders on Paw Paw's prized heifer.

Today marked my third day in Rose City, Oregon, and it was a far cry from Charleston. More like a holler, really.

"Quit your bellyaching, Clarke," I whispered into the cup of coffee in my hands. Maybe if I closed my eyes and counted to ten, it would magically turn into a macchiato. I hadn't had a shot of espresso in days. To say I was struggling to lift my feet would be a bit of an understatement. I'd never felt the effects of gravity so strongly until now.

Steam rolled off the top of the mug, a black-and-blue ceramic piece decorated with hand-painted trees and the phrase *Oregon makes me wet* in delicate handwriting.

You got that right. I only wish it weren't so literal.

It had been raining for two weeks straight, from the moment I'd left Charleston. It had rained during my drive through Louisiana. It had rained during the entire trip across Texas—do you know how big that state is? And it had rained every day since I'd crossed the Colorado River.

Buying a brand-new, water-resistant wardrobe was at the top of my to do list. As soon as I got my first paycheck.

What little money I had saved had gone quickly during my trip out west. At least I had gotten a good deal on a used Honda HR-V when I traded in the Range Rover.

"Morning, Clarke." I turned toward the melodic voice, immediately regretting my move when a series of raindrops pelted my face.

"Sugar!" I shouted, scolding myself more than the rain. I stepped back under the protective layer of wood shading the porch and only then did I wave to June. "Morning, June."

The statuesque blonde waved back from two porches over, a bucket of cleaning supplies in her hands. "Are you finding everything okay?" Her imposing height and square shoulders reminded me of Brienne of Tarth, the tall drink of water from *Game of Thrones,* aka my sister's, Viv's, "hall pass." If Brienne of Tarth wore crop tops and pierced her belly button, that was.

"Just fine," I told her. It was hard to imagine not being able to find something in such a small dwelling. June owned Bed of Roses, Rose City's very own vintage trailer resort and the place I currently called home.

Home.

Maybe another sip of coffee would wash down the bitter memory. I suppressed a sigh and put on my twenty-watt, pageant queen smile.

"Have you met your new neighbor yet?" June asked.

"Not yet."

"Just wait 'til you see him," she said around a smirk.

My eyes shifted to the hand-lettered sign hanging above her head. *The Golden Girl.* The six trailers were named after famous women and characters named Rose. Rose Nylund from *The Golden Girls,* Rose Tyler from *Dr. Who,* and silver screen icon, Rosemary Clooney. I'd already met the newlyweds staying in *Rose McGowan*—their new year's resolution was to get married in every state—and the PhD student staying in *The Riveter.* Ironically, she was working on media portrayals of women in the workforce during World War II. That just left me in *Rose DeWitt Bukater.* My life up until now had been somewhat of a sinking ship, so it was more than appropriate that I'd ended up in the Tiffany-blue tin dwelling named after *The Titanic* heroine.

And of course, the mystery man in *Moira Rose.*

I had a newfound appreciation for *Schitt's Creek.*

"Hey, listen," June started. "Why don't you join me and a few of my friends for drinks sometime?" She smoothed her thick-rimmed glasses back into place. Personally, I thought a round, wire frame might suit her face better, but I'd never tell her that.

Mama always told me that a "good wife" only gave her opinion when asked.

Sweet Pete, I really needed to call that therapist that Viv recommended. The two-thousand miles of distance and fresh Pacific Northwest air just weren't cutting it.

"Or maybe dinner would be better?"

June had mistaken my silence for indifference.

"Oh, I'm so sorry!" I waved my hand toward my coffee cup and pajamas. "I'm not myself before at least two cups of coffee. But please don't feel like you need to entertain me. I start my new job tomorrow."

"Let me guess." She set down the bucket of supplies, only to lean forward and rest her elbows on the makeshift porch railing. "The Roasters."

"How'd you know?"

"Oh, I don't know. The recent influx of hot, new residents to Rose City kind of gave it away." She winked before adding, "You won't hear me complaining, though."

"Want to know a secret?" I asked, bolder than usual. Confidence was a key ingredient in my recipe to reinvent myself.

"Always."

"This is my first job. Like, first *job* job."

Her eyes widened, not with disapproval but rather with interest. "Wow. Congratulations."

"I'm a little nervous, but also very excited."

I blamed the whirring buzz in my belly for my lack of sleep the last three nights, not the twin-sized bed my trailer offered.

She nodded. "I'm sure you'll do great. How about my friend, Nessa, and I treat you to happy hour tomorrow? Sort of a 'congrats on making it through your first day' kinda thing."

My first day.

It was hard to believe that just two weeks ago, I'd been crying into a plate of hashbrowns. What had started as my bachelorette party had ended with me updating my resume on my new friend Trixie's phone, and applying for a social media coordinator position in a town I'd never heard of, in a state I'd never been to. I hadn't expected to hear back from them at all. I certainly couldn't have predicted them hiring me on the spot during my first ever job interview.

So, yes, I did want to have lunch with June and her friends. My contract with the Roasters lasted until October, so it'd be nice to meet some new people. Maybe even make some new friends.

Who am I kidding? It would be nice to make any.

"That sounds great," I told her.

"I'll meet you here and we can walk over together."

After we said our goodbyes, I changed into my practically indecent bathrobe and grabbed my shower caddy. Not since my sorority days had I used a communal shower, and even then, it'd been with eighteen- and nineteen-year-old girls. And yet, here I was, a twenty-seven-year-old woman, dressed in nothing but a hot-pink bathrobe covered in adorable piglets, preparing to take my first public shower. Outdoors. In February. But what other choice did I have?

Rose City had no hotels. No motels, no hostels, not even an Airbnb. No, the only option for nearly forty miles was Bed of Roses, and since I'd be working in Rose City, it only made sense to stay here. Which meant it was time to pull up my (metaphorical) big-girl pants, pull down my robe before . . . bits started to show, and take on the outdoor, all-gender shower.

I could do this.

Thankfully, the chances of running into anybody were nil. It was still fairly early, especially for a Sunday, and I had yet to see any of my neighbors emerge from their houses before ten a.m. June would be busy cleaning for new visitors, so that only left the elusive Mr. Moira.

Probably still sleeping.

I nudged the door open, enough to peek outside but not enough to let in the brisk air. I was a Southern girl. By nature, we did not do well in colder climates. After checking to see if the coast was clear, I slipped out the door and made a mad dash for the showers. Thankfully, I didn't have far to go. That didn't stop me from muttering a long line of curses as I trudged through the cold, down the grassy hill and across the gravel path. It didn't help that the last time I'd worn this robe was in college, when I'd been a size or two (or four) smaller. Certain areas had filled out (and then some) since then.

"You could stand to lose a little weight, darling."

But despite what certain people—my mother, my ex-fiancé, *People* magazine—had said, I loved my curves. What I did not love were the icicles trying to take up residence in my nether regions.

I threw open the door to the first shower stall, practically knocking the dang thing off its hinges, and made a beeline for the hot water nozzle. "Please, please, please . . . ," I begged, cranking the shaft as far left as it would go. Modesty be damned, I removed my robe and tossed it over the wall dividing the stalls. I was committed now. It was either a shower or hypothermia.

Warm water trickled out of the nozzle. A few seconds later, a geyser erupted from the holes above, drenching my hair and scalding my naked body in the best way possible. So much so I did what anybody who hadn't had a shower in three days (er, maybe four) would do.

I moaned.

"Oh, *gawd*," I cried, closing my eyes and letting the water rush over my face. "*Sooo* good."

"I can come back later, if you want?" a deep, gravelly voice asked from the shadows.

I screamed and then immediately regretted my reaction as soon as my mouth filled up with water.

Death by communal shower. What a way to go.

Soren

*G*reat job, fuckhead. *You drowned the woman.*

The incredibly sexy, incredibly naked woman.

So much for lying low and avoiding trouble.

I turned my attention to a nonexistent plane in the sky. Maybe if I stared long and hard enough—*shit, don't say "hard"*—I'd lose sight of the rosy-colored nipples burned across my retinas.

"Are you alright?" I called out across the barrier between us. Her chaotic sputtering drowned out the sound of the still-running shower.

"Are you crazy?" she choked. "You can't just sneak up on a woman while she's showering."

"I wasn't exactly sneaking. It's communal." I kept my gaze averted. From my peripheral vision, I could tell she was rustling with some kind of fabric, a towel or robe maybe. "Besides, I didn't realize you were having a . . . private moment."

"Now wait just a minute." She huffed, her voice full of irritation. I tried to suppress a grin.

I waited until the shower faucet squeaked to a halt before turning toward her. I looked down and came face-to-face—well, more like head to chin—with the most stunning woman I had ever laid eyes on. Even half-showered, blonde hair askew, and nipples now (sadly) tucked away behind a ridiculous robe decked out in cartoon pigs, this woman was a sight to behold.

Judging by her furrowed brow, it was safe to say the feeling wasn't mutual.

"I was not—" She stopped. "That is, I was just excited."

My eyebrows rose.

"Not like that. You . . . You . . ." She trailed off when I removed my shirt and tossed it to the bench just outside of the shower stall. Probably a dick move considering the fact that she was clearly uncomfortable. Sometimes I forgot that not everybody was fortunate enough to shower next to forty sweat-drenched, hairy-assed guys six days a week. In this case, I couldn't be bothered to care. Not when her chocolate-brown eyes were licking over every line, dip, and curve of my sculpted torso. I was suddenly thankful I'd taken the extra time to do my upper-body workout this morning after my run.

"Do you want me to remove the towel, too?"

She sobered. "Excuse me?" Today's eye-fucking session had officially come to a close.

"You know, so you can get the full picture." I smirked when her cheeks reddened.

"Ah, Moira, I presume?" she asked.

It took me a minute to realize what she was talking about. The first thing I'd done after checking into Bed of Roses was connect to the Wi-Fi. If there was another shitty tabloid write-up about Monica and me, I wanted to know about it. The second thing I did was text my sister, the biggest fan of *Schitt's Creek*, a photo of my trailer.

As someone who had spent the better part of their adult life living out of hotels, I'd seen my fair share of themed kitsch. Famous Roses were a lot easier to swallow than pirates or Disney characters. Then again, my bias against Disney was less about Mickey Mouse and more about the "Disney adult" I'd dated once. She'd replaced my entire wardrobe with pastels while I was out of town one weekend and used *my* credit card to buy us both season passes to Disneyland. I'd been living in Dallas at the time. Never again.

"The name's Soren."

I waited for some flicker of recognition, but it never came, and there was something refreshing about that. Then again, ninety-nine percent of the world knew me as Sin. Something told me the buxom blonde across from me knew nothing of sin. But I'd be happy to rectify that.

"Well, *Soren*," she grumbled. Damn, I liked the way she said my name—my real, legal name—with her subtle, Southern twang. "Would you mind?" She motioned toward the row of trailers behind her. I was too busy eyeing the bead of water dripping down her neck, traveling into the opening of her robe.

"Not at all," I said around a smile, the first one I'd had in days. I stepped farther into the shower stall and turned on the water. "Don't leave on my account."

And with that, I removed the towel from around my waist.

The wall between us was tall enough (and she was short enough) that she'd need to lean over the top to get a glimpse of "the goods," but she knew I was naked. And like the Grinch, that made my smile (and my now semihard cock) grow three-sizes bigger.

Exhibitionism had never been my thing before. The general public already knew too much about my private life as it was. But fucking with blondie here was just too fun.

I lathered my body with soap, daring her to call my bluff. Instead, she gathered her shower supplies, slamming them back into her plastic carrying caddy one by one. Why any person would need that many products to take a shower was beyond me, but nonetheless, I was enjoying the show. The last to go was the mug she'd set on the edge of the shower. I squinted to read the text on the side, which said . . .

Damn.

"Nice mug."

That had to belong to the resort. There was no way this girl had a sense of humor, let alone a penchant for dirty puns. No, if her trailer was anything like mine, it came fully equipped with a tiny kitchen, chock full of appropriately sized appliances, cutlery, and dishes (with inappropriate sayings).

She stormed out of the stall, stomping her sandal-clad feet across the gravel, and back up toward her trailer. The higher she got up the hill, the better view I had of the milky, lush cheeks peeking out from beneath her robe. Just as she reached the main path, I called out to her.

"See you next time, blondie." She stiffened and then, in a move rivaling only *The Exorcist*'s Linda Blair, slowly pivoted her head until she was glaring at me. And only then, when I knew she was watching, did I snake my hand down to grip my cock. I couldn't help the groan that escaped if I tried.

Her eyes widened. Her cheeks flushed until they were practically the color of the fire burning through my groin. And then, as if conjured by own sex-starved imagination, she was gone.

The slam of the door leading to the trailer marked *Rose De-Witt Bukater*—which, just my luck, was the one right next door to mine—was the only indication she'd been there in the first place.

You can run, blondie, but you can't hide.

My mother would have my ass if she knew what I'd done. That was nothing compared to what Ward would do to me if he even knew I was entertaining the idea of another woman right now. But none of that was enough to sour my mood. Or my erection.

I'd never rubbed one out in a public shower before. Showering with your teammates was one thing; jerking off in front of them was frowned upon. Then again, there was nobody around. Nobody but me and the stacked blonde. And maybe, just maybe she'd be watching.

I dragged my fist down my shaft, giving it a rough squeeze when I reached the base.

I hope you enjoy the show, blondie.

Clarke

Starting a new job was nerve-racking enough. Starting a new job after a sleepless night of pornographic dreams about your infuriatingly handsome neighbor, and what he was hiding underneath his terrycloth towel, was something else entirely. So much for waking up bright-eyed and bushy-tailed for my first day.

More like sleepy and sex starved.

Nobody was going to stand in my way of making a good first impression today, last of all my new neighbor. With chiseled abs. All eight of them.

Sugar.

I shrugged off my fatigue—and horniness—and reached for my compact mirror. It had taken an extra layer of concealer to cover up the dark circles under my eyes this morning, and by the looks of it, the makeup was holding up well. My nerves on the other hand . . .

Thankfully, today was supposed to be all onboard paperwork and orientation, plus a tour of the Roasters' facility. All one million square feet of it. Even though I'd barely made it out of the parking lot, I was already feeling miles out of my league—baseball pun intended.

I tilted my head back, staring up at the titanium structure in front of me. Panel after panel of glass was stacked on top of each other, like an endless pile of Legos. It was overwhelming.

"I can do this," I whispered to myself before glancing self-consciously to the side. The last thing I needed was for one of my new co-workers to spot me talking to myself.

My stomach roiled. I should never have had that second cup of coffee this morning.

Why did I wear this shirt?

Was my Drop Dead Red lipstick too much for the office?

The doubts ran rampant through my brain, repeating themselves like a record stuck on repeat. I matched my steps to their beat as I approached the door.

I don't belong here. This is a mistake. I—

"Clarke!" a bubbly voice called out from behind me.

I turned to find a petite, sprite-like woman waving me down from the parking lot. I recognized Dani immediately, though this was my first time seeing her in person. It would be hard to forget that ear-to-ear smile, not to mention the electric blue, pixie haircut and neck tattoos.

And to think I was worried about my lipstick.

As the Roasters' social media director, Dani was single-handedly responsible for interviewing, and ultimately, hiring me for my coordinator position. From what I'd gleaned during my interview with her, Dani was somewhat of a genius. Not only did she have two master's degrees—one in sports psychology and another in multimedia journalism—she had also played an instrumental role in creating the team's initiative for mental health. Every Roasters' employee—from the top-tier management down to the part-time custodial staff—was required to take one mental health day per month, specifically to better their personal well-being. It was a model that several other teams in the league had decided to employ as well.

"Great to meet you in person, Dani." I extended my hand to her. "I mean, Ms. Bernal. Or do you prefer—"

"Dani is fine," she said. "And I'm more of a hugger, if that's okay with you?"

"Um, I suppose—"

Before I could finish my sentence, she'd already hauled me into an all-consuming hug. For such a small person—she had to be at least two or three inches shorter than my 5'6"—she sure packed a punch. Her tight squeeze tempered all my insecurities better than any prescription or pint of praline crunch ice cream.

"Alright," she said, pulling away. "Now that that's out of the way, let's get started. Paperwork, coffee, tour. In that order."

From teddy bear to top dog, just like that. She walked while she talked, and I did my best to meet her pace. Dani reminded me of my sister-in-law, Ellie. The type of person who was always in motion, always busy thinking about the next step, literally and metaphorically. An *in-betweener,* as my sister called it.

Together, we walked the three floors of offices and facilities before taking a lap around the stadium's concourse level. When Dani had mentioned a tour, I hadn't expected a full-on hike. Truthfully, I was a little embarrassed by how winded I was. It'd been a while since I'd hoofed it for more than a block or two, especially in my favorite wedge heels. I'd pick a more sensible pair of tennis shoes tomorrow.

What impressed me most was the way the designer had seamlessly incorporated the natural wonders of the Pacific Northwest in with the modern architecture. Solar panels lined the west side of the building, a one-hundred-foot waterfall cascaded behind the centerfield bleachers, and about eight thousand square feet of the roof over the press box had been converted to an organically maintained rooftop farm. The plan was to grow herbs and seasonal vegetables to be used in dishes served at the stadium during games and at private events throughout the year.

My favorite feature, though, was the beanery. That was right. The Rose City Roasters had their own coffee roasters on site, just fair of the left field foul pole. Which meant visitors could take home a fresh bag of Rose City Roast on game day, and more importantly, I had access to a lifetime supply of upside-down, quad-shot caramel macchiatos. A glass-enclosed atrium full of

Oregon flora and fauna, and Ponderosa pines tall enough to breach the ceiling ran through the center of the beanery. According to Dani, the building had literally been built around the trees, to preserve as much of the wildlife as possible.

And *I* got to work there.

"I'll never get sick of that smell," Dani said. She took another sip of her chai latte with oat milk. Oat milk was apparently very big in Oregon.

"I know what you mean."

"We should get some content with the guys ordering coffee. Like, videos of their favorite coffee orders."

A lightbulb went off in my head. "What about—"

I bit my lip. Maybe it wasn't my place to make any suggestions. Dani was the social media director, my superior. I didn't want to step on any toes.

"What? Say it." She waved her hands excitedly.

I swallowed my nerves whole, then washed them down with the dregs of my coffee. "Well, what if the players took turns acting as baristas. Not during the games of course, but for special occasions, maybe even birthday parties, corporate events. Sort of a new take on meet and greets."

A slow smile spread across her face. "I love it."

"Really?"

"Fans will love it, too. Great idea!" She nudged my shoulder with hers. "Why did you hesitate?"

"Oh, I don't know," I said. "I guess I don't have the best history of voicing my ideas and opinions."

She pursed her lips and nodded. Something told me that despite her cool, confident demeanor, Dani had firsthand experience with suppressing her ideas, too. Then again, I didn't think there was a woman alive who didn't.

"That ends now," she said firmly.

"Sorry?"

"You said it yourself." She must've noticed the blank look of confusion on my face because she added, "It's history. So, let's leave that shit in the past. Deal?"

"Deal."

"Alright. Let's go. We've still got one more stop."

Ten minutes and one elevator ride later, we stopped outside a pair of bright red doors that matched the shade of my lipstick. *Rose City Roasters Red.* Hmm, maybe there was some kind of MLB x Maybelline collaboration to be had. I could practically hear the jingle now . . .

Maybe it's MLB.

"Final stop: the locker room."

Dani crossed one boot over the other and leaned against the wall. I longed to be as effervescently cool as she was.

"You make it sound like a horror movie."

She snorted. "It definitely can be."

"Are we even allowed in there?"

She arched her brow. "Don't tell me you're afraid of some nasty, naked boys." She leaned in and added, "Most of whom probably don't wash their own butthole properly."

I couldn't contain the giggle that escaped.

"Locker room is off-limits the hour before and after a game, thirty minutes for practices, and anything else needs to be cleared with Coach Ward beforehand." She pulled the phone out of her back pocket to check the time. "It's still pretty early, so we should be good."

I twisted my mouth sheepishly. "Maybe we should ask first?"

Dani yanked on the handle, pulling the door wide and holding it there with nothing but the heel of her ass-kicking boots. "I'm more of an ask for forgiveness, not permission kinda gal." She punctuated her statement with a wink.

When I grow up, I want to be Dani Bernal.

I took two tentative steps forward, careful to keep my eyes shielded from any surprise peen that crossed my path. I could count on one hand the number of penises I'd come eye to, well, penis with. I wasn't currently in the market for more. Unless, of course, that penis came with a certain pair of gray-green eyes and soapy-covered abs, and even then . . .

I tried shaking off the memory embossed on my brain. I'd just broken off an engagement, moved clear across the country, been cut off by my parents, and started a brand-new career. The last thing I needed to think about was men. Especially men with roguish grins and zero inhibitions.

I just had to do my job, make new friends—both of which were off to a good start—and everything would work out fine. *It had to.* I stepped farther into the room, listening half-heartedly as Dani pointed out each of the players' lockers. Feet shuffled from somewhere behind me. To my left, a bag zipped closed. Nonetheless, I kept my eyes averted.

That was, until a pair of well-worn cleats—the *biggest* pair of cleats I'd ever come across—stepped in front of me, stopping me dead in my tracks. I slowly lifted my head, skimming the lines of the intruder's well-defined body, from the ankles clad in red-striped socks—a staple of the Roasters uniform—all the way up to the thighs, which were thick enough to crush a watermelon, and finally, the, um, package. If the rumors were true about men with big feet, then this guy must have a huge—

"Oh, for the love of Pete."

"It's Soren actually." His lips twitched. *Bastard.*

What the hell was he doing here? In all of his bearded, smart-ass glory.

"Soren Sinclair, Dani Bernal," Dani said, introducing herself. "Social media director."

Soren held out his hand, but I knew better. A handshake wasn't going to cut it.

"Do you hug?" she asked him.

He wrinkled his brow, studying her like she was some kind of riddle. "I might be a little sweaty, but okay."

She wasted no time throwing her arms around his waist, nearly knocking him off his feet. That was the power of a Dani Bernal hug.

Soren's eyes widened. *Did I detect a hint of embarrassment from my annoyingly sexy neighbor? Interesting.*

"Are we doing hugs? I want hugs." A blonde man with a baby face and the number zero on his jersey sidled up to Dani. He didn't look old enough to order alcohol, let alone play professional baseball. "I'm Jared."

A smile split Dani's face. "Jared Pink. 3.1 ERA. 125 strikeouts your rookie season at Baltimore."

"Well damn, now *I'm* gonna give *you* a hug."

Jared tugged Dani into his arms. She didn't seem to mind. Something told me the two of them were cut from the same cloth. When they unwound themselves, he turned toward me.

"And you are?" he said, arms still stretched wide, closing in on me.

I opened my mouth. Before I could say a word, the big lug beside him growled, "No." And yes, I do mean *growled*. And yes, I'd be lying if I said that rasp of his didn't make me—or my vagina—feel a certain way.

His eyes locked on mine. "Pink," he said, gaze never wavering. "Why don't you show Ms. Bernal your bear?"

"Your what?" Dani asked.

"My bear," Jared explained. "My little sister gave me her favorite stuffed bear before the state championship my sophomore year at Penn. We won the title and ever since, I've carried it with me to every game, at every stadium."

"Okay, that's adorable. Show me the damn bear."

Jared led Dani to the other side of the locker room. As soon as they were out of earshot—and she was already mid-hug with another player named Wu—Soren set his sights on me.

"What, no hug for me?" He smiled. The smug bastard probably thought the sun came up just to hear him crow.

"Did you do this?" I gestured wildly, nearly smacking him right on the number four across his chest. "Last night, did you know—"

"Know that my new shower buddy was also going to be working with me?"

"How dare—"

"If anything, I would say *you* knew."

Outrage zipped through me. "I most certainly did not."

"I don't know. You show up there as my neighbor—"

"There's nowhere else to stay in town—"

"And then you hop into my shower—"

"I was there first!" My voice hitched as reality set in. We were in a locker room, surrounded by *his* team and *my* boss. How dare this man get such a rise out of me. I lowered my voice. "I was there first. Besides, it's a communal shower."

"And now, here you are. Hired to follow me around and what? Take a few pictures?"

Says the man who swings a stick around all day.

Just when I was about to let him have it, onlookers be damned, he adjusted his belt, drawing my attention—yet again—to his crotch.

"You're wasting your time." My eyes shot back up. I couldn't tell what pickled my herring more—his stupid smirk or the challenge in his eyes. "There are plenty of pictures of *that* already out there."

I hated the way my cheeks warmed, one of the many hazards of having such fair skin. *"Like a porcelain doll."* I shuddered as the memory of Walden's grating whine rolled through me.

No, that was another time, another day, another asshole.

This asshole, the infuriatingly handsome one dressed in a Rose City Roasters jersey and standard issue baseball pants that (gulp) left little to the imagination, had another thing coming. And I'd be all too happy to give it to him.

In a wicked move that would without a doubt give my mind—and my vibrator—a workout tonight, he leaned down until his face was just inches from mine and whispered, "For what it's worth, you look just as good with your clothes on, blondie."

Fortunately, Dani had already covered fire safety equipment with me during our tour. Because my panties combusted then and there.

He studied me with an air of amusement, though I couldn't imagine why. The downward curl of my lips should've been enough to tell him I was anything but amused. Little did he know, I was silently plotting his demise. And thanks to the catalog of "murder shows" I enjoyed—*Deadly Women, Dateline,* and *License to Kill* to name a few—I knew of at least a dozen ways to dismember and dispose of a body.

"Woah, what'd we miss?" Jared asked.

I stepped back, needing to put some distance between Soren and me. What was it about this man? Never had someone sucked me so deep into their orbit while simultaneously driving me to contemplate homicide.

My attention shifted to Dani, whose eyes were flickering between the two of us. *Sugar, how much had she heard?*

"Nothing," I said, pasting on a saccharine smile. I knew all about fake smiles. From my debutante days to my sham of an engagement, I'd had years to perfect them. "*Soren* and I are . . . old friends."

"I'm touched you remember my name, *blondie.*"

"It's Clarke, actually."

"Like Clark Bar?" he teased. How painstakingly unoriginal.

"Like Clarke Gable," I told him. "My mama had a thing for *Gone with the Wind.* I have a sister named Vivian."

"I'm more of an *It Happened One Night* kind of girl," Dani added.

"*Manhattan Melodrama,*" Pink said. All three of us pivoted to face him. "What? Turner Classic Movies," he explained. "I spent my summers at my grandma's house until I was sixteen."

Soren stared dazedly, which made me smile. It was refreshing to see him—and not me—out of sorts for once. Plus, it wasn't every day you came across a group of millennials so knowledgeable about black-and-white movies.

"Well, Ms. *Gable*—"

"That's not her name, dumbass," Soren grumbled. He crossed his arms over his chest like a toddler not getting their way.

"—and seeing as we're both new to town, we can get together and, you know, explore." Jared winked. In the history of winks, nobody had ever looked cuter—in that adorable little brother kind of way—than Jared Pink.

"No, you can't," Soren interrupted. For heaven's sake, who licked the red off his candy? "We have team photos in five."

"That's right," Dani said. "I forgot about that."

"It was nice meeting you, Jared," I told him. If the rest of the team and staff were as pleasant as he was, I was sure we'd get on swimmingly. Mr. Sourpuss, on the other hand, didn't deserve my pleasantries. No, I had something extra special reserved just for him, the most searing Southernism of them all.

"Soren," I said, smiling sweetly, *"bless your heart."*

Elated that this time, *I* had the final words—and a deadly combination at that—I turned to the door. I had left him speechless. Maybe Rose DeWitt Bukater had rubbed off on me because suddenly, I was feeling like the king of the world. Like for the first time, nothing or nobody could possibly get in my—

"It suits you," he mumbled, startling me.

Close, but no cigar. How dare he ruin my *Titanic* moment.

I looked over my shoulder. "What?"

He tugged the bill of his hat down, low enough to nearly block out his piercing gaze. "Your name. *Clarke.*" He drew out my single syllable name. Never had I heard every letter enunciated so clearly before. "It suits you."

My vision blurred. My heart beat wildly. Dangerously so. Distantly, I heard the door to, presumably, the field close behind him, the sound barely intelligible over the thumping of my vagina. My fresh start was beginning to feel more like a sticky mess.

"Okay, what was that about?" Dani asked.

Pull yourself together, Clarke. Despite our casual candor, Dani was still my boss. That meant maintaining professional boundaries. "What was what?"

"The . . . *tension*," she said, wagging her eyebrows. "Between you and Soren Sinclair." It was all too clear what kind of tension she was talking about. And I was having none of it.

"There is no . . . *tension*," I answered, mimicking her exaggerated brow movement.

"Yeah, no," Dani countered. "That was fight me or fuck me kind of energy."

So much for professional boundaries.

I gasped. Not because of what she said, but rather the way she said it. I wasn't used to people swearing in front of me. Heck, I only swore in my head. And I definitely wasn't used to hearing that kind of language in the company of women, other than my sister. I had a sudden flashback to the first (and last) time I'd brought up the topic of blow jobs with my bridesmaids, the women who supposedly knew me best. So, sue me for wanting some tips on how to deep throat my soon-to-be husband.

Sigh. I would've made a great wife.

They'd all looked at me like they'd seen their granddaddy's ghost on Christmas morning. Dani's frank demeanor was refreshing, to say the least.

"He should count his blessings that it didn't come to blows."

She snorted. "Ha, blows."

Dang it, I'd stumbled into that one.

"You know what I mean."

"And *you* know about his reputation, right?"

"Soren?" I asked her, drawing a blank.

"Soren 'Sin' Sinclair." She blew out her breath. It wasn't ringing any bells. And *Sin* wasn't exactly a forgettable name.

"Well, I know what we're going to be doing this afternoon. Research."

Soren

"Sin, have you apologized to Monica? Are the cheating rumors true?"

"How are you and your teammates getting along?"

"Who's got the biggest bat in the locker room?"

Jesus Christ. The vultures were at it again.

This was the part of the job I fucking hated. It didn't matter what I said or wore or how many personal questions I answered. Somehow, I always walked out of these interviews looking like an asshole.

"Woah, one at a time, please."

A thirty-something blonde guy who looked like he belonged by the beach serving up daiquiris stood up. "Brock Heller, *Portlandia Press*." Of course his name was Brock. "How are you settling in with your team?"

"So far so good." As good as things could be considering we had only been practicing together for a week or so. "The guys are great, coaching staff knows their stuff. I'm in good hands."

It wasn't the team or coaching staff I was worried about. It was the the Southern bombshell leaning against the back wall.

"Meena Patel from *Cascade Chronicle*," a South Asian woman with magenta hair said from the front. "Rumors are circulating that your ex-fiancée, Monica J. is seeing her bodyguard, Kieran Kline. Do you have a response?"

I resisted the urge to roll my eyes. Barely.

"Who Monica sees is entirely up to her. You said it yourself, she's my *ex-fiancée.*"

My eyes flicked to our team social media director, the one with tattoos and blue hair that reminded me of cotton candy. Dani something. She was a stark contrast to blondie—I meant *Clarke*—both in size and stature. Her outgoing personality more than made up for it.

She waved at me from the back of the room, miming an exaggerated smile. I caught the hint.

"And I wish her nothing but the best, in all professional and personal endeavors."

Phones and cameras clicked when I flashed what was hopefully, a charming smile.

I could handle it, though—any shit they slung my way. I'd dealt with it for years. There wasn't anything these gossip mongers could say that would throw me.

"Are you nervous about a repeat of your performance in Atlanta?"

Except maybe that.

There was no hiding the twitch in my eye or the clench of my jaw. Knowing my luck, some recap podcast probably captured the sound of my molars grinding together in high-resolution.

Last Halloween, I had taken my sister's kids trick-or-treating. Her three-year-old, Penny, had gone as Mirabel from *Encanto,* her favorite movie. A movie that we had watched together over and over and over again, to the point where I memorized every line of every song. And just as, "We don't talk about Bruno," I didn't talk about Atlanta.

"No."

"Care to elaborate?"

"No." I stood abruptly, the scrape of my chair echoing throughout the press room. "I've got a practice to get to."

So much for keeping my cool.

Tense silence descended over the room. I wasn't about to wait around for somebody to break it. Instead, I tore out of the press room, careful to keep my focus rooted on the door in front of me and not the blonde beside it.

I knew a thing or two about bad news. My career, or what was left of it, was living proof of that.

Clarke had bad news written all over her.

Every. Mouthwatering. Inch.

We were on our third set of sit-ups when Pink opened his big mouth. Honestly, I was impressed he had waited this long. "Did you guys hear that Sinclair got *bless your heart*-ed this morning?" he asked on his next up.

"Fuck, seriously?" Tuck asked.

"That's embarrassing." This from our first baseman, Roman Garcia.

"Sh-it," Matty said, drawing the word out into two syllables. "What did you do, man?"

Matty Miller was Mr. Irrelevant, aka the very last pick in this year's draft. But as the only Southerner on our team, hailing all the way from Scratch Ankle, Alabama—and yes, that was the real name of a real town—his opinion was perhaps most relevant. At least in this circumstance. I might have a decade on him, but he spoke Southernisms fluently.

On my next up, I draped my arms around my knees. "I didn't *do* anything to her."

"But you want to," Pink said before lying back. On his next up, he added suggestively, "Don't you?"

Nosy fucker.

I rolled my eyes. Pink wasn't a bad guy, but he was predictable. I'd dealt with guys like him my entire career. Hell, I'd *been* that guy back in my early twenties. They craved attention, fed off it really. They weren't looking for a fight—not most of them anyway—but rather a response, recognition.

But I wasn't going to feed his already overinflated ego.

"Who exactly are we talking about?" Tuck asked. Like me, our second basemen, Johnathan "Tuck" Tucker, had seen his fair share of the minor leagues. The only difference was the Roasters marked Tuck's first time in the big leagues. I had been given a shot at the majors before. Twice.

"Our new social media girl," Pink told them. He was a worse tattletale than my two sisters.

"She has a name," I snapped, immediately regretting it when Pink smiled. The kid was a pro at pressing my buttons.

"Is this the stacked blonde or the tattooed pixie?" Tuck asked.

"Blonde," Pink and I answered at the same time.

"So, the tattooed chick is free, then?"

Before anybody could respond, a dark cloud settled over the gym. One much heavier than any of the weights we'd been lifting. "If you can talk this much, then you're not pushing hard enough."

None of us needed to look up to know it was Coach Ward grumbling from the doorway. That man needed to come with a warning, or at least a bell around his neck.

We resumed our respective workouts. We'd long since ditched the uniforms after team photos this morning, swapping them out for casual gym clothes, or in Pink's case, a lavender pair of mesh shorts. The kid was either extremely proud of his massive cock or more secure in his sexuality than any man I'd met before. Knowing Pink, it was probably both.

Mondays during the preseason were reserved for strength training exercises—sit-ups, hand weights, wall sits—which meant come Tuesday, I'd be sore as hell.

Outfielders had the machines across the hall for another few minutes, which meant the infield squad—me, Pink, Roman, Tuck, Matty, and our catcher, Bennett—had the weight room.

When I finished my final set of crunches, I moved over to the wall, taking the free spot next to Matty. I pretended not to notice the way my knee creaked when I slid down until my thighs were parallel to the ground.

Fucking hell. This is going to be what kills me.

"Sinclair, this is very important." Matty checked the doorway. None of us wanted another Bailey-Ward scolding. "Did she say *bless your heart*?" he asked, his inflection light and playful. "Or was it *bless your heart*?" The second time around, he said it more condescendingly. Like he'd just told a joke and I was the only one who hadn't gotten the punchline. Or in this case, that I was the punchline.

"Definitely the second one."

He whistled. "Aw, hell, man. You're fucked."

Damn right I was. I still had twenty seconds to go in this wall sit and already, I felt like my stomach was gonna fall out of my ass.

"Doesn't matter," I huffed, clenching my core muscles. "I'm not looking for anything right now. Just trying to stay focused on my game."

"Time," Roman called out. He tapped Bennett's shoulder and signed the same to him. Bennett was deaf and even though he had cochlear implants, he turned off the external speech processor sometimes during workouts or practices.

My body crumpled, sliding the rest of the way down until I met the floor. Damn, I shouldn't be this winded after a thirty-minute training circuit. I dropped my head back against the wall, straining to catch my breath. My legs were going to feel like mashed potatoes by dinner time.

Fuck, I'd kill for some mashed potatoes.

Matty used the ends of his tee to wipe the sweat from his brow. "It's probably for the best."

"Huh?" I asked him. My brain, along with the rest of my muscles, was mush.

"Focusing on your game and not on—"

"Clarke Myers," I finished for him.

He nodded. "Cute name."

Cute woman, I thought to myself. Scratch that, cute didn't even begin to cover it.

Clarke was a fucking smoke show.

I couldn't lie. She'd shocked the hell out of me when she'd strolled into the locker room this morning. She'd traded her robe for the standard PNW getup: jeans, a flannel shirt, and a raincoat. I'd done a double-take when my eyes landed on her very impractical, open-toed shoes. I guessed the saying was true—you could take the belle out of the South, but you couldn't take the South out of the belle.

I bit my tongue and tried not to smile. I didn't know why I irritated her so much. I didn't know why I liked it so much either.

It was hard enough—emphasis on *hard*—that we were going to be neighbors for the foreseeable future. Now we had to work together, too.

Fucking awesome.

"What'd I miss?" Bennett asked after he'd switched his processor back on. A part of me envied the fact that he could tune these clowns out whenever he felt like it.

"Sinclair's in love," Pink announced. He narrowly dodged the sweat-drenched shirt that Matty hurled at his head. "What? It's true. You didn't see the way he looked at her before."

"He's full of shit." I rubbed the back of my neck.

"Or the way she looked at him."

That gave me pause. I wasn't sure what unnerved me most about Clarke. Perhaps it was the fact that I didn't have a clue what she was thinking. Not that I would ever claim to be an expert at understanding the female psyche, but it wasn't like I was starting at ground zero. I had sisters; I'd dated. We'd barely exchanged a few sentences, though, and I was already feeling miles out of my depth.

Maybe it was the fact that, by all accounts, we had nothing in common. Hell, we barely spoke the same language. She was a Georgia peach. I was a Brooklyn bialy. Extra onions. I lived in ripped joggers and Costco brand T-shirts. She matched her candy-apple-red manicure to her lipstick. *Fuck.* It was going to take more than a couple of cold showers to wash away the vision of her sucking my cock, leaving a ring of red lipstick around the base.

Marking me as hers.

"Sinclair, you in?"

I looked up to find five sets of eyes on me. At some point during my musings on lipstick and blow jobs, the guys' conversation had shifted away from my infatuation with Clarke and onto—

"M&M night at Bennett and Diaz's," Roman said. "You in?"

Bennett and his roommate, our left fielder, Peter Diaz, shared a house in North Portland. Their place had become the unofficial gathering spot for team barbecues and M&M nights, aka movies and margaritas. Diaz was what you'd call a movie buff. He'd even turned the third bedroom of their house into a screening room, complete with a floor-to-ceiling projector screen—because according to Diaz, the *only* way to watch a movie was on the big screen—and a legit movie theater popcorn machine. The margaritas were just the free-booze incentive for the rest of the guys, who didn't give a fuck about whatever movie he picked that week.

Diaz, and only Diaz, got to pick the movies.

Typically, I wasn't much for "team bonding" activities, and how much bonding could really happen during a two-hour, quiet, movie-watching experience? Because, yes, Diaz demanded complete silence while the movie played. But I'd been to a couple M&M nights already and, admittedly, they were a pretty good time.

"That depends. What's playing tonight?"

I'd missed last week, but the week before had been *Knives Out,* one of my personal favorites. I had a thing for murder mysteries, and Diaz had a thing for Chris Evans in cable-knit sweaters.

"*Groundhog Day,*" Bennett said. He shrugged. "Seems appropriate."

It was only the second week of February and yet, it felt like I'd aged ten years in the past few weeks. A breakup had the power to do that.

"Works for me."

"I'm in," Tuck echoed.

"Me, too," said Matty.

"I'll be there with bells on." *Fucking Pink.*

"Can I crash with somebody?" I asked. "Pink, don't bother. There's no way we're having a sleepover." I couldn't help but chuckle when his mouth opened and closed wordlessly. It was nice to know that he *could* shut up if he wanted to.

"You can stay at mine," Matty offered.

"Thanks, man."

The drive between Portland and Rose City was less than an hour, but driving that alone at night, when it was raining—and in February in Oregon, it was always raining—was fucking miserable.

I climbed to my feet, wincing at the stiffness that had already set in in my upper thighs. While the rest of the guys packed up their stuff, I leaned over to Matty. "Think I can use your tub for an ice bath, too?"

"Sure thing." He slapped me on the shoulder. *Fucking ouch.* "But I get it first."

"Deal."

"Can y'all stop making out so we can go?" Pink called out from the doorway, jumping foot to foot. Oh, to have the energy of a twenty-three-year-old again. "I call dibs on the elliptical."

Matty smiled when I rolled my eyes. "Are you jealous, Pink?" I asked our pitcher.

"Please," he protested. "We all know that I'm the most lovable one here. If anybody's getting kissed, it's gonna be me."

Roman and Tuck smirked. Bennett looked like he regretted ever turning his speech processor back on. Together, we trudged down the hall toward the weight room, some of us—namely me—moving slower than the others.

"I hate to break this to you, Pink," I said as I limped across the linoleum until our shoulders were square. Only then did I deliver my parting blow that would, no doubt, crumble his ego. "Matty's much more my type."

The smirk fell clean off his face.

"Excuse me?"

I clapped his shoulder and rounded the corner to the weight room. I didn't have to look over my shoulder to know that Pink was hot on my heels. "Why am I not your type, Sinclair?!"

Clarke

"**L**et me get this straight." June narrowly dodged a puddle. We were already nearly ten minutes late for cocktails with her friend, Nessa. Mostly because I'd insisted on changing my shoes before we left. I was already *this* close to throwing out my favorite wedges. "You're part of the Roasters' social media team, yet you didn't know a thing about their star third baseman? The bad boy of baseball? Lothario to the stars?"

Apparently, I was the only person in the Western Hemisphere who, until today, hadn't heard of Soren Sinclair. Or *Sin,* as they called him.

"I'm not a sports fan," I told her.

"You work for a baseball team."

I shrugged.

"Okay, but surely you know Monica J.?"

That was a name I did recognize. Even the farthest corners of rural South Carolina knew Monica J., the chart-topping pop princess and Grammy nominee. Celebrity news had never been my thing—the circles Walden and I ran in didn't exactly dabble in idle gossip, at least not about celebrities—but I'd heard her music on the radio a time or two.

And based on this afternoon's research, I now knew that until recently, Soren had been dating her. Their breakup had been front page news on every tabloid and blog in America. And the string of bad press about Soren didn't stop there.

"I know they dated."

"Oh, they more than dated," June said. "Supposedly, he broke her heart. She thought they were going to get married and then he dumped her when the Roasters traded for him."

That didn't surprise me, but I'd be lying if I said I wasn't a little disappointed. Soren had all but ogled me in the shower the first time we met, and then he'd teased me about it the second time. The guy dated pop stars, supermodels, and, *allegedly*, his ex-teammate's wife. There was no way in hell I'd get mixed up with a guy like that. Not that I was looking to get "mixed up" with any guy anytime soon.

"What's that look?" Her eyes lit up on a smile. "Oh my god, do you like him?"

Her question stopped me in my tracks just outside of a storefront called Green Goddess, which, judging by the logo, sold cannabis. *Toto, we aren't in South Carolina anymore.*

"Of course not."

"Uh-huh." Her eyes narrowed. "I wouldn't blame you if you did. He's a good-looking guy, clearly charming. He even helped remove some fallen branches off the outdoor kitchen after last week's storm."

Now *that* did surprise me. Despite every blog, article, and Reddit thread detailing Soren "Sin" Sinclair's illustrious past, I couldn't help but feel like there was more to him than met the eye. Or, in this case, met the internet. That didn't help *me* any, though. If I had my druthers, it would be a lot easier to avoid him, so long as I could pretend like he was a bad person. Anything to protect my heart.

Then again, I'd pretended like bad people—some of the worst people—were good for years, and where had that gotten me?

"Doesn't matter," I said, tossing my hair nonchalantly over my shoulder. "He's not exactly my type anyway."

I winced at my haughty tone of voice. The one I'd fine-tuned so frequently over the years, until it was just right. Until even I believed it. Almost.

But June didn't know me. Nobody here did. *That's not who I have to be anymore.* Rose City was my opportunity to do better. To be better. The last thing I wanted was to alienate my new friends—if I could even call them that—or mislead them into thinking I was too good for them. I knew I wasn't.

"Sorry," I told her. "What I meant is that I'm not looking for anything romantic with anybody. I just ended an engagement."

I didn't know what prompted me to tell June the truth. She certainly hadn't asked for an explanation of any kind. That was what friends did though, right? Share their secrets, insecurities. *Celebrity crushes.*

"Oh, I'm sorry to hear that."

"Don't be," I told her. I swallowed my pride, along with everything my mama had taught me about sharing personal business with strangers, and added, "It wasn't the healthiest relationship. Rose City is sort of my fresh start."

She smiled weakly and placed her hand on my shoulder.

"I know people say this all the time, but trust me when I say that I understand *exactly* what you're going through."

Those seven words told me everything I needed to know.

Somebody had hurt June, in one way or another. And despite the sad realization, I smiled back. Because for the first time in a long time, I didn't feel so alone.

"Not to interrupt, but are you coming inside?"

I turned toward the low, honeyed voice.

Goodness gracious. Nessa Gibbs had the body of a Botticelli painting and the voice of a nine-hundred number. Her layered, reddish-brown locks cascaded halfway down her back. A vintage, checkered peacoat covered her, shoulders-to-knees, and yet somehow, at the same time, clung to every curve of her body. Whereas I carried most of my weight in my midsection, Nessa was all hips, in the best way possible. She had the quintessential hourglass figure most women dreamed of, with an emphasis on the bottom half.

Clearly, there was something in the water in Rose City, because their cup ranneth over with big, beautiful women.

"C'mon," Nessa said, waving us forward from outside Thorn Tavern, the local watering hole. The only one in Rose City, as far as I knew. "It's freaking freezing, and I am in desperate need of wine after the day I had."

I'd rather drink muddy water.

"Sounds great," I lied.

I despised the taste of wine. Red wine, white wine, even rosé. Everyone had told me I'd develop a taste for it eventually, and considering the number of dinner parties and functions I'd attended over the years, I probably should have. Maybe it was my one act of rebellion. Maybe wine just sucked.

In any case, I had years of experience choking the swill down, so I was sure I could manage another glass or two. Especially if it put me in Nessa's and June's good graces. What a perfect way to commemorate this new phase of my life, full of new opportunities. And who knew?

Maybe Rose City Clarke would like wine.

Rose City Clarke did *not* like wine.

"Clarke," Nessa said, giggling from behind her glass. "You don't have to drink it. I promise, you won't hurt anybody's feelings."

"Speak for yourself." Nero, the proprietor of Rose Tavern and Nessa's older brother, topped off Nessa's glass. "That's my award-winning merlot."

"Hush, Ne," Nessa scolded.

"It's not . . . that bad." I smiled politely.

"You should put that on the label, Ne," June teased. "Thorny for You: 'Not that bad.'"

They both laughed, but not at my expense. No, as far as I could tell, Nessa and June were as genuine as it came. They'd also been friends for years and, as I'd learned over the past half-hour, were some of the only remaining locals born and raised in Rose City.

"Wait, you made the wine?" I asked Nero, June's joke finally registering.

"I did," Nero said proudly. "I—"

"We," Nessa interjected.

"*We* inherited the bar when our mom passed a few years ago."

I swallowed, embarrassment and guilt washing over me. Suddenly, my problems didn't feel so big after all. "I'm sorry to hear that."

"Thank you. The grapes are more of a passion project. When Mom left us the bar, Nessa the mess-a here," he said, pointing a thumb at his sister, "didn't want anything to do with it. I bought her out and she opened the bookstore."

That was another thing I'd learned during our first round of drinks. Not only was Nessa on the town council—because Rose City was too small for a mayor—but she also owned and operated Smutty Buddies, a bookstore dedicated to romance novels and erotica. I could practically hear my God-fearing, Southern Baptist mother screaming, "*No, you can't read those filthy sex books,*" three-thousand miles away.

"A *lot's* changed in Rose City over the last few years," June added.

"Especially since 2020," Nessa said.

She didn't need to explain further. A lot had changed for everyone during the Covid-19 pandemic. I'd finished the final days of my college career from my living room couch. Finding a job had proven next-to-impossible, and by the time I started dating Walden in early 2021, my priorities had shifted.

"We've had an influx of almost *two times* our population since 2021," June bragged like a proud parent. "Most of whom are folks under forty. It seems like there's a new business popping up every day."

"And now, we have the Roasters," Nessa grumbled. It was clear she wasn't thrilled with the latest business to grace Rose City.

"That's a good thing, Ness."

"It's only a matter of time before our sleepy little town turns into a condo-covered tourist trap," Nessa argued. "Not that I'm not thrilled you moved here, Clarke. Just saying."

"Well, I'm happy to be here," I told them, bringing a smile to Nessa's face. "And for what it's worth, I think Rose City is lovely as is. As my gran always said, the rest will all come out in the wash."

Nessa's smile fell faster than one of Gran's chocolate soufflés. Gran was always better with savory eats, not sweets.

"What I mean is, these things tend to work themselves out."

Nero brought us our food after that. We'd all decided to forgo dinner in favor of some smaller, shareable plates. Roasted brussels sprouts with a lemon-garlic aioli, an assorted spread of meats and cheeses, and something so sinfully delicious that it could only be the work of the devil himself called fried cheese curds.

Never had I felt so at home in the company of other women. Viv and Ellie were the only exceptions, and even then, I'd always functioned more like a third wheel than a friend. It was clear to me now that I'd spent the first twenty-seven years of my life *competing* with women. For what exactly, I didn't know. Approval, maybe. Or affection. As if either of those were a prize.

I scoffed into my Long Island iced tea. Nero had long since replaced the bitter glass of wine with my drink of choice.

"How about you, Clarke?" Nessa asked, sloshing her wine.

"Sorry?"

"Are you single?"

"Nero's free, if you want him," June added around a wink.

"Oh, please," Nessa begged. "Please take him. That would make my life so much easier."

"Well, I don't—"

"Actually, no. I like you and I want to keep it that way. My level of respect drops exponentially for anybody who fucks my brother." She leaned over, gently knocking herself into June's side. "Just ask this one."

Woo boy. Smells like trouble.

My eyes flicked between June and Nero. "The two of you—"

"In high school," June said, following it up with an exasperated sigh. "It's a small town." She leaned over to knock Nessa back, only this time with a little more force. "And you have a big mouth."

Nessa giggled. "Only when I drink. Oh! That reminds me."

She reached for the oversized purse at her feet and rummaged inside. Mama had been strict about my movie watching habits growing up, but one I was allowed to watch was *Mary Poppins*. I waited with bated breath to see if Nessa would pull out a magical measuring tape or coatrack.

After a moment, she found what she was looking for, and much to my disappointment, it was a candle, not a coatrack. "Check out the new candle I'm stocking at the store."

June's eyes lit up with excitement. "Oh, Clarke, you'll love it. Seriously, Nessa gets them from a local artist, and once you try a Rose City Candle, you'll never step foot in a Bath & Body Works ever again."

Nessa deposited the glass-wrapped candle in my lap. It was beautiful, that was for sure. A deep magenta adorned with flower petals and small crystal shards on either side of the wick. At one point in high school, my sister had gone through a "woo woo" phase, as my mama called it. From then on, Viv had taken the label of the "weird sister" and worn it like a badge of honor. I knew that every crystal had some kind of special meaning or power. You know, if you believed in that kind of thing.

I turned the candle over to read the label on the side.

"Unfuck—" I bit my lip. Nessa nodded, goading me to continue. "Unfuckwithable," I said, louder this time but still soft enough that the rest of the bar wouldn't hear me. "A positive energy manifestation candle for your inner bad bitch."

I'd never said so many swear words in one breath before.

"Smell it," Nessa said.

I brought it to my nose and took a whiff.

Sweet Mary's Molasses.

It smelled like the first days of summer. Like cool, crisp air after an unexpected sun shower, with a hint of hand-churned ice cream. Lemon. No, lemonade. With a spot of moonshine. It smelled like sex. Not sweaty, bedroom sex, but "our picnic turned to rolling around in the meadow and rinsing off in the creek" kind of sex. Not that I had any firsthand experience with that, but a girl could dream.

"Judging by the sounds you're making, I'm gonna guess you like it?" Nessa asked.

I opened my eyes—I didn't even realize I'd shut them—to find them both staring back at me, utterly amused. *Oh lord.* Had I made noises, too? I slapped the hand not cradling the lemonade sex candle over my mouth.

"Oh my gosh," I said from behind my palm. "I'm so sorry."

"I'm not," June muttered. "That was pretty hot."

My cheeks flamed.

"But honestly, it's been so long since I got laid that literally just the idea of *somebody else* having sex is enough to set me off."

"Same," Nessa added.

"Yeah, but unlike you, I'm not on some self-imposed sex ban."

"It's a sex *cleanse*, thank you very much."

My eyes ping-ponged back and forth between the two of them. They bickered like siblings, and I would know. To this day, my sister was the *only* person I spoke openly-ish with about sex. And even then, we generally kept it fairly PG-13—blame it on two decades of purity culture in the Deep South.

"Clarke, please tell Nessa that sex isn't supposed to *cleanse* you." *Hells bells.* I could already tell this was heading down a dangerous path. "It should be dirty, sweaty, and full of fluids."

"Clarke," Nessa said, smiling sweetly. I knew from firsthand experience that the sweeter the smile, the more deadly the venom. "Please tell June that my body is a temple. Only I control what—or who—comes inside, and right now, I'm exorcising some bad spirits out of it."

I took another sip of my drink. Surely, they couldn't expect me to mediate if my mouth was full.

"I didn't realize your pussy was full of demons."

I sputtered, trying to contain my gasp? Laugh? It didn't matter because it all came spilling out of my mouth, all over me and the bartop. Before I could even contemplate what had happened, Nero was already there, mopping up my mess with a hand towel.

"Jeez Louise," I choked, "I'm so sorry, Nero."

"Please." He rolled his eyes. "You think it's the first time somebody spit up on my bar?" He leaned over the top, rocking forward on his heels and showcasing some fairly detailed tattoo work on his forearms in the process. "Plus, you're rolling with these two troublemakers now. It's only a matter of time before you're dancing on top of it."

"That happened one time," June protested, watching as he walked away.

Nessa flipped off her brother before turning to me. "We should be the ones apologizing. I forget that not everybody is as . . ."

"Crass?" June suggested. "Aggressive? Horny?"

"Open. Not everybody is as *open* as we are."

I pulled the sleeves of my flannel down to cover my hands. Even inside by a roaring fire (which only added to the cozy, cottage-like feel of the tavern), I was freezing.

"It's okay," I told them. "I'm just not used to it. Things are a little less . . . progressive in South Carolina. Heck, my mama and daddy never even gave us the birds and the bees talk. Everything I know about sex I learned from back issues of *Cosmo*, Tumblr clips, and my sister, Viv. And she's a lesbian."

"Bisexual," Nessa said, raising her hand.

"Demisexual," June echoed.

They high-fived across my body and then turned their attention back to me, an unspoken question in both of their eyes.

"Oh, I'm not . . . That is, I've only ever been with the one guy."

"For reference, it's not who you're with," Nessa said, matter-of-fact.

"Or how many people you've been with," June added.

"It's who you're attracted to. But that's okay!" Nessa swung an arm around my shoulder. "You don't have to be queer to hang out with us."

"Yeah, you can be our token straight friend."

That made me laugh. I'd been around Viv, Ellie, and their friends for years, but they'd never labeled me as the "token straight friend." At least not to my face. Typically, labels made me uncomfortable—probably because they'd always come from a place of insecurity or ignorance—but this was a title I could get on board with. It also didn't slip by me that these two incredible women had called me their friend, welcomed me in, no questions asked. For that reason alone, they could call me whatever they liked.

"And as our token straight friend . . ." June cleared her throat, slipping into a lower octave—one usually reserved for serious or explicit phone conversations. "It's our duty to *initiate* you into the most sacred, secret society in all of Rose City."

I didn't miss the mischievous grin she flashed Nessa. The two of them were cooking something up, and dang it, I wanted to know more.

"Alrighty, let's hear it."

Soren

*R*ight there. Oh god, that's good.

Pleasure and pain rocketed down my spine. My biceps protested, working overtime to hold up the weight of my body. I welcomed the pain. Embraced it, really.

Hold on. Just a little bit longer.

Easier said than done. Even after a year of practicing yoga, I could honestly say it still kicked my ass every time. In the best possible way. Much like baseball, yoga required practice and discipline, two things I knew all too well. However, yoga also *stretched* me mentally—pun intended—in a way that baseball never had. That wasn't to say that it didn't take years and years of training to get to where I was with my game. It had. Hell, I still had to work at it every day. But physically, at this point in my career, I operated mainly on instinct rather than forethought. The same couldn't be said for yoga.

I breathed through the final few seconds of the twisted lunge before releasing my hips and stepping forward until my feet were together. From there, I dropped my upper body, sliding into the next position—forward fold ragdoll. My deep exhalation mingled with the calming sounds of nature.

Inhale fresh air and pine trees.

Exhale tabloid bullshit and sexual tension.

Part of me felt like a piece of shit for even entertaining my attraction to Clarke.

From the outside perspective, I was the callous bastard who had just dumped America's sweetheart. Then again, nobody knew the true nature of my and Monica's relationship. Nobody except a few record execs and the team of publicists who had woven a tale of two industry-crossed lovers. Her music label had eaten it up; the press had eaten me alive.

Breathe.

My breath echoed through the trees. It had taken a few days, but I'd finally found the perfect place for yoga in Rose City. A clearing tucked away in the surrounding wooded area, far enough from Bed of Roses to avoid wandering eyes but still close enough to walk to. No distractions, no lights, nothing but me and the moonlight.

You know who would look great spread out under the moon?

I choked on my next exhale. This was the problem. Here I was, more worked up over a woman I barely knew than the one I'd dated for the past year. She had reduced me to a sputtering, hormonal teenager.

Well, the buck stopped here.

Clarke wasn't going to be the reason I lost focus. Nobody was. Not now. Not when I was so close to getting everything I'd spent years working for, sacrificing for. And I wasn't the only one who had sacrificed. I could spend a lifetime counting the ways my family had made concession after concession to support my dream. They deserved some kind of payoff. I owed them that.

Because what else can I offer them?

My phone buzzed beside the yoga mat, interrupting my not-so-peace of mind. Normally, I'd ignore it, but when I saw my oldest sister's name pop up on the screen, I got curious. It was a little late for her to be calling, especially on a Thursday. Aside from the monthly Zoom call (cue eye roll here) with the entire family, she and I usually reserved our communication for the weekend when she wasn't teaching.

"How's my older but not-so-wiser sister doing?"

"Talk to your nibling, won't you?"

Shelby might've been two-thousand miles away, but her frustration echoed through the phone loud and clear.

"Why? What'd they do?"

Shelby's kid, Monty, had started using they/them pronouns a few years ago. At the time, I hadn't known much about what it meant to be gender fluid. Three books, two online classes, and one year of family counseling later, and I was now the proud uncle of a *nibling*—a term we had all agreed fit best.

"It's what I won't let them do. Here."

And then, after a brief fumbling with the phone and a muffled, "Mo-om!" with two syllables . . .

"Uncle-sorus!"

"Mont-star!" I mimicked their enthusiasm. "What are you doing up so late?" It was almost midnight in Milwaukee, on a school night no less.

"We just got home from the Harry Styles concert! And guess what?" I could practically picture them jumping up and down in my sister's apartment. I bet the downstairs neighbors loved that.

"What?"

"Harry liked my sign. He pointed to it and read it aloud and smiled and now I'll never be the same ever again." They squealed, all without taking a breath. Oh, to be fourteen again.

"That's amazing. Have your mom send me pictures, okay?"

"Only if you tell her I can get my nose pierced."

Ah. That must've been what had irked Shelby. Beat me why though. Monty was fourteen, and like most teenagers, this wasn't the first time they'd wanted to experiment with their look. Shelby had fully supported their decision to color their hair pink last year, and again when they'd wanted to buzz the sides. From the sound of things, she drew the line at body piercings.

"Now you know that's up to your mom, not me."

"But—"

"You're not winning this one, kid."

Silence. "Fine."

I could practically hear the lightbulb go off over their head. "And please"—I lowered my voice—"whatever you do, don't have a friend do it for you behind her back. Trust me, that is a fight you do *not* want to have with your mom."

They released an aggravated sigh of defeat. "Fine."

And then I did what any good uncle who didn't want to disappoint the kid he loved most would do. I told them, "Wait until you come to visit this summer, and we'll buy you some clip-in nose rings."

"Really?!"

"*Temporary* nose rings," I stressed, because I knew firsthand that you did not want to be on Shelby's bad side.

"Oh, Uncle-sorus, you're the best!"

"Tone down the excitement," I whispered. "Otherwise, you'll give us away. Now, say goodbye and put those acting chops to use. Seriously, I expect some Oscar-worthy pouting."

"O-kay," they said, really milking it. *I knew sending them to that drama camp in the Catskills would be worth it.* "Thanks for nothing, Uncle-sorus." I caught the hint of a giggle before they passed the phone back to my sister.

"Did you back me up for once?" Shelby teased.

"I'll always back you up, Shelb." I smiled to myself. "You know that."

"Of course, I know that, you little shit."

I'd never given much consideration to fatherhood, but I loved being the "fun uncle." Spoiling my sisters' kids with trips and gifts and, apparently, piercings was a role I'd never get tired of.

There wasn't a thing I wouldn't do for the people I loved. If Shelby called and asked me to bury a body tomorrow, I'd book the first flight out of PDX and bring my own shovel. She and her ex had had somewhat of a heinous divorce when Monty was just starting kindergarten. In fact, the last any of us had seen or heard of Thayden—fuck any dude whose name ended in "ayden"—was the day he'd packed up his overpriced golf clubs that had been collecting dust for going on a decade, and climbed into his twenty-two-year-old girlfriend's mint green Ford Fiesta.

Meanwhile, Shelby and Monty had packed up their lives, including their pet rabbit, Bernard, and moved in with me. It had been a tight squeeze for the three of us—well, four, including Bernard—in my one-bedroom loft. For eighteen months, we'd fought over the one tiny bathroom, built forts out of empty mac and cheese boxes, and had countless "campouts" on the rooftop deck. It had been hectic, to say the least, and yet, I wouldn't trade those eighteen months for anything.

"So, do you want to talk about it?" Shelby probed. "Or should I say *her*?"

Her questions sparked a vision of a voluptuous blonde with a face made for fucking and an ass made for eating.

Great. Guess I'll be jerking off for a second time today.

And then it clicked. I hadn't mentioned blondie—I mean, *Clarke*—to Shelby. That meant there was only one other woman she could be talking about, and I really didn't want to talk about her.

"Seriously, Sor. What happened?"

Apparently, I couldn't even go a day without being reminded of Monica. Of whom the world, including my family, thought I really was. All *Sin*, no substance.

"The same thing that always happens." I gritted my teeth. "I fucked up."

She sighed. "I don't believe that."

"Well, you'd be the first."

She sighed. "I don't think you're being fair to yourself, Sor. You signed up to be a pro athlete, not tabloid fodder."

That was very true. Sports media had changed dramatically over the last decade, largely because of social media. Facebook had only been around for a few years when I was first drafted. I still didn't have any social media accounts, much to the dismay of my agent. That didn't stop the media (or my so-called "fans") from skewering me left and right any chance they got.

"It doesn't matter because I don't want to talk about her anyway. Remember?"

She sighed. The deep, elongated sigh of an older sister who thought she knew better, and truth be told, she probably did. I still needed a few more days to lick my wounds though.

"Okay."

"Thanks, Shelb."

After we said our goodbyes, I did a quick twenty push-ups to work out my frustration. *So much for releasing my tension.* It was either sweat it out or jerk it off, and I did not want to take that kind of frantic energy out on my dick. I'd already jacked off once today and when I'd come, it hadn't been my ex's name on my lips, but instead, the southern bombshell next door.

When I got back to Bed of Roses, I traded my yoga mat for shampoo and body wash, wrapped a towel around my waist, and headed for the showers. I second-guessed myself halfway there. The sun had set hours ago, so it was already pitch black out, save for a couple strands of twinkle-lights strung across the lot. Was it too late to shower? I didn't want to disturb any of the other residents.

I eyed the rest of the houses, looking for any sign of life. So what if I spent an extra minute or two watching the trailer next door?

Are you awake, blondie?

Something told me there was a fiery minx hidden under that fluffy-robe and gruff exterior, and that was something I wanted to further explore. At another time, when the frigid temps weren't tickling my balls. There was good ball tickling and bad ball tickling, and this was most definitely the latter.

I started the shower in my go-to stall, the same one I'd used every day since I'd arrived in Rose City, and dropped my head to my chest, rolling it side to side to release the tension that had set up camp between my muscles.

The field was my church, but this was my sanctuary.

I'd never been a man of faith, but I worshiped at the altar of bathroom-tiled bliss.

There wasn't much I was certain about: Dominic DiMaggio was better than his brother Joe, you should always add extra butter regardless of what the recipe called for (thanks, Mamaw), and showers were the cure-all for just about anything.

Can't sleep? Feel sick? *Page Six* hounds you after your pop-star girlfriend dumps your ass? Take a shower.

So maybe it wasn't a cure-all for *everything*, but generally speaking, there wasn't much that couldn't be solved with a good, long, melt-your-skin-off shower. It was where I did some of my best thinking. And jerking off.

"You've got to be kidding me."

Speaking of jerking off . . .

I smiled into the stream of water currently cascading down my face. I'd know that pissed-off drawl anywhere. I cleared the suds from my face before turning to the sprite that'd haunted my dreams as of late. My very explicit, sweat-inducing dreams.

"Oh, good, you're up." I leaned my head back into the spray. "That makes two of us," I added, wagging my brows suggestively.

I couldn't help myself. It didn't take much to get her riled up, and there was something sexy about the way she slipped deeper into her accent when I ticked her off. Or when her nostrils flared. *Great, now I'm turned on by her nostrils. What a freak.*

Blondie lifted her shoulders before letting out an almost pained breath. My eyes raked over her body, admiring the way her thick ass jiggled with every step. I didn't care if she noticed me staring. In fact, I hoped she did. She was wearing the same ridiculous (or ridiculously cute) robe as the first night we met, only this time, she'd tied her hair into a messy bun atop her head. What I wouldn't give to unravel it and knot my hands through it while she . . .

"You know what? No." She marched toward the stall on the opposite end, the one farthest from mine. "You are not ruining showers for me. If I want to shower at 10 p.m., then by golly, I'm gonna do it."

Well, shit. I'd expected her to turn tail and stomp off like she had during our last shower encounter. Instead, she flung open the curtain of the last stall.

"That one's out of order," I told her.

Her nostrils flared again. I half expected them to emit to flames. Maybe I'd gotten her wrong all along. She wasn't the damsel in distress; she was the fire-breathing dragon.

She tried the next stall, only to find that the water only ran cold.

"You did this, didn't you."

I scoffed. "How's that?"

"I don't know, but it's still your fault."

"That seems to be the case more often than not."

She trudged toward the next stall, the one directly across from me. "There, happy now?"

"Ecstatic."

She turned away from me, but not before glaring over her shoulder and scolding, "Just keep your eyes to yourself, okay?"

She still hated me. *Thank God.* It was a blessing in disguise if you asked me. I'd come to Rose City to get away from temptation. That didn't make it any less fun to flirt with danger.

"Whatever you say, blondie."

As much as I enjoyed teasing her, I didn't make a habit of spying on women while they showered. Unless they asked me to, of course. I turned away from her, wincing when the scalding spray hit my back. My traps were aching from that extra set of push-ups. Hopefully, the hot water would loosen them up. Otherwise, I might have to make a pitstop at the pharmacy in the morning to pick up some Icy Hot, and—

The sound of glass shattering followed by a loud, "Fuck!" snapped me out of my musings. I was already wrapping a towel

around my waist and rushing around the divider before she finished the expletive. I'd just tucked the edge of the towel into my
waist when I rounded the corner and flung open her curtain.

"What are you doing?!" She gasped.

"What happened?" I asked, ignoring her question and scanning her body for injuries. She'd only partially untied her robe,
and I did my best to ignore the way it parted, exposing her ample
cleavage. My eyes zeroed in on the blood pooling around the
drain. "What. Happened?" I asked again.

"It's my salt scrub," she said, her voice waning. "It's too dark
out. I thought I had a hold of it, but obviously I didn't and
I—oof!"

She half-squeaked, half-grunted when I scooped her up, one
hand under her bare legs, the other cradling her back, and carried her out of the stall.

"Put me down!" she cried. "You can't—" She lowered her
voice. Even in the limited light, I could tell she was blushing
again. "You're going to hurt yourself."

"Please," I said when her eyes met mine. "Don't insult me."

So, she didn't have a rail-thin, size-six body. *Who cares?* She
didn't realize she was talking to someone who benched three
hundred on a bad day and hip-thrust four hundred every day
that ended in y.

"Wrap your arms around my neck." When she opened her
mouth, no doubt ready to protest further, I tightened my grip
on her thighs. My hand was nearing dangerous territory, inches
away from her bare pussy. "Don't make me say it again."

She squeaked but did as I asked. Er, ordered. There wasn't a
peep the entire walk back to my trailer.

As much as I wanted to relish the feeling of her in my arms,
I was too caught up in medic mode. Even though I'd always
envisioned a career in pro baseball, my mom had encouraged me
to take some college courses as a backup. I'd chosen mostly bi-
ology and kinesiology-based classes—something I could apply

toward baseball—but I'd also become EMT-certified. It wasn't something I talked about with people, not even my teammates.

The sight of blood had never bothered me. It came with the territory of being a lifelong athlete. What did bother me was a woman in pain.

I carefully deposited Clarke on the lounge chair outside my trailer. Her muffled whimper had me dropping to my good knee in front of her. "Are you okay?"

"You really don't need to do this," she said, avoiding my gaze. "I'm sure it's just a small cut, nothing more."

"But are you okay?" With the tips of my fingers, I tilted her chin up until her eyes met mine, tears collecting in the corners. It didn't escape my notice that she hadn't answered my question the first time I'd asked. I got the feeling that people didn't ask about Clarke's well-being often.

Her lips parted. "Um, yes. I'm fine."

Her eyes had doubled in size when my gaze met hers, and I'd be lying if I said I didn't love it. She kept them on me even after I reluctantly withdrew my hand from her face and came to my feet. I pretended not to notice when her attention drifted downward. I couldn't blame her. She had a front-row seat to my towel-covered cock that was getting harder by the second.

Anything to distract her from crying, right?

I opened my door. "Stay here," I said gruffly over my shoulder before shutting it behind me. This woman had ruffled my feathers more than I cared to admit in the last few days. No way was I bringing her inside my place. Not that the trailer had the space for multiple bodies to begin with. It was a struggle fitting my 6'4" frame through the doorway.

It only took a minute to find my travel-sized first-aid kit, another to throw on a pair of sweatpants that did nothing to hide the state of my arousal, and one more to catch my breath. Once I had my heart rate (and erection) somewhat under control, I opened the door.

Surprisingly, I found her in the exact spot I'd left her.

Good girl.

She scrunched her face up. "You couldn't have put on a shirt, too?"

"Too distracting, blondie?"

"It's *Clarke*," she said through gritted teeth. Annoying her was officially my new, favorite hobby. She waved her hand toward my torso. "And yes. You know darn well it's distracting. You're . . ."

"Cut?" I offered, a shit-eating grin on my face. Being a smartass had always come naturally to me, but Clarke brought it out of me in spades. "Chiseled? Rock-hard?"

Even in the dim lighting, I could make out her pinkened cheeks.

"Impossible. You're impossible."

"Unfortunately, I think you might be right about that one, blondie." She raised a brow. "*Clarke,*" I amended.

It wasn't that I didn't like her name. I did. I hadn't been lying when I told her that it suited her. In a strange, "we call him Tiny even though he's the biggest dude on the team" kind of way. Despite the soft Southern belle demeanor, this woman had sharp edges and a wicked tongue.

I squatted in front of her, wincing when my quads objected. I must have audibly groaned because she asked, "You alright down there?"

"Fine," I grumbled. "Hang on a second."

I pulled the side table closer and took a seat, praying that the thing wouldn't break apart beneath me. Her brows furrowed when I lifted her bloody foot onto my lap.

"What do you think you're doing?" she asked, her eyes tinged with suspicion.

"Hold still and let the doctor look at your feet."

"You're not a doctor."

"Close enough."

"I wasn't born yesterday. I know you didn't finish college, so you couldn't have gone to medical—" Her lips turned upside down. I didn't miss the way her eyes widened. *Caught.*

"Ah, so you've done your research. What else did you find out about me?" She kept her mouth shut. "Shoe size? Hometown? Favorite food?"

I raised a brow, challenging her. And judging by the conflicting emotions washing over her face, I had a hunch she wouldn't be able to resist.

"Twelve. Long Beach, New York. Spaghetti."

I smiled. "Impressive. But your research left out the fact that I'm also a licensed EMT." Her eyes widened. "So, no, I might not be a doctor, but I do know what I'm doing."

She pursed her lips. *I can think of at least three better uses for those, blondie. No, wait, four.*

"I also know that you're getting blood on the chair, and I don't think June will appreciate the mess."

It might've been a low blow, but as expected, Clarke relinquished the last bit of control she'd been clinging to.

I'd never been a betting man per se, but reading your opponents, judging whether they were going to bunt the ball or steal a base or if they were just good at bluffing was a major part of baseball. From what I could tell, Clarke was a terrible bluff. She wore every emotion front and center, fully transparent. She was also far more concerned about what a virtual stranger *might* think about her staining a twenty-dollar lounge chair than any physical pain she was experiencing. Which was concerning to say the least.

I carefully gripped both her ankles and drew her toward me, sliding her down the chaise until she was practically flat on her back with her feet on my lap. Right on my dick.

She was patient while I inspected her feet and lower legs. Thankfully, her wounds were relatively superficial. Nothing some saline solution and gauze couldn't fix.

"What about you?" I asked her.

"What about me?"

"Doesn't seem fair that you know just about everything about me and I know nothing about you." I grinned wolfishly. "So, spill."

She hesitated.

"C'mon," I pressed. It wasn't like I was asking for her deepest, darkest secrets, though I wouldn't complain if she decided to unburden herself. What was holding her back?

"Seven. Mt. Pleasant. Tom Kha soup."

"What?" I looked up from her foot.

She lifted her head, smiling nervously. "Shoe size, hometown, favorite food. Seven, Mt. Pleasant, South Carolina, and Tom Kha soup."

"Tom Kha, really?" I had her pegged for more of a kale salad kind of gal.

"Minus the carrots. I hate carrots."

I nodded before turning back to her wounds. After that, we were quiet. In fact, I thought she might've dozed off until I felt her flinch when I rubbed Bactine over one particularly nasty scrape.

"It's okay," I whispered before blowing lightly on the spot.

"You better not kiss it, too."

"Well, now, that would be unsanitary," I said as I placed one last bandage on the top of her foot, just under her perfectly polished toes. She'd swapped out the red on her hands and toes for a bubblegum pink. Why did that not surprise me? "Besides, I prefer blowing."

"Okay!" She removed both her feet from my lap and jumped to stand, nearly plowing into a nearby plant stand. With a hand wrapped through her terry-cloth belt, I drew her toward me until her back was flush with my front, save for the robe and sweatpants between us. Disaster averted. Well, one disaster at least.

She gasped. There was no missing the thick cock that was doing its best to burrow through her robe and into her heat. "Careful, blondie."

She swallowed and looked back at me, her defiant gaze meeting mine. *Ooh, I knew there was a brat in there somewhere.* "Thanks," she whispered, her voice huskier than before, "*Sin.*"

And just like that, my dick deflated.

Her words numbed me more than an ice bath after a doubleheader. Painful, piercing shards embedded themselves under every inch of my skin until all that was left was nothing. Hollowness. I couldn't move. I couldn't breathe. All I *could* do was hope that my facial expression—the one I'd spent years honing specifically for blindsiding moments like this—wouldn't betray me.

At some point, I must've let her go, because it was only the slamming of her trailer's door that snapped me out of my impromptu paralysis. It was amazing how one word could hold such power over a person. Even more amazing when that one word was the person's name.

Sin.

Clarke

Four Weeks to Opening Day

"Okay, Peter." I pressed the record button for the umpteenth time today. "How do you take your coffee?"

"I don't think you're going to like my answer."

"There's no wrong answer," I encouraged. "This is just for fun. Something to share on the Roasters' Tiktok."

"Dude, we all did it," Jared Pink said from behind me. His voice was by far the most recognizable on the team . . . mostly because the guy rarely stopped talking.

"Yeah, it's no big deal," Roman told him.

I looked over my shoulder to find that a small crowd of players had gathered to watch our interview. Peter Diaz was one of the last players I needed to film. For someone who loved movies so much—at least, that was what the other players had told me—he sure hated being in front of the camera. The rascal had done his best to avoid me all day.

That was nothing compared to Soren. I hadn't heard a peep from him for going on a week now. Ever since our great shower debacle—the second one.

Ever since he'd almost kissed me. Ever since I'd (stupidly) almost let him.

What was it about that man that fried my brains like bacon grease? What was it about him that made me want to throw caution to the wind and smash my body against his, sweat and grass stains be damned?

"This guy giving you trouble?" Matty Miller asked. His unmistakable drawl made me smile. Leaving almost everything and everyone I knew behind had taken a toll on me these last few weeks. Regardless of how bad the circumstances were, making a clean getaway was easier said than done. Even though Matty and I had next to nothing in common except the region we came from, I still took comfort in the way he elongated his vowels.

"Nothing I can't handle," I told him.

I turned back toward Diaz. His arms were still crossed over his chest, his eyes combing the dirt on his shoes. He wasn't the first obstinate man I'd dealt with—he wasn't even the first one this week—but I knew exactly how to handle him. "I apologize, sugar," I said to him, turning my twang up to an eleven.

"I know this might seem silly to you, and you know what? It is. But you know who loves silly? Your fans. All two-hundred thousand of them." I racked my brain for the mental file on Peter Diaz. "They love it when you post movie reviews. They love your rock-climbing videos. Heck, your most-liked Tiktok is from that event y'all do every Monday night."

"By the way," Pink interrupted while also raising his hand. He did it for attention, not permission. "Who do I submit my movie requests to? Because my self-esteem drops dramatically whenever we watch a Chris Evans movie. The dude is too handsome."

Matty slugged Pink's arm. Everybody else ignored him entirely.

"My point is, your fans *love* the silly side of you." Diaz's arms lowered to his sides. It was time to play my final card. The queen of diamonds—baseball diamonds—if you will. "Besides, you know who else people adore because he's silly? Because he's so confidently sexy, but also hilarious? Chris Evans."

And just like a scoop of peanut brittle swirl by the beach on the Fourth of July, he melted.

"Roll the tape," Diaz said.

I smirked. If there was ever something to thank my mother for, this was it. *This* was my superpower. For years, I'd been well-schooled in the art of observance and manipulation, though Melanie Lynn Myers would *never* call it that. That'd be uncouth. You didn't give your opinion unless you were asked for it, and nobody asked for your opinion when you were Pat Myers's daughter. Not when they could go straight to the source.

So, I listened. I observed and absorbed. I studied social media profiles and wedding announcements. I attended ribbon cuttings and yacht parties. Most importantly, I built a metaphorical catalog of profiles—for every senator and socialite south of the Smoky Mountains—to have at my disposal, as needed. Every person had their stressors, their buttons just waiting to be pressed. *But* they also had to be pressed in specific ways.

It was clear to me that unlike many people, Diaz didn't operate out of fear or insecurities. No, his button was idolatry. And if he worshiped at the altar of Chris Evans—an excellent choice of a deity, if you asked me—then by golly, I was going to exploit that.

I lifted the phone and pressed the record button again. "Alright, Peter. How do you take your coffee?"

He smiled, wider than I'd even seen before. "To be honest, I take it right back to the counter because clearly, I've taken somebody else's drink." He shrugged. "I much prefer tea. Earl Grey, one cream, two sugars. I don't know, maybe I was British in my last life?"

His sideways smile perfectly punctuated the message, like icing on a cake. "Perfect!" I told him as soon as I turned off the camera. "Was that so bad?"

He kicked the dirt. "No," he said softly, like an embarrassed child.

"You've got to be kidding me."

My confidence waned. I'd know that voice anywhere. I pivoted to face my neighbor and just about swallowed my tongue when I spied him leaning against the left-field wall, his gloved hand tucked under his armpit, his hat backwards on his head. An image flashed quickly across my brain of him fucking me wearing nothing but that hat.

Gulp.

"That worked?" he asked, stalking toward us. "Diaz, she manipulated you."

"I didn't manipulate him," I said, looking up at him when we were nearly toe to toe. "I . . . encouraged him using the resources at my disposal."

"To get what you want."

"To get what I needed, yes."

"That's manipulation, blondie."

"Call it whatever you want, Sinclair."

His attention drifted to my suddenly dry lips. "Whatever. That's not going to work on me." I knew a challenge when I heard one.

"Good thing I didn't ask you," I countered. I knew he was right. There was no point trying to win him over with pleasantries or guilt. No, that wouldn't work for Soren Sinclair.

"I'm not doing it," he said defiantly.

"As I said, I didn't ask you to." From the intel I'd gathered, one thing was clear: Soren's biggest enemy was himself. *That* was his button. "I've got everything, and *everyone,* I need here." I turned on my heels. "Thank you, boys!" I called out over my shoulder.

It would take me thirty seconds to reach the dugout. I'd give him ten. *Nine, eight, seven, six—*

"Wait."

I smiled confidently and spun to face him. There was no prompting him when I lifted the phone and hit the record button again. He already knew the question.

"Americano. With milk," he said gruffly. "Soy."

I stopped the recording. "Thanks."

"What about you?"

"Sorry?"

He stepped closer. "Your coffee, blondie. How do you take it?"

I swallowed. There he went again, challenging me when I had the upper hand for once. This was a recipe for disaster.

"Upside-down, quad-shot caramel macchiato," I told him. Regardless of how much he annoyed me, it would be rude not to answer his question.

He wrinkled his brow. "And that's . . . got coffee in it?"

I rolled my eyes and walked away. He was either clueless or purposefully making fun of me, but I didn't care to find out which. What was it about society looking down on anything that gave women joy? Movies, music, coffee beverages. Sex.

In any case, I was riding the high of a successful first couple of weeks in the workforce, and I wasn't going to let anybody ruin it. Last of all Soren Sinclair.

Later that day, I found an aluminum, reusable tumbler with the Roasters logo on it. The sweet smell of caramel wafted through the lid. "Aw, you didn't have to do this," I said to Dani.

She smirked knowingly. "I didn't."

Tanya, our social media intern, had already gone home for the day. And only one other person knew my coffee order, which meant . . .

Damn him.

Soren Sinclair had found *my* button.

"You see Brogan approach the wall behind the tavern. Only, it isn't a normal wall. After a few whispered words, the ivy pulls away from the bricks and they begin to separate. A section disappears, leaving behind an opening, a doorway into the unknown. Brogan looks around before disappearing through the space, which closes almost immediately behind him. You turn to each other, stunned, confused, and say—"

"Are we going to ignore the fact that he bought you coffee?" June squealed, practically bouncing in her seat.

Nessa sighed. This wasn't the first time she'd been interrupted tonight with talk of my and Soren's latest interaction. It had happened when we crossed the haunted bridge and then again when we followed Brogan, the priest's guard, to the tavern.

As promised, I had been inducted to Rose City's "most secret and sacred society," otherwise known as *The Salem Bitch Trials*, June and Nessa's Dungeons & Dragons game. *Campaign*, I mentally corrected myself, *not game.*

I hadn't known what to expect when they'd first invited me to join. Sure, I'd heard of Dungeons & Dragons, but I'd always assumed—naively so apparently—that it was a game meant for teenage boys, not millennial women. Add that to the growing list of things I'd mistakenly prejudged over the years.

"Not to interrupt you, *mi amor*," Jo said, weighing in. Like me, Jo was a transplant to Rose City. He'd moved here from Puerto Rico two years ago, as part of the new business initiative, to open his bakery, Would Smell as Sweet. The branding in this town was unmatched. Seriously, between Bed of Roses, Thorn Tavern, and Would Smell as Sweet, I had some competition cut out for me. "I don't think any of us are going to be able to concentrate until we get through the latest *Cloren* drama."

My brows furrowed. "Cloren?"

"Your couple name."

Oh, for heaven's sake.

My stomach churned. I suddenly regretted that second Tequila Sunrise.

"Personally, I'm kind of partial to *Saren*," June said.

"Isn't that a chemical weapon or something?" Jo asked.

"Enough!"

Nessa's frustration echoed through the bar's private event space. The irony of an erotic bookstore owner being our campaign's "dungeon master" wasn't lost on me.

"We're never going to get through this if we don't focus."

"You're right," June told her. At the same time, Jo said, "*Perdón.*"

We all sat in silence after that. A silence that lasted approximately five seconds until—

"But it has to mean something!" June cried out. Nessa buried her head in her hands. "First, he carries you to safety—"

"He carried me out of the shower."

"Then he tends to your wounds—"

"A couple of Band-Aids. That's it." Judging by her theatrics, you'd think June was the one penning and selling romance novels.

"You almost kiss, and now he's buttering you up with your favorite coffee. What's it all mean?"

"Clarity check," Nessa said, peeling back her hands. Our matching looks of confusion made her add, "You want to talk about it, you roll for it." She held up the twenty-sided die. "Roll for a clarity check."

June and Jo both rolled their respective dice.

"Seven," Jo whined.

"Nat twenty," June said, pumping her fist in the air. Nothing beat a natural, or *nat* twenty.

"Fine," Nessa grumbled. "You have two minutes to gossip about Clarke's sexy neighbor."

"There's nothing to gossip about," I protested.

"He clearly likes you." June smiled wide, cupping the mulled wine in front of her.

"He does not," I said emphatically.

"He doesn't *want* to, but he does. You have that in common."

My cheeks warmed, and I couldn't even blame that on the alcohol. Dang it, she was right. At least about me. I didn't want to like Soren, and truly, I didn't know if like was the right word. Nonetheless, I was drawn to him. Reluctantly so, but still.

"It doesn't matter," I told them. "I just got out of a relationship. The last thing I'm looking for is something as crude and complicated as Soren Sinclair."

"I don't know," June said. "Crude and complicated sounds pretty good to me."

"One minute," Nessa warned.

"*Chica,* it's only complicated if you make it complicated."

My head swiveled to Jo. "What do you mean?"

"Sex is simple," he told me, very matter-of-fact. "Feelings are complicated."

My eyes widened. "Surely, you're not suggesting I—"

"Suck his baseballs and ride his rock-hard bat until you explode like the pop of a mitt?" Nessa's suggestion shocked us all into silence. "Yes, that's exactly what June's suggesting."

"Wow." June's breath whooshed out of her. "That was graphic."

Nessa scrunched her lips together. "Look," she said, directing her words to me, "there's nothing wrong with a mutually agreed upon fling."

"All-out fuck fest," June amended.

"Whatever you want to call it. You're both recently single, you clearly have chemistry, and there's no rule prohibiting the two of you from exploring that."

"With your bodies." June wagged her brows.

"If you want to fuck to his brains out, then do it. Nobody's stopping you." Nessa sat back in her seat, composing herself. "Now, do you want to cast a spell or not?"

And just like that, we were back to the game, er, campaign. Physically, at least. My mind was on other things. They were right. Despite what Mama might say, there was nothing wrong with pursuing a strictly physical relationship with Soren. We were both attracted to each other, that much was clear. We were both unattached. We'd be seeing a lot more of each other in the coming weeks, when we all headed to Arizona for Spring Training. Why shouldn't we enjoy ourselves?

Scratch that.

Why shouldn't *I* enjoy *myself* for once?

I swallowed my nerves before downing the last of my drink. I swallowed that, too. "Fuck it," I said, louder than before. June and Nessa's eyes widened. The fact that I'd said the expletive aloud—probably for the first time in my life—didn't escape my notice. "Let's cast a spell."

"Huzzah," they both squealed.

I channeled that same energy for the next few hours as my character, Heralda the hedge witch, navigated the ups and downs of East Salem. I channeled it even when together, we faced our first fictional foe, a demon unleashed from the gates of hell by Brogan and his army.

And I channeled it later, after we'd finished playing for the night, all the way back to Bed of Roses.

I knocked on the door, the sound reverberating through the otherwise quiet campsite. When he swung it open, I didn't expect to find him clad only in a towel, water droplets clinging to his bare chest.

"Did you come for the show, blondie?"

He grinned wickedly. I'd been caught, yet again, ogling his well-defined body—a stark contrast to Walden's limp figure. Not that there was anything wrong with a slimmer man. On the contrary, I'd always been attracted to men with "gamer boy" bodies, as Viv called it. But Walden's body insecurities had rivaled those of most nineteen-year-old coeds. Whenever we'd gone to luncheons or fundraisers, it had always looked like he was playing dress-up, trying to fill out his daddy's suit rather than one made for his smaller frame.

Something told me that Soren only wore custom.

He'd have to with a body like that, one practically sculpted from marble. That chest. The deep V, like an arrow pointing straight toward his . . .

"Keep staring like that and it might just do a trick."

My eyes snapped up to meet his. And in a moment of pure, unadulterated confidence, I asked, "Is that a promise?"

His nostrils flared.

Blame it on the spell. Blame it on the tequila. Blame it on the fact that I hadn't had sex in nearly six months—and I hadn't had *good* sex in twenty-seven years. Whatever the reason, this midnight train had already left the station, passed Georgia, and was rambling full speed ahead toward *Sin.*

Rather than give him the time to come up with some smartass response—and before I lost my momentary burst of sexual prowess—I took the two remaining strides across the threshold, threw my arms around his neck, and yanked his lips down to meet mine.

The moment our mouths met, everything stopped.

If I'd known a kiss was all it took to shut Soren "Sin" Sinclair up, I might've done it sooner.

Soren

I'm kissing Clarke Myers. I'm kissing Clarke Myers.

Correction, Clarke Myers was kissing me. And it was even better than I had imagined.

Not that I'd spent *a lot* of time imagining this moment. Oh, who was I kidding? I had been fantasizing about Clarke's lips on mine since we met. And reality fucking kicked my fantasy's ass.

Her hands drifted to my shoulders before tracing a downward path over my torso. Down farther still. A shiver rippled through me when her nails scratched at each of my abs. Methodically, almost as if . . .

My god, she's counting them.

Things were moving dangerously fast. She was already closing in on my throbbing cock—only two abs left to go—and we hadn't even made it to the bedroom. Then again, the bedroom wasn't so much of a bedroom as it was a double bed tucked behind the kitchenette.

Airstreams weren't exactly made for rollicking sexploits.

Even though I knew I'd probably regret it later, I dragged my lips away from hers and caught both her hands up in one of mine. "What are we doing, blondie?" I pressed her hands against the wall above her head.

Her eyes popped open at the sound of my strangled voice. "Isn't it obvious?"

She anchored her pelvis forward until she was practically riding my bare thigh. *Fuck.* I was suddenly thankful I hadn't put on sweats after my shower because I could feel her heat through the thin barrier of her panties. The flimsy material of her dress did nothing to hide it.

"I'm gonna need your words, sweetheart. How far do you want to take this?" I buried my face in her neck, dotting a trail of kisses from ear to collarbone. My hand snuck down her spine. "What do you want?" I asked when I reached the hem of her dress. *Inches from heaven.*

"Um . . ."

I reluctantly pulled away when she trailed off. After one more delicious whiff of her hair, that was. *Fucking peaches.*

"Clarke." She squirmed beneath my penetrating gaze. "What do you want?"

She swallowed. "I don't know."

Well, shit.

I loosened my hold on her wrists immediately. When I stepped away from her, she followed, as though her body were drawn to mine by some magnetic pull.

I reversed our positions, leaning back against the wall and drawing her hands into mine. That was the safest option, one where her hands couldn't wander up and down my naked torso. The woman had arms like a goddamn octopus.

"What's going on, blondie?"

Her eyes avoided mine. I dragged a finger across her jaw, torturously slow, until finally, she had to tilt her head back to look up at me. My eyes searched her face. There wasn't a trace of the confident sex vixen who had knocked on my door just moments ago. No, this was a side of Clarke I hadn't seen before. One that I didn't care to either. Hurt, embarrassed, and, worst of all, afraid. *Of me?* The thought hit me harder than a punch to the gut.

"Did somebody . . ." I swallowed, preparing to ask the question that no man ever wanted to ask any woman. "Did somebody hurt you?"

I was already calculating all the ways to fuck this dude up—whoever he was, wherever he was—without damaging my hands before Spring Training.

"Not in the way you think." She spoke softly, barely louder than a whisper.

"I'm gonna need more than that."

She bit her lip and shook her head, blinking away the tears that were already brimming in her eyes. "Let's just say that up until about a month ago, I was engaged to a . . . not-so-great guy. Who said a lot of not-so-great things to me."

I nodded, blowing out a breath. "Go on."

"He was never really interested in *me*. Just my family's name and everything that came with it." My confusion must have been evident, because she added, "Myers, as in Myers Hotel Group."

Sweet fuck. Myers Hotel Group was one of the biggest luxury hotel franchises on the East Coast. Clarke was a freaking heiress.

At least I knew she wasn't a ball girl—a term often used to refer to women who chased after baseball players. She wasn't going to be swayed by status or checkbook. Hell her bank account probably rivaled the team's owners'.

"I broke off our engagement when I found out he cheated on me. Apparently, I wasn't . . . enough for him"

Oh, hell no. "Blondie—"

"It's fine! I'm sorry. I don't know what I was thinking coming over here and mauling you like this." She pulled away, brushing off my hold. "I thought that you might, um . . . That we might . . . Because I really do . . ."

I tried not to smile. She made it impossible to resist her, even when she was flustered and stuttering her words. "I hope the ends of those sentences are good."

Her cheeks flushed. I longed to see that shade of blush color her freshly spanked ass. Right before I bent her over and fucked it. Would she let me do that?

Would she trust me to?

"I should go."

She turned toward the door, ready to run. What would it take to show her that I wanted to be the one she ran to, not away from?

Where the fuck did that come from?

One kiss and I was spiraling down a vortex of dangerous thoughts. I needed to get my shit together.

Before she made it more than a step or two, I snaked my hand out to catch hers. "Come back when you know."

"Huh?"

"Come back when you know what you want from me."

I lifted away from the wall and bent down until we were eye to eye. With her hand still in mine, I lowered my lips until they were inches from hers. Close enough to feel her sharp exhalation of breath while still maintaining the space between us.

"And please, let me give it to you."

This wasn't a kiss; it was a promise. And while Clarke might not know it yet, I delivered on all my promises.

Sleep was impossible after that.

What was the point of sleeping, of dreaming, when the reality of kissing Clarke Myers far outweighed my fantasies?

Even now, hours after she'd left my trailer, hours after I'd watched her walk back to her own—because Rose City might be a small town, but shitty things happened to women at night in small towns, too—I was still trying to wrap my head around what had transpired.

The woman I'd been lusting after for weeks—the same woman who lived no more than a stone's throw away—had been lusting after me, too.

She'd kissed me. *Fuck.*

I'd kissed her back. *Double fuck.*

I'd also ended our kiss. *Fucking idiot.*

A war was waging between my brain and body, and judging by the way my dick was throbbing against my thigh, it was safe to say my brain was losing. More concerningly, my heart didn't know which side to join. Then again, it was a losing battle either way.

Despite what my fans, friends, and even family assumed, I hadn't been with anybody in nearly six months. Hell, I hadn't *seen* a woman's naked body (beyond my phone screen) for almost twice that. That was the only way to explain my intense, physical reaction to Clarke's kiss.

A kiss that shouldn't have made my dick harder than granite. I was thirty-four, for fuck's sake.

Part of me was pissed at her for reducing me down to a grunting Neanderthal. But that paled in comparison to the anger I felt toward myself for missing the signs that beneath that sweeter-than-sweet tea persona, Clarke was hurting. Maybe we had more in common than I'd originally thought.

I'd done a little research of my own after she left. About her, her family, the piece of shit she'd been engaged to who had clearly done a number on her. I wasn't the only one who had had my fair share of scrutiny from the press.

By the looks of it, Clarke had been living under a microscope even longer than I had.

I shouldn't have pushed her like that, shouldn't have teased her. Maybe if I had I known more about her past . . .

Who was I kidding? I still would've gone for it, greedy bastard that I was.

I snaked a hand under the band of my briefs and palmed my throbbing cock, cursing under my breath. The calluses on my palms didn't stop me from imagining a smoother set of hands wrapped around me, fisting my cock up and down. Squeezing me tightly, to the point where pleasure met pain.

Fuck.

I hadn't jerked off more than once a day since I was a horny teenager. Not until I met Clarke. It was easy, too easy, to close my eyes and succumb to the scene I'd concocted weeks ago. There had been many Clarke fantasies as of late, but this was by far my favorite—satisfaction guaranteed, fast and efficient release.

I pictured her on her knees—in the locker room, in the shower, wherever—one hand stroking my cock while the other fingered her clit. I'd tell her to tease herself, but not enough to make herself come. No, the first time she came, it would be with my tongue buried in her pussy and my name on her lips.

Her eyes would peer up at me. For approval, maybe. Or instruction. And as I promised her tonight, I'd be happy to give her either.

I'd be happy to give her everything.

That was a dangerous thought.

My abs contracted as I pumped my hand faster, dragging a pearl of precum down my shaft.

I imagined her bare, her perfect, heavy breasts pushed together by the press of her arms. They'd bounce wildly with each pump of my cock, each ragged exhale of breath as she rode her own hand. Would she let me fuck those, too? I could die a happy man if Clarke Myers let me fuck her tits.

That was for another day. For now, her hands would do.

And her mouth.

My balls pulled tight when I envisioned my hands winding through the soft strands of her hair, tugging her head back tight enough to make her gasp, but not rough. Because Clarke deserved nothing short of worship. Her eyes would darken when

I'd tell her to put me in her mouth, then water as she worked herself up and down my cock until it nudged the back of her throat. Fuck, just the thought of her throat constricting around my cock had me practically seeing stars.

I fucked my hand mercilessly, wishing it were her mouth, her pussy. *Her pert, rounded ass.* Each thought pushed me closer to release.

What would she do, I wondered, if I pulled her to her feet and painted her lips with her own pussy juices before licking them clean? How about if I bent her over and fucked her from behind, one hand wrapped around her throat, the other strumming her clit like Prince's guitar?

I wanted to claim her.

To mark her.

To make sure she felt me between her thighs long after we said goodbye. And goodbye was inevitable.

But not before I made her mine.

Blistering heat pooled at the base of my spine just before my release erupted across my stomach and chest.

Sometime later, after I caught my breath and washed the cum off myself, a staggering thought crossed my mind. For the first time, it wasn't the vision of Clarke on her knees, taking my cock that had made me come. It wasn't the memory of our kiss nor the laundry list of fantasies I'd scripted for us. No, it was something else entirely, something new . . .

It was the idea of making her mine.

Clarke

"What do you want, Clarke?"

Soren's words had played on repeat in my mind for the last forty-eight hours. The question itself was simple enough. Five words, five syllables. Something even a child could understand and, dare I say, answer as well.

But not me. No, not this fully-grown woman.

I could detail the full history of the house of Versace and list the name, age, and marital status of every hotel mogul in the country, but I was still struggling to answer Soren's question. The same question that Trixie had asked just last month at Waffle House.

I'd had an entire month to think it over and still nothing.

Well, not nothing. Progress had been made in that department, but as it turned out, I'd spent a lot more time thinking about what I *didn't* want these last few weeks instead of what I *did*.

I twisted the knob and pushed the door open to Smutty Buddies. I smiled when I spotted Nessa behind the counter at the back, chewing on her drink straw, fully engrossed in whatever book she was reading. I doubted she would've noticed me had the bell over the door not chimed.

"Well, hello stranger!" She dogeared her book and jumped to her feet. I made a mental note to ask her what size shoe she wore because dang it, her floral-printed ankle boots were to die for. "Fancy seeing you here."

"I promise I haven't been avoiding y'all. We leave for Spring Training next week and there's still so much to do."

When I'd accepted the job with the Roasters, nobody had thought to mention the prospect of spending two days on a bus with thirty guys. I wondered why.

"Did you come to stock up on reading?"

"Kind of." She lifted her brows, waiting. "Maybe?"

I bit down my lip, a chronic habit of mine that Mama had tried—and failed—to correct for years. *Better that than your nails, I suppose,* she would say to me.

I sucked in a breath and promptly word-vomited all over my new friend. "Soren and I kissed the other night after we cast a spell, and by that I mean that *I* kissed him. Although he definitely kissed me back. He *more* than kissed me back. And I thought we were going to do a whole lot more than that, only he asked me what I wanted, and I didn't know what to tell him because no man has ever asked me what I wanted . . . *that* way. Or in any way, for that matter. Not that there have been many men. Just the one. Well, two, if you count my senior prom date, although we never went beyond third base."

Nessa blinked. She opened her mouth then shut it again.

Heavens, I broke her.

Just as my breathing finally returned to normal, she asked, "You kissed Soren Sinclair?"

I nodded. "I did."

"And he kissed you back?"

"That's right."

"But things were moving a little quickly, so he stopped to ask you what you wanted?"

"That's the long and short of it."

"But you didn't know what you wanted?" I swallowed and shook my head. She must have recognized the anguish on my face because she added, "You still don't know what you want."

It didn't escape me that this time, she wasn't asking. I nodded again. The first step was admitting you had a problem, right?

"Okay." A slow grin spread across her face. "Okay!" she repeated, this time with a little more pep in her step. I didn't know whether to love or fear the glint in her eyes.

Nessa placed her hand on my shoulder and walked me over to a colorful table display. "Here's what we're going to do," she said. "I am going to load you up."

"With what?"

"With research." She gestured at the books piled high in front of us, a sea of pinks, blues, blacks, and reds. Many of the covers featured illustrated representations of the stories' characters—of every age, size, and ethnicity—while others showcased a male model's chiseled abs.

Soren could model for book covers.

I regretted the thought even as it crossed my mind.

"I don't understand. How . . ."

"Look," Nessa started. "You don't have a lot of experience, and that's nothing to be ashamed of. Some people are perfectly happy to go their entire lives without a romantic or sexual relationship, and that's fine . . . for them. But I think there's something brewing between you and Mr. Sin. And I think you owe it yourself to explore that. But first . . ."

She trailed off as she placed a book in my hands. I almost choked when I read the title. "*Puck Me, Daddies.*"

"That's a 'why choose' romance. One woman, three hockey players." She wagged her brows. Before I could protest, she handed me another.

"*The Bear Shifter Next Door*?"

"There's a great oral scene in that one where he eats her out from behind."

My cheeks warmed. I resisted the urge to look around and make sure nobody else heard us talking about this. "I'm not sure what I'm supposed to take away from . . . bears."

"Ideas, Clarke." She winked. "You might not like all of them. Hell, there might be some things in here that ick you out. But just remember, your yuck is another person's yum."

I couldn't contain my giggle. I'd just never heard it put quite so bluntly before. It was refreshing, knowing women who spoke so openly and positively about sexuality.

"Okay."

"Consider these guidebooks for your journey to sexual enlightenment."

"Got it, Yoda."

"Hey," she said, playfully chastising me. "It's not easy being green."

And so, it went on. For nearly thirty minutes, Nessa led me around the store, adding book after book to the stack in my arms. When it was taller than my head, I set it down by the register, and we started again.

Paranormal romance. Prince in disguise. Marriage of convenience. That one hit a little too close to home and I told her so.

"No problem, how about enemies to lovers?" she asked, swapping one book out for another without missing a beat.

And with every recommendation, Nessa bookmarked particular pages, scenes, and/or chapters she thought I should read. Passages she hoped would give me a little more clarity as to what I might want out of my sexual relationship with Soren . . . er, anybody.

"Not to rush you, Nessa, but my lunch break ends in ten minutes."

"Got it."

As we carried our haul to the register, a new concern arose. "I have to be honest," I told her. "I can't afford all of this."

I'd only received my first paycheck last week, and though I wouldn't be living off Ramen noodles anytime soon, I certainly couldn't afford two dozen new books.

"It's alright," she said. "Consider these a loan."

"You don't have to do that."

"It's fine." She smiled as she bagged up the books. "Besides, what's the point of having a smut peddling friend if they don't share it with you?"

Friend.

I blinked back the moisture in my eyes and took the bags from her. Lord, maybe I needed to start using that gym membership that came with the job. Who knew paper weighed this much?

"One more thing." She'd already given me nearly two-hundred dollars' worth of merchandise. What more could there be? "I think you should make a list."

My brows scrunched together. "A list of what?"

They lifted clean off my forehead when she answered, "Of all the things you want him to do to you. To do with you." She leaned over the register, resting her head in her hand as if this were some casual conversation between clerk and customer, when it was anything but. "That way," she said, smiling confidently, "the next time he asks you what you want, and there will be a next time, you know exactly what to tell him."

Little did Nessa know that was all the motivation I needed. Because if there were two things I knew how to do—and dammit, I knew how to do them well—they were research and list making. In that order.

Which meant I had some reading to do.

Soren

"Tucker, you should be hauling ass the second that batter shows bunt. Run it again." Coach Ward cupped his hands around his mouth. "And if Wu doesn't back up first this time, we're all doing stadium stairs."

I could practically hear our right fielder mumbling obscenities under his breath all the way in the outfield. Ward was right, though. Wu was a great batter and a decent fielder, but he slacked at backing-up first on the bunt.

Ward kicked the dirt with his toes and signed to Bennett to go again. We had an ASL interpreter on staff, but Ward was adamant that all of us know some rudimentary sign language to communicate with our catcher. That included him, too. Ward intimidated the hell out of me, but I'd give the guy credit for practicing what he preached. Something told me that when he said *we'd* all be doing stadium stairs if Wu fucked up again, that included him, too.

He stepped closer to my bag. It was unnerving having him mere feet away from third base. Call me paranoid, but it felt like he was always watching me, judging me. At least this time, I wasn't the one getting my ass chewed out at practice. How refreshing.

"You should be on him more."

I knew it was too good to be true. I turned to him over my shoulder. "Sorry?"

"Wu. You should be on him when he fucks up." The lens of his glasses did nothing to dull his penetrating stare. "You knew he wasn't where he needed to be."

It wasn't a question, so I didn't bother coming up with an answer.

"That's part of being a team. A well-oiled machine." He crossed his arms over his chest. "When one part fails, the others work overtime to make up for it. Better to fix it now then wait for the implosion."

Damn. The man certainly knew his way around a metaphor. I wasn't convinced that Ward, himself, wasn't a machine. Between his constant grimace and lack of blinking, the guy had cyborg written all over him.

"Speak up," he said. "That's what leaders do."

There was a bad idea if I ever heard one.

"No offense, coach, but you've got the wrong guy. I'm not exactly leader material."

I could tell by his silence that that wasn't the answer he wanted. Disappointing others, especially my coaches, was a feeling I knew well. He popped another handful of sunflower seeds into his mouth. Sucking, chewing, all without taking his eyes off me. When he spat them out, he did so with grace and precision, landing them millimeters from my feet. Fuck, Ward's legacy was intimidating enough. I didn't need him using me for target practice.

When I finally tilted my cap down to cover my eyes—and block out his stare—he shouted, "Again."

Wu and Tucker both hauled ass after that. We all did.

Later, while the guys wrapped up batting, I ditched out early to get my fingers taped. I was halfway down the tunnel to the locker room when she appeared. Like a shadow from the mist—or maybe the steam room—a siren calling to me. The lighting in the tunnel was shit, but I didn't need it to know it was Clarke. I'd memorized every line, dip, and curve of her body weeks ago.

We moved in slow motion. At least, that was what it felt like, her magnetic pull drawing me closer until we were nearly face-to-face.

God, that lipstick.

If there was one thing I'd learned about Clarke, it was that she wore her lipstick like a coat of armor. Painted to perfection, ready for battle. And oh, the shades. She had more than enough to wear a different one every day if she wanted. I didn't know the actual names for them, so I'd given them my own. There was Bubblegum Pink, the lightest of her shades. Pink Lemonade was a little bit darker but still light enough that it probably wouldn't leave a ring around a glass. Or something else.

Pink was clearly Clarke's comfort zone, though she dabbled in darker neutrals from time to time. A Caramel Kiss here, a Cookie Crisp there, both equally delicious. But none of them compared to Cherry Red. Roasters Red. My personal favorite and hers too, based on how often she wore it.

It was Clarke's power color.

It was also the color I pictured staining the base of my cock after fucking her mouth. She could leave her mark on me any day of the week.

This wasn't the first time we'd seen each other since the night we kissed. We'd made pleasantries on the field and in the locker room. I'd watched her come and go from her trailer more than once, usually with June by her side or the woman who owned the bookstore. Come to think of it, she'd been doing a lot of reading lately. It seemed like every time I saw her, she had a book in her hand.

"Soren," she said coldly.

I nodded. "Clarke."

"Got a minute?"

Every rational part of my being said I should keep moving. That I should make up some excuse and walk away. Unfortunately, "rationality" had no place when it came to my feelings for Clarke Myers.

"That depends."

"On what?"

"Is this about business or pleasure?"

My lips kicked up when she sucked in a breath.

"It's about the other night."

My smile grew. "So, pleasure, then?"

"I think we should talk about it."

"Talk about what exactly?"

"You know what."

I spun the cap on my head until the brim faced away from her. I needed to see her, needed her to see me when I said this.

"Maybe about how wet you were for me. So wet that I could feel you through that innocent floral skirt."

Her eyes widened, darting around the tunnel.

"Don't be embarrassed," I told her. "I loved it. I think you did, too."

She licked her lips, painting them with moisture. As if it had a mind of its own, my hand reached forward, tucking a wayward curl behind her ear before trailing it down her neck. Her pulse thumped wildly against my fingers, matching the beat of my heart. It was reassuring to know that I wasn't the only one affected.

"Or maybe," I said, lowering my voice, "you want to talk about how after you left, I fucked my hand until I came." I softly squeezed her throat, carefully gauging her face for any signs of distress. There weren't any. Only longing, pleasure. A silent plea for more.

"And do you know what I thought about, blondie?" She shook her head. Barely. That was all she could manage with my hand holding her in place. "I thought about you. About us. How I wished it were your hands, your pussy wrapped around me. Squeezing me tight just like this." She shivered when my hand tightened around her throat. "Is that what you want to talk about, blondie?"

Fuck, I love this.

The way her throat vibrated against my hand when she swallowed. The way her lashes drifted shut as I lowered my head. I couldn't believe this was happening again. I couldn't—

A sudden clanging had us both nearly jumping out of our skin. This wasn't a position either of us wanted to be caught in. Thankfully, it wasn't the sound of some surprise interloper, but rather a fallen clipboard.

When she wordlessly knelt to gather her papers, I came back into myself. It only took a second for me to realize just how inappropriate it was to be having this discussion in the tunnel to the locker room of all places. Not only that, but I'd had my hand wrapped around her throat like a fucking serial killer. If that didn't have HR disaster written all over it, I don't know what did.

"Fuck, I'm sorry." I sighed, righting my hat back into place. "I shouldn't have said that."

I bent down to help her retrieve the fallen papers, then immediately regretted it when both of my knees cracked. *Fuck, when did I get so old?*

"No, it's okay." Clearly, it was anything but. She was nearly out of breath.

That makes two of us, blondie.

"No, it isn't. You don't deserve that." I picked up what I could reach. "Not that I didn't mean what I said, but this isn't exactly the time and place to—"

My eyes stopped on a piece of pink legal pad paper, zeroing in on a particularly heart-stopping line.

7. Tie me to the bed and blindfold me.

"What the fuck is this?"

I almost couldn't believe the animalistic growl that came out of my own mouth. Judging by the widening of Clarke's eyes, she couldn't either.

"Oh, that's, um—"

"Clarke." My eyes skimmed the paper in front of me. *Holy fuck.* I asked her again, "What. Is. This?"

"I made a list."

Boy, did she ever. I scoured her checklist.

1. Do it with the lights on.
2. Somewhere we could get caught.
3. Use my vibrator on me.
4. Fuck my face.

"You asked me what I wanted."

"Excuse me?" I asked without looking up. Jesus fucking Christ, there were sixteen things here. Not only that, but she'd titled the thing like a fucking school essay. *Clarke's Sex List.*

"The other night. You told me to figure out what I wanted." She shrugged. "So, I did."

Of course you did.

It all made sense now. Clarke wasn't a fly by the seat of your pants kind of gal. No, she was organized. She made lists and plans and rules. Fuck, I bet she loved rules.

"What am I supposed to do with this?" I asked, holding up the piece of paper.

She snatched the list out of my hands. Not that I needed it. The words on the page were forever tattooed on my brain. I'd be fantasizing about number twelve for weeks to come.

"Give me that."

"What were you thinking carrying that around at work? What if one of the guys saw it?" A sudden thought stopped me cold. "Unless that's what you wanted."

"Don't be ridiculous," she said defensively. "I made it for you, you . . . jackass."

I didn't know which of us was more surprised by her outburst. She looked like a child who'd been caught sneaking sweets from the cookie jar.

"Feel better?"

"Hardly."

I tilted her chin up until her eyes met mine. "About this list. As much as I would love to do . . . that to you, *with* you, do you really think it's a good idea?" Her expression soured. "What you're talking about here is more than a random one-night stand. This is, um, detailed."

Fucking idiot.

I was sure I'd regret this in the morning. Or, more likely, ten minutes from now. Clarke deserved more than the night or two of passion I was prepared to offer her. It was better to cut our losses now, lest we both get burned.

"Fine," she grumbled. "Your loss."

She turned on her heels to strut back down the tunnel. Watching Clarke walk away had become my favorite hobby as of late. I was so entranced by the sway of her hips, by the embroidered flowers on the back pockets of the denim that cupped her ass like a second skin that her words barely registered.

"What's that supposed to mean?"

"Exactly what it sounds like."

Just as she reached the end of the tunnel, she flipped her hair effortlessly over her shoulder, a devilish glint in her eyes. "I'm going clubbing tonight in Portland."

"Clubbing? You?"

I could practically see the steam coming out of her ears. "That's right, Sinclair. If you won't give me what I want, I'll find somebody else who will."

My vision blurred. I suddenly understood why they called it "tunnel vision." Here I was, stranded in the tunnel between the clubhouse and dugout, staring at a vision of Clarke messing around with some random fuckhead from the city.

And I didn't like it. I didn't like it one bit.

"Hold up, Sinclair."

Roman clapped my shoulder, jolting me out of my fog. The rest of the team trudged in from the field. All except Pink, whose incessant yammering echoed through the tunnel.

When I turned back, she was gone. Not a trace of her, minus the lingering scent of peaches. *That fucking smell.* It haunted my dreams at night. Literally. Bennett, Matty, and I had had this conversation last week. Bennett dreamt without sound, Matty dreamt in black and white, and me, I dreamt of smells.

Freshly mowed grass. My mom's homemade chicken parm. Clarke's peaches and cream shampoo.

"You good man?"

"Yeah," I groused, running a hand across the back of my neck to work out the kinks. Fat chance. My kink was Clarke Myers.

I followed Nuñez into the locker room.

"My lats are killing me," Tuck whined, already tugging his shirt over his head. "Seriously, I hope none of you fuckers plan on showering because I'm going to stand under the spray for the next hour."

"All yours." Bennett smiled wolfishly. "I've got plans elsewhere tonight. No point in showering."

Roman snorted. The rest of the guys ribbed him.

While Pink showed off his best *Magic Mike* moves and the rest of the guys groaned because, well, we weren't all twenty-three anymore, I considered my next move. I was thirty-four years old, well past the game-playing stage of my life. I didn't gamble, didn't play pickup basketball like some of the guys. Hell, the only games I enjoyed playing were *Super Mario,* America's national pastime, and the occasional round of mini golf with my oldest sister's kids. They kicked my ass every time.

This back-and-forth with Clarke needed to end, and it wasn't going to with her coming on some other guy's dick. Not unless she had a threesome on that list of hers, and even then, it would be a hard sell. I'd never been good at sharing. Youngest child syndrome.

I wanted her all to myself.

If she wanted to check off some kind of fuck-it list, then she was going to do it with me and only me.

"If you won't give me what I want, then I'll find somebody else who will."

Oh, I'd give her what she wanted, and she'd love it. We both would, I had no doubt. But giving her what she wanted wasn't enough for me.

I was going to give her what she needed, too.

Even if she didn't know it yet.

I stood abruptly from the bench, my thighs protesting.

"How about you, Sinclair?" Roman asked. "You down for a beer at my place?

"No. We're going out."

The team stared back at me, their faces washed with equal parts surprise and confusion. It wasn't any secret that I preferred to keep my private life just that, private. A movie or beer at Roman's place was one thing, but a night out in Portland's newest club was another.

"Say that again," Matty drawled.

"We're going out," I repeated. "To a club in Portland."

"For reals?" Pink asked, his eyes lighting up like a kid in a candy shop. One where the sweets and treats came in blonde and brunette. So long as he kept his distance from one specific honey-voiced blonde . . .

I bet she tastes like honey, too.

Typically, I avoided sweets, but tonight, I wasn't going to settle for anything less than Clarke on my tongue.

And my name on her lips.

Clarke

"How about him?"

I eyed the dirty blonde Nessa pointed out, emphasis on dirty. He had that sweaty, rugged, "I just got back from a ten-day camping trip," kind of look. Which, now that I thought about it, was entirely possible. This was the Pacific Northwest.

"Too messy."

Sweat-soaked after sex was one thing. Lack of personal hygiene was another.

"How about him?"

June's suggestion was safe, predictable. He reminded me of the guys I'd grown up with. Uptight nepo babies who blew their trust funds on the three b's: bumps, boats, and babes way too young for them.

"Too preppy."

Despite the dim lighting, I could see Nessa's eyes roll back in her skull. "Who are you, Goldilocks?"

"Goldi-cocks," June corrected. I clapped a hand over my mouth. I might have been out of the dating game for quite some time, but something told me spitting out my drink was a surefire way *not* to attract a man. "Are you sure you want to do this? I'm all for you getting out there and meeting somebody new, but a random guy at a club?"

"Would you prefer she meet a random guy on the internet?" Nessa offered.

"Fair point."

I sipped my drink, basking in the burn of tequila and rum. The first Long Island had taken the edge off; the second had been for liquid courage. I was happy to report that the liquid was indeed . . . courage-ing.

"No, this will be good." I gestured toward June. "Like you suggested, I need to get out there and meet somebody new." The remix of Britney Spears's "Toxic" and Ginuwine's "Pony" vibrated aggressively through my bones. It was so loud, I could barely hear myself, let alone my two friends. I pivoted to face Nessa. "And I made a list. So, now I know what I want when Soren asks."

Nessa smiled. "You mean when *somebody* asks."

Crap on a cracker.

"That's what I meant."

"I want to see this infamous list," June whined.

I sucked the last of my drink through the straw and shook my head.

"C'mon, please?"

"The list is for her, June."

"But—"

"Let it go, June."

Nessa hit her with a scorching look, effectively ending the conversation. Watching the two of them fight like sisters never got old.

"Are you ready to drop it like it's hot?" June asked.

I eyed the dance floor. Admittedly, my experience with bumping and grinding was limited. They never played much Snoop Dog or Megan Thee Stallion at the cotillions I attended, and Mama hadn't allowed me to go to any school dances.

"You should ask somebody to dance." Nessa nudged my arm with hers.

"Maybe later."

Maybe I needed a third tea first.

This was part of being a single, independent woman. Flirting with a sexy stranger at a nightclub, buying them a drink. People did this all the time, and most of them were a lot younger than me. I'd organized black-tie galas for four hundred at the Ritz Carlton. I could ask a man to dance. Maybe.

"What about if somebody asks you to dance?" Nessa asked.

"Well, then good thing I wore my dancing shoes." They were actually Nessa's. She'd let me raid her closet for something to wear tonight and my eyes had lit up when I'd spotted the chunky platform heels hidden in the back.

"In fact," I told them, emboldened by my liquid courage. "I'll dance with the next guy that asks."

Nessa and June's attention drifted to something—or some-one—behind me.

Nessa opened her mouth then shut it again.

June's magenta-painted lips curved into a smile, one that said she knew something I didn't. "You promise?" she asked.

"Cross my heart. Might as well get on with it, right? Because let's face it, ladies. None of these guys hold a candle to Soren Sinclair." June's smile widened. "He makes me crazier than a bessie bug, but he's got abs meant for shredding cheese."

Nessa choked on her drink.

"I'm serious," I told them. "What I wouldn't give to lick butter off that man's body."

"Is that a fact, blondie?"

Hells bells.

Every part of me froze. I'd know that voice anywhere.

"Ladies, how are we doing tonight? The name's Pink. Jared Pink."

Oh no. That made two voices I recognized. Which meant Soren wasn't alone. Which also meant . . .

I swiveled my head, coming face-to-face with half of the Roasters' starting roster. Pink, Matty, Tucker, Roman, and, of course, the object of my (apparently) dairy-covered fantasies. Pink wasted no time in sidling up to Nessa. That boy was bark-ing up the wrong tree, and I, for one, was looking forward to seeing her knock his confidence down a level or two. Right after I recovered from my embarrassment.

I resisted the urge to cover my face. They'd all heard me; that much was clear. The shit-eating grin on Soren's face was a dead giveaway. There wasn't any point in hiding from reality.

"Can I buy you a drink, gorgeous?" Pink asked Nessa.

"I don't know," Nessa told him. "Are you old enough to drink?"

Tucker and Roman chuckled. Matty rounded the table, striking up a conversation with June. But all of that blurred into the background when faced with Soren Sinclair.

"Need a refill, blondie?" he asked. "Maybe some butter?"

My cheeks warmed. "Thank you, but no."

"How about a dance then?"

"I—"

"Clarke." I turned back to June, who lifted her brows expectedly. "You promised."

I rolled my eyes, cursing myself and my big mouth. I might be chicken shit, but a promise was a promise.

Soren rested his hand just above my ass, his fingers flirting dangerously with the exposed skin at the base of my spine. From the front, the romper I'd chosen to wear was relatively modest. A short-sleeved, color-blocked number with a built-in belt that perfectly matched my heels-on-loan from Nessa. The back, however, was a different story. Open, bare, held together by nothing more than a flimsy string at the base of my neck.

It wouldn't take much for him to untie it. To bare me completely from the waist up. And when I said bare, I meant bare. There was no way to wear a bra with this one. Judging by the Cheshire Catlike smile on Soren's face, he knew that, too.

"Fine."

He leaned down until he was close enough for me to smell the minty freshness wafting off his kissable lips. "Sorry?"

"I said, fine. Let's dance."

He tightened his hand on my waist and guided me toward the dance floor, deeper and deeper into the throng of sweaty bodies. When we reached the center, he turned me toward him, gently tugging on my belt until I had no choice but to step closer to him. Any closer and I'd be on top of him. Not that that would be a bad thing . . .

Before I could decide what to do next or where to put my hands—because something told me my two years of ballroom dance lessons wouldn't serve me well this time around—we were moving once again. I gasped when he spun me away from him, then squealed when my back met his front. His ridiculously hard front.

"Okay, blondie?"

At this point, I could barely breathe, so forming coherent words and sentences was out of the question. Instead, I nodded.

He held me just like that, one hand on my hips, the other resting on my stomach, as we began to sway to the beat. I let him take the lead. Our bodies molded together, moving as one. With anybody else, this closeness, this control would've been too overwhelming. I'd endured enough control to last a lifetime. But with Soren, I felt safe. Warm, comforted. Like nothing could penetrate the invisible force field surrounding us.

One song flowed seamlessly into another until eventually, I found myself leaning back, relaxing into him. His grip on my hip tightened when I rolled my body against his.

"I reconsidered your offer," he grumbled against my neck.

"What?"

It wasn't that I hadn't heard him. I had, despite the thumping of Usher's "Love in this Club" vibrating through the dark room. But if he was saying what I thought he was, he needed to be crystal clear.

He turned my head until I was looking up at him over my shoulder.

"*Your list.* I'm in."

"I thought it wasn't a good idea," I said, throwing his words back in his face. On an especially slow swivel of my ass against his already burgeoning erection, he groaned. "You know, mixing business with pleasure?"

"It's not a good idea." He stopped us from moving altogether before adding, "But if the choice is an awkward work relationship or getting fired for fucking up anybody that touches you, I'll choose messy any day."

My eyebrows shot up into my hairline just before he lowered his head and claimed my lips. I returned it with fervor, moaning into his mouth when his hand moved from my chin to the back of my neck, holding me to him for a deep, voracious kiss. There was no turning back now.

We'd sealed our fate.

Soren more than lived up to his nickname. *Sin.* His mouth alone should come with a warning label.

And his teeth. The man was a goddamn vampire.

Even now, I could feel a hickey blooming on my neck and another on my ear lobe. I'd double-up on concealer tomorrow, but tonight . . . Tonight, he could eat me up. He was already doing a fine job of it.

Our make out session on the dance floor had moved to an alcove by the bathroom. Then the fire escape. Then the coat room. Until finally, we were asked to leave by a nice member of the security staff.

Holy hell, I was asked to leave an establishment. Mama would have a fit.

A giggle bubbled out of my mouth, vibrating against his lips.

"What?" he asked when he came up for air.

"Nothing."

"Blondie, if you're laughing, I must not be doing it right."

My laugh turned into a gasp when he drove his thick thigh a little higher, spreading my legs wider for him. I tugged his mouth back down to mine.

After we were asked to leave Sanctuary—the irony of the club's name didn't escape me—Soren had called us a Lyft while I'd said my goodbyes, assuring June and Nessa that I was safe with him. Nessa had driven us to Portland and, much to Pink's disappointment, she and June were planning on driving back to Rose City tonight.

Which led to here and now—me gyrating against Soren Sinclair's rock-hard thigh in a dark alley, moaning into his mouth while he gave me the best damn tongue-fucking of my life. I'd never gotten off from dry humping before. I didn't have the greatest track record of orgasming with a partner in general, but already, I was a few strokes away from exploding.

"Ride, blondie."

"I am," I told him, rubbing myself against his thigh, closing in on oblivion.

He smiled against my lips. "No, our ride is here." My face flushed. "But I like where your head is. Keep it there."

He punctuated the order with one final peck on my lips.

I followed him into the back of a gray Subaru, aka the Oregon state bird, according to Nessa. Even after we buckled up, he kept a hand on me, cupping my knee, toying with my hand. Who would've guessed Soren Sinclair's love language was physical touch?

"Where are we going?"

"Matty's place."

"You told him we were . . ."

"He didn't ask for details." His knuckles traced my inner thigh, inching higher under the hem of my romper until he was just inches from my already-drenched thong. "He did have one request, though," he whispered against my neck.

"What's that?"

"To change the sheets after we're done." He bit down, eliciting a surprised yelp. I tried to cover it with a cough, tried to conceal it behind my hand, but it was too late—and he was too good. All I could do was hope that our Lyft driver was too caught up in whatever podcast he was listening to.

"One more thing, blondie." Soren gripped my chin, turning my head until I had no choice but to meet his penetrating gaze. His pupils dilated to pools of black, pulling me deeper into the dark, out of my depths. The slight upturn of his lips made me swallow. "When we're alone, I don't want you to muffle those sounds. I want to hear you scream when you come. And Clarke, it better be my name you're screaming."

Soren

We barely made it through the door before I had her shoved up against it, burying my hand so far up her shorts, I was fingering the edges of her already-drenched panties.

It was hard to believe that this was the same woman who had tormented me for weeks with her cherry-red lips and sunny disposition, that she reserved for everyone but me. Yet here she was, wet and wanting, putty in my arms.

"Lights on, remember?" I nipped her neck, making her shiver. "I want to see all of you."

She had it on her list to fuck with the lights on, and I aimed to please. I had a feeling we'd be checking off more than one item before the sun came up tomorrow.

Clarke continued to maul my mouth while I reached for her back, desperate to get her naked. When I found a bow at the nape of her neck, I knew I was onto something. Deftly, I untied the material, until the entire front of her romper peeled away, leaving her top half bare.

"Fuck me." As if they had a mind of their own, my hands dropped to her tits. "You're the most beautiful thing I've ever seen."

She lowered her lids, avoiding my gaze.

"You don't think so?" I couldn't hide my surprise.

"I like the way I look," she told me, "But I know I'm not perfect. I've got cellulite, love handles, a muffin top."

"Yeah, you're fucking gorgeous." I cupped her tits, my mouth watering when the fleshy mounds more than filled my hands. "You've got the body of a woman, Clarke."

I tugged her romper down the rest of the way until it fell to the floor. "And these?" I grabbed the thick, fleshy hips she was so self-conscious about. "You know why they call them love handles, don't you, baby? They're for me to hold onto while I make love to you."

"Oh."

"Except this first time, I'm going to fuck you." Her eyes widened with interest. "I'll make love to you later, okay?"

"Okay—"

I didn't give her a chance to finish before I had her in my arms again, fingers digging into her bare ass. I was still fully dressed, but her lacy thong was all that separated me from nirvana.

Her tits bounced when I dumped her back on the mattress. I tried not to think too hard about the fact that I was about to fuck her sideways in my teammate's bed. Then again, it wouldn't be the first time, and I wasn't about to pass up the chance to spread out in a king-size for the first time in weeks.

Bed of Roses was a good spot to hang my hat for now, but I couldn't fuck Clarke the way I wanted to in a tin can on wheels.

Her hips leapt off the bed when I ran a finger over the seam of her panties. "Is all this for me, blondie?" I asked, testing her wetness.

"*Yessss*," she hissed, tossing her head back and forth on the comforter.

I slipped a finger beneath the scrap of lace, tracing her slit. *Damn.* If the way she was soaking my hand was anything to go by, I was going to have to buy Matty new bedding altogether.

"Ah! Soren!" she shouted when I slipped first one, then two fingers inside her.

"Fuck, you're tight."

Forget Matty's bedding. I was going to need new pants. I was already close to busting and I wasn't even inside her yet. There was still one thing I needed to do before I fucked her. Something I'd dreamt about for weeks.

I needed to taste her. Now.

My bad knee screamed in agony when I knelt on the wood floor in front of her. Fuck, I was going to feel that tomorrow.

"Wait," she cried before reaching back. She dragged a pillow down the bed and held it out to me. "For your knee."

Well, that's a first.

"You really did do your research," I told her around a wink. "Thanks, blondie."

I made myself comfortable before tucking my fingers under the elastic of her panties. I looked up to make sure she was still with me. She nodded vigorously for me to continue, her eyes full of fire and need.

She lifted her hips, helping me slip the panties off her body. *Fuck, what a view.* Better than any box seat in any stadium across America. And she was all mine, at least for a little while.

She was also a natural blonde.

My eyes raked her top to bottom, taking my time—we had all night, after all—memorizing every scar, curve, and freckle. Clarke squirmed under the weight of my gaze.

"Is it—it everything okay?" she asked nervously.

Aw, baby. She thought I didn't like her perfect pussy, her luscious body. Well, she was wrong. And I would tell her so every chance I got until she believed me.

I framed her pussy with my hands. "Mm. Everything's perfect."

"I . . . usually wax." She kept her eyes trained on the ceiling. "But I haven't had a chance to do it recently. So, um, sorry."

I shook my head. I had the sudden feeling that some jerkoff had made her feel a certain way about her body. Also, what grown ass man gave a fuck about a little pubic hair? You might as well just walk around, holding up a sign that says, "I don't know where the clit is."

"Quit thinking so much." She yelped when I tugged her down the bed until her ass met the edge. When I threw her legs over my shoulder, burying my face against her mound, she moaned. "Now lie back, relax, and let me eat this pretty pussy that I've been thinking about for weeks."

She tasted like sunshine and sweet tea.

I licked a line between her pussy lips, lapping up her juices like a man who hadn't eaten in weeks. If this was my reward for avoiding gluten, I'd never eat bread again.

She bucked her hips when I drew my tongue over her clit. That only motivated me more. When I flattened a palm over her stomach, pinning her to the mattress, she whimpered. There was no escaping this torture. I took my time, gliding my tongue up and down her slit, stopping to suck on her clit.

At one point, I started drawing my jersey number through her wetness. That had her clutching my hair, rolling her hips to meet my mouth.

"That's it, blondie," I growled against her thigh. "Fuck my mouth. Take what you need to come all over my face."

She whimpered when I dove back in again.

When I knew she was close, I worked my hands up her stomach to cup her breasts. Her nipples were sensitive. All it took was a slight pinch of each nub to have her back arching off the bed. I massaged the hurt away, all the while stroking her cunt with my tongue before doing it again. And again. Until she was a panting, sobbing mess.

"Soren," she moaned. "God, please."

"Tell me what you want, blondie."

I could keep this up all night. It might mean coming in my pants, but sacrifices often yielded the best rewards.

I slid two fingers between her pussy lips, splaying her open for me. My fingers tunneled deeper, curling up to massage her

G-spot. She was already drenched, but I wanted more. I needed her dripping, gushing all over my face.

"Please, please," she chanted, spasming around my fingers. It wouldn't be long now. Thank fuck, too, because my cock was practically crying to be inside her.

"Say. It."

"Please make me come, Soren. *Please!*"

"Good girl."

I worked her harder, faster, and this time, when I pinched her nipples, I sucked her clit, too. Hard. The combination of pain and suction was enough to set her off, screaming and thrusting against my face until I thought I might suffocate in her pussy.

What a way to go.

By the time the waves of her orgasm receded, I had already removed my clothes and slipped on the condom Matty gave me at the club. He'd also told me where to find the rest of the box should tonight go well.

Talk about friend of the century.

"You ready for more, blondie?" I crawled up her body, holding myself up with a hand on either side of her head.

I hovered above her, waiting for an answer while soaking up how beautiful she looked, her makeup a mess and hair askew. The glazed look of desire in her eyes told me she was hungry for more, but I needed to hear her say it.

She passed a hand through my hair, curling it behind my ear and sending shivers down my spine. Fuck, Clarke was dangerous. She made me want things I had never thought about before. Things people like me didn't deserve.

"I'm ready for everything."

That was all the invitation I needed to nudge myself against her opening and thrust forward, one inch at a time until I bottomed out inside of her.

"*Fuck.* You feel like heaven."

I gave her a minute to adjust to my size. I wasn't swinging around a horse cock like Pink, but I'd had enough sexual partners to know that I was above average. On top of that, Clarke's experience was minimal. All she had to do was say the word and I'd pull out. I could just as easily spend the night eating her out and cuddling.

She rocked her hips the tiniest bit forward, allowing me to slip in farther.

"Jesus. Fuck."

The sensations were overwhelming. Her pussy stretched around me, squeezing me tight like a warm, wet hug. Her pebbled nipples pressed tight against my bare chest. Fingers raked my back, digging into my ass to pull me closer, deeper. I wasn't going to last. And as much as I wanted to pretend that was due to the fact I hadn't had sex in nearly a year, I knew it was because of her.

"Baby," I grunted. "I promise I'll make this last longer the second time, but you feel too good. I can't hold back."

"Don't," she all but screamed. "Give me everything."

You asked for it, blondie.

Unable to stop myself, I bent down to take her mouth in a searing kiss. After that, it was a race to the finish. I hammered into her over and over, an endless soundtrack of bodies slapping together bouncing off the walls.

This wasn't making love. It wasn't even sex—there would be plenty of time for both later. No, this was primal, chaotic fucking.

"So fucking good," I huffed in time with my thrusts.

"So." *Thrust.* "Fucking." *Thrust.* "Good." *Thrust.*

I set a furious pace, but Clarke didn't complain. Instead, she snaked her arms around my neck and held on tight, matching me in rhythm and fervor.

"I'm going to come again," she gasped.

"Fuck yes," I grunted, slamming into her hard enough to shift her up the bed.

Her teeth sunk into her plump lips, biting back a deep, guttural moan. When her eyelids drifted shut, I wrapped a hand around her throat. "Uh uh, baby." Her eyes widened—with fire, not fear—when my hand slightly tightened. "Eyes on me. Watch me while I fuck you. While I make you come on my cock."

That was all it took to send her over the finish line, with me following closely behind.

"I swear, I usually last longer than that."

Clarke laughed against my chest, her warm breath tickling my skin. "Did you hear me complaining?" When I grabbed a handful of her ass, she quickly added, "Besides, you more than made up for it the second time around."

That was true. The first time had taken the edge off. After that, I'd fingered her to orgasm again before swapping out the spent condom for a fresh one and taking her from behind.

That time, when she came, it had been with my name on her lips and my handprint on her ass.

"That wasn't too much, was it, blondie?"

She tilted her head back until her eyes met mine. "Which part?"

"Any of it. The choking?" I gulped. "The spanking?"

She buried her face in the pillow next to her. "No."

"What's that?"

I wrestled the pillow away, pinning her hands together in one of mine above her head. It was playful, not forceful. Loose enough for her to break free if she wanted to. She knew that, too.

"I said no." She giggled nervously. "I liked that."

"Which part?" I asked, parroting back her question.

"All of it."

I used my free hand to trace her eyebrow, down the curve of her freckled cheeks, over the bow of her reddened lips—this time because of my lips and teeth, not that lipstick I loved.

"What am I going to do with you, blondie?"

"I've got a few ideas." She kissed my finger then licked it. It looked like somebody was ready for round three. "In fact, I wrote them down."

"About that."

"Oh." And just like that, the saucy minx had left the building. Clarke bit her lip. "Did you— Did you change your mind?

"Not at all," I told her, hoping to assuage those lingering doubts. "I just want to make sure we're both clear on the . . . terms of our arrangement."

She quirked a brow. "Should I have papers drawn up? Something for you to sign or take to a notary—"

"Okay, that's enough of that."

She yelped when I folded her legs back until they rested on either side of my head.

"Great, now that you're done talking, I want to be clear that *this*," I said, rocking forward until I nudged her opening with my tip. "*This* is only until the season starts, okay?"

"Okay."

"I'm serious. We'll check off as many filthy, fucked-up fantasies you've got, but once the season starts, it's back to business."

"I said okay."

I could feel her trying to adjust her hips to notch me inside her. There was no use, not at this angle. An adorable crease formed between her eyes when she realized she was stuck, held at my mercy.

"Agreed?"

"What?" she cried desperately.

"Are we agreed?" This time, I punctuated the question with a thrust of my hips.

"God, yes. Yes." She tugged my head down to hers. "Now, please shut up already and make me come again."

"If you insist."

Clarke

Spring Training: Week One

"The obvious answer is 'Party in the U.S.A.'"

Diaz snorted. "Of course it is."

"What's that supposed to mean?" Pink huffed.

"Just that you have the maturity of a teenage girl."

"Fuck you, guys. It's my little sister's favorite song."

Matty leaned over the seatback. "Don't pretend like you don't know every word. We all heard you singing it in the shower last week."

I smiled as the guys teased Pink about his chosen walk-up song, all in the name of good fun. We were about five hours into our twenty-two-hour bus ride to Scottsdale, and so far, the topics of conversation had ranged from celebrities on their "freebie lists" to whether hot dogs should be categorized as sandwiches. Obviously not. If anything, they were tacos.

We'd moved onto walk-up songs. Every player in the league got to select the music that played when they walked up to bat, hence the name.

I'll take "Things I Never Knew About Baseball" for two hundred, Alex.

"'25/8' by Bad Bunny," Diaz announced, interrupting my musings.

"You can take the boy out of Puerto Rico, but you can't take Puerto Rico out of the boy?" Roman asked from across the aisle.

"Si, mi pana."

"Alright, Matty." Bennett tipped his thermos toward Matty. Our catcher had a thing for hot cocoa. He was already onto his second batch today. "Let's hear it."

"Wait, wait," I interrupted. I couldn't resist this one. "Let me guess. 'Sweet Home Alabama.'"

The corner of lips quirked up, giving him away.

"Such a stereotype, bro." Tuck shook his head, feigning disappointment.

"You couldn't have chosen any country song from this millennium?" Diaz asked.

"Y'all don't get it," Matty rebutted. "It's not just a song. It's an anthem."

The guys laughed. Matty and I exchanged a glance, one that said, *These dang Northerners never get it.* I had no doubt this wasn't the first time he'd had to defend his walk-up song of choice.

It didn't escape me that there was one person who had been strangely quiet through this entire conversation, and he was currently sitting next to me. Stroking my lower back.

Goosebumps prickled when I felt Soren's fingers toy with the hem of my hoodie before flicking over my skin. We had both agreed not to flaunt our temporary relationship. Neither of us were interested in anybody's questions or opinions, and frankly, it wasn't anybody's business but ours. None of that had stopped him from touching me throughout our trip.

A twirl of my hair here, a brush of my thigh there. All subtle enough to evade his teammates' notice.

Which, somehow, made the whole thing even hotter.

I tilted my head to the side. "How about you?"

He smirked. "'Sin City.' AC/DC."

Curiouser and curiouser, Mr. Sinclair.

For someone who shied away from his nickname, he sure did enjoy living up to it. Something told me we might have more in common than I originally thought.

"Is that a band?" I asked. Silence descended amongst the bus. Soren looked at me like I'd grown a second head. They all did.

"AC/DC?" he asked. "You're kidding, right?"

All I could do was shrug.

"'Back in Black?' 'It's a Long Way to the Top?' 'Highway to Hell?'"

The guys fired off (what I could only assume was) song after song, each one more foreign to me than the next. When they finally ran out, I told them the truth.

"I've never even been to a concert."

That launched them into a completely new discussion, this time on their most memorable concerts.

Soren leaned over until his lips grazed my ear. "Oh, blondie," he said. "There's so much I have to teach you."

My cheeks warmed. Damn this man and his silky voice. The one that made my vagina flutter and my body vibrate.

"Um, I'm going to go check on Dani," I said, removing myself from his orbit. He turned toward the window to hide his smile.

I made my way to the back of the bus, carefully sidestepping discarded clothing and empty water bottles. Boys were gross.

If the soft snores were anything to go by, Wesley Nuñez, our center fielder, was already deep into his REM sleep. How he could sleep through this mayhem was beyond me.

Finally, I plopped down into the seat across from Dani.

"You doing alright?"

"Just peachy." Dani smiled weakly.

I wasn't so sure about that. Frankly, she looked like death warmed over. Scratch that. I'd seen ghosts with more pink in their cheeks. *Poor thing*.

Dani was prone to motion sickness. The kind that went well beyond feeling a touch queasy. She'd spent the first couple of hours laid out across Pink's lap, and the next couple locked in the bathroom.

"Can I get you anything?"

"No." She tucked her knees up to her chest before slumping over in her seat. "Just let me die here in peace."

Pink turned around in his seat, crossing his arms over the seat back between the two of them. "How's she doing?"

Dani groaned.

"Not too great," I said, translating for him.

"Don't be sad, D.B." He rubbed a hand over her side. "Because sad spelled backwards is *das,* and *das* no good."

She groaned again.

"Jared, would you mind grabbing her some Gatorade?"

"Sure thing, Clarke Kent."

I rolled my eyes. Pink and Dani had become fast friends, and even though I knew his heart was in the right place, his relentless golden retriever energy might not be the best thing for her right now. What she needed was electrolytes.

My attention wavered between Dani, still curled into the fetal position, and the rest of the bus. A few of the guys had scattered throughout, tucking their faces behind books, tablets, and sleep masks. Some of them, Soren included, seemed to be caught up in a heated debate about . . . pizza toppings?

Jeez Louise.

All these guys thought about was food, sex, and baseball.

Pink exchanged a few words with Coach Ward at the front of the bus before grabbing a Gatorade from the team's cooler. I was too far away to hear their conversation, but Ward's eyes tracked Pink's movement all the way to the back of the bus.

"Distract me."

I turned back toward Dani. "Hm?"

She lifted her mouth from behind her knees, just long enough to repeat herself. "Distract me. Please." Her eyes shifted to the floor. "Before I barf all over your cute shoes."

"Alrighty." I blew out a breath, cocked my hip, and told her the first thing I thought of. The thing I hadn't been able to take my mind off since we boarded the bus at five a.m. this morning.

"Here's a fun one for you. I was supposed be leaving for my honeymoon today."

Her eyes widened from behind her knees.

"You're married, Clarke Kent?"

I made room for Pink in the seat next to me. I knew I was taking a risk by sharing my sordid past with the biggest gossip on the bus, but they were all bound to find out anyway.

"I said *supposed* to be. I called off the wedding a month ago when I found out he was sleeping with our wedding planner."

"Woah." Dani groaned.

"Yup."

"That's . . ."

"Surprising?" I finished for her. "Irresponsible? Heavy?"

"Brave," Pink said, matter-of-fact.

I turned to face him. Apparently, Soren wasn't the only Roaster full of surprises.

"Thank you, Jared."

"I just call it like I see it." He winked before passing Dani her bottle. "Drink up, buttercup."

I'd been watching the bond develop between Pink and Dani for some time now. At first, I thought Soren and I might not be the only ones having an interoffice fling. But the more I saw them together, the more I realized that their relationship wasn't flirtatious or romantic in the least. More like brother and sister.

"By the way, what's up with your friend Nessa?"

I smiled coyly. That was another reason I knew Pink's relationship with Dani was platonic. He was smitten with Nessa.

"I'm not sure what you mean, Jared."

"She totally blew me off at the club the other night. And *then* . . ." He paused for dramatic effect. "She rejected my friend request on Facebook."

"I hate to break it to you, Jared, but I don't think you're her type."

His face fell. "But I'm everyone's type."

"Sure you are, stud," Dani said around a giggle.

"Whatever," he grumbled. "Oh, coach said we're stopping in ten minutes."

"Why?" we both asked.

According to the schedule we'd all received from Coach Ward's assistant, there were only two planned stops during the ride to Spring Training, and the first was still two hours away. Still, it'd be nice to stretch our legs. And Dani, more than anyone, could use the break.

Pink shrugged. "Beats me. Ask coach."

I scanned the bus for the man in question, but he was slumped over in his seat, facing the front. When my focus shifted right, I nearly combusted on the spot.

Soren was staring directly at me. And oh lord, he was wearing his hat backwards again. I couldn't help but wonder how he might react if I asked him to eat me out again, this time wearing his hat. *And only his hat.*

Judging by the wicked smile that spread across his face, he had a vague idea about what I was thinking.

And suddenly, making an early pit stop didn't seem like such a bad idea after all.

Soren

Like most athletes, I'd learned early on in my career that discipline was just as important as talent. You could have all the raw talent in the world, pitch the ball a hundred miles per hour, hit it out of the park anytime, but unless you had the discipline to harness that energy and develop those skills, you'd never make it to the show.

My concentration might have wavered over the years, but the same couldn't be said for my discipline.

Until now.

If I didn't get my hands on Clarke soon, I was going to lose it.

And I wasn't talking about the light, covert touches we'd exchanged on the bus or the "accidental" grazing of her thigh. Those were temporary fixes, Band-Aids if you would. No, I needed a handful of Clarke Myers, and I needed it now.

"You might want to stop looking at her like that."

I turned toward Matty, who had apparently snuck up on me sometime between me perusing the snack aisle and watching Clarke like an obsessed stalker.

We'd stopped at the gas station twenty minutes ago to "stretch our legs," according to Coach Ward. Personally, after catching the coach eyeing the back of the bus more than once, I figured it had more to do with giving our social media director a break from her nausea.

"Not sure what you mean."

His pointed stare told me he knew that I was full of shit.

"It's pretty obvious," he said.

"What is?"

"That you want to swallow her whole. You're looking at her like she's Little Red Riding Hood."

I guessed that made me the Big Bad Wolf.

"I take it that things went well the other night."

Matty didn't have to say it. We both knew he was talking about when Clarke and I hooked up in his apartment. He'd caught me mid-changing the sheets the next morning, after I'd called her a car back to Rose City.

"We're keeping things casual," I told him, tucking a couple packs of turkey jerky into my shopping basket. "It's just temporary, until the season starts."

He scoffed before adding a handful of sunflower seeds to my basket. "Yeah, okay."

"We both agreed. Work comes first."

"Sure."

"Why is that so hard to believe?"

"Keeping things casual is one thing. Keeping things casual with a woman like that?" He nodded his head toward Clarke. "Impossible."

She looked so out of place in a gas station convenience store, somewhere outside of the Nevada desert, and yet completely unbothered. I couldn't look away as she chatted up the middle-aged cashier. It was probably nothing more than casual conversation, but with Clarke, that was all it took. The cashier's eyes lit up with genuine interest, like he was hanging on her every word, and he smiled when she tilted her head back to let out a bellowing laugh.

Forget Mary. There's something about Clarke.

Some effortless, hypnotic air about her that never failed to make somebody's day a little bit brighter. Or the world a little bit better.

"Just be careful." Matty clapped me on the shoulder.

"Look, dude, you don't need to worry. She knows exactly what she signed up for."

He looked me dead in the eye. "She's not the one I'm worried about," he said cryptically. "I'll meet you back on the bus."

My brow furrowed in confusion and maybe a hint of annoyance. Then again, it was hard to stay annoyed at someone with that dreamy drawl. Did I have a Southern accent kink?

"I'm not buying your seeds," I said to his already retreating form.

"I gave you my apartment," he called back. "You owe me sunflower seeds for life."

I couldn't argue with that.

After I paid for my snack loot—plus Matty's sunflower seeds—I stepped outside for some air. Maybe the frigid temperatures would clear my head . . . and numb my greedy dick.

Just as I reached for my phone to text my sister, a glimpse of honey blonde curls rounding the back of the building snagged my attention. I'd know those curls anywhere.

I snuck a glance to make sure nobody was around before I followed her around the back. When she emerged from the single stall restroom a few minutes later, I pushed my way inside, closing the door behind both of us.

She yelped when I reversed our positions, backing her against the door. Any nerves she was feeling fled when my lips met hers. I dropped my snacks to the ground, trading the bag for two handfuls of Clarke's ass.

"*Fuck*," I groaned into her mouth. "I've been dying for a taste of you all day."

"So, taste me," she said breathlessly before dragging my lips back to hers.

There was nothing like this. The first few weeks, or sometimes months, in a new relationship when you couldn't keep your hands off each other. When you had to have each other three, four times a day, regardless of the time and place. It was the same rush, same thrill I got from hitting a homerun or knocking the catcher on his ass at home plate.

Clarke and I had already rounded the bases—once at Matty's place and then again in my trailer—but that hadn't quenched my craving for her any less. On the contrary, now that I knew what I'd been missing, it only made me want her more.

I hoisted her farther up the wall, aligning her pussy perfectly with my throbbing cock. It would be so easy to just dry fuck her until we both came in our pants like teenagers. I'd never hear the end of it from the guys if I came back to the bus with stained joggers, but it might be worth it.

I, however, had something else in mind.

I snaked a hand down between us, flicking open the button of her jeans. She tore her mouth away when I eased her zipper down.

"We can't do this here," she protested, her fingernails digging half-moons into the base of my neck. A part of me hoped they would leave a mark. I'd more than marked up her neck and shoulders the last few days, so turnabout was fair play. "Anybody could catch us."

"Isn't that the idea, blondie?"

Number two. Somewhere we could get caught.

My eyes searched hers. If she wanted this to continue, she was going to have to learn to start using her words. This was her list, her fantasy, and while I was more than happy to fulfill it, I would never pressure her. If she wanted me to zip up her pants and get back on that bus, I'd do it.

An adorable crease formed between her brows, a clear indicator that her brain was waging war with her body.

"What do you want, Clarke?"

"I-want-you-to-make-me-come," she blurted out before turning her face away.

You can run, blondie, but you can't hide.

I caught her chin between my fingers, tilting her head back until eyes met mine. They glittered with desire. I smoothed a thumb along her lower lip, tracing the length of it back and forth painstakingly slowly.

"Try again," I ordered, tucking my thumb ever so lightly between her lips. A shutter rippled through me when she closed her lips around it, sucking, tasting the heat of my skin. "What do you want?"

This time, her words were slow and direct, edged with hunger.

"I want you to make me come." Her eyes twinkled before she tacked on, "Now."

That was all I needed to hear.

My fingers breached her panties, sending her head thudding back against the wall. Fuck AC/DC; I'd take a soundtrack of Clarke's moans as my walk-up song any day of the season. But-toned-up Clarke was one thing, but sex-starved, wanton Clarke was something else entirely. Especially knowing that I was the one that brought it out of her.

I pressed two fingers deep inside her, curling them to rub against the spot that I knew would drive her crazy. Her hands tightened on my shoulders as she struggled to lift herself up and off my fingers, only to force them deeper again. It was cute, the fact that she thought she was the one running the show. That I might just *let* her ride my fingers until she came.

Time to change that.

She closed her eyes, savoring the thumb swirling around her engorged clit while the other gauged the ragged pulse at her neck. My hand slid around her throat until finally, I fisted the back of her neck, forcing her face down.

"I love how wet you are for me," I whispered against her lips. Her pussy clenched in response. "Imagine what people would think if they knew you were letting me get you off in a dirty gas station bathroom."

Her hands slid into my hair, tugging my lips down to hers. I smiled into our kiss.

Mm, my girl gets off to dirty talk.

I had to stop thinking of her that way. Clarke wasn't *my* girl. She wasn't *my* anything. This was just a short-term fling, something to get Clarke out of my system before the season started.

Matty was right. We were both playing with fire.

But *god,* if the fire burned as hot as Clarke's pussy . . .

She gasped when I added a third finger.

"You have to be quiet, baby." I knew it wouldn't be long now. For either of us. The sounds of my heavy breathing and her squelching cunt were enough to set me off. "You don't want the whole team to hear me finger-fucking you through the door, do you?"

That had her squeezing the absolute hell out of my fingers.

"Such a naughty girl."

"*Yesss . . .*"

"You're so fucking beautiful like this." I nipped at her bottom lip, swallowing her cry. "Are you going to come for me, Clarke?"

She bit her lip, nodding rapidly.

"Are you going to come all over my hand, you dirty fucking girl?"

When she shattered, I swallowed the sound, crashing my mouth down on hers. I crushed her against the door, rubbing her through the endless waves of orgasms, until finally, one of her hands covered mine.

"Too much?" I trailed a path of gentle kisses up her neck as she came down from her high.

"Just sensitive," she choked out in between uneven breaths.

She tangled her fingers with mine, still covered in her juices, and removed them from her pants. Together we buttoned and zipped her pants, laughing when our foreheads accidentally knocked together. When she reached for the erection tenting my sweats, I looped my fingers through hers again.

She looked up at me with apprehension. "What about you?"

"Later. We've got a bus to catch."

"But—"

"Believe me, blondie. The things I want to do to this pussy—this mouth—can wait until we reach the hotel."

She tried (and failed) to hide her flushed face against my chest. I kissed her forehead, relishing the taste of sweat . . .

And peaches. *Fuck me.*

It was going to be a long bus ride.

Clarke

"And with that, Roasters lead the Gulls three-one, heading into the bottom of the ninth."

As it turned out, I had severely misjudged just how long and boring baseball games were. And no number of tight buns in tighter baseball pants made up for that.

Well, maybe a little.

We'd been in Scottsdale for five days now, which meant five days of glorious sunshine, seventy-plus degree temperatures, and a hotel dresser full of shorts that showed off my legs—even if they were paler than usual.

Now that I was making a steady paycheck, I'd treated myself to a few new wardrobe pieces. Mostly shorts, a couple of skirts, and even a spaghetti strapped romper, each more colorful than the next. Gone were the days of my mother ranting like a lunatic about dresses with ice cream cones on them, as if the devil invented them himself. I was a color girly now.

These last few months had been exhilarating, to say the least. Full of firsts, adventures, and the highest of highs—without actually getting high because even now, I didn't think that was something that interested me. Whereas some people might have called it a quarter-life crisis, I knew better.

It wasn't a crisis. It was an awakening.

There wasn't a doubt in my mind that I had made the right choice to reset my life two months ago. I had friends, a job. I was making my own money. I had even grown quite fond of the little trailer I called home, though my hotel room in Scottsdale was temporarily a nice change of scenery—one that came with a soaker tub.

I was exactly where I needed to be.

And even though baseball wasn't the most riveting game, I had certainly learned a lot the last few days.

First, Spring Training games didn't even count. As Dani had tried to explain to me, they did technically *matter,* in that they gave each team the opportunity to try out different players—some of whom were fighting for their spots—but at the end of the day, the wins and losses made no difference to the team's overall record.

Second, the Roasters were pretty damn good. Sure, I had seen the team practice together dozens of times, but batting practice and fielding drills weren't full-on games. These guys played like they'd known each other for years. I was already looking forward to the real deal come April, and even better, so were the fans. That was right. The Rose City Roasters already had fans.

Third, and perhaps most importantly, I *loved* hot dogs. Songs could be written about my borderline pornographic love affair with ketchup-covered wieners. According to Matty, Soren had almost thrown a tantrum in the dugout after he caught more than a couple of his teammates watching me devour my third one during yesterday's double header. I'd gotten an earful about it—plus an ass spanking to remember—last night in his bed.

That was something else—entirely non-baseball related—I had learned about myself. I enjoyed my pleasure with a side of pain, and Soren, bless his heart, was more than happy to deliver on all of the above.

And boy, did he deliver.

"Pink and I are hitting a rooftop bar tonight." Dani looked up from the phone in her hands. "Want to join?"

It took a few days to get there, but between Dani and me covering the on-the-ground events at Spring Training and Tanya managing the content calendar back in Rose City, we had finally found our rhythm. Dani and I took turns with game coverage, giving the other time to rest or explore Scottsdale, which, surprisingly, had a lot to offer. Hot air balloon rides, spa treatments, and as Dani had mentioned, a rooftop bar on every corner.

"Thanks, but I already have other plans."

Her eyes narrowed. "Mm-hmm, I bet you do."

My attention caught on my favorite player as he took the field for the final inning. More specifically, on his behind. It should be illegal for somebody *that* talented to look *that* good, especially in knee-high socks.

And he was sleeping with little ol' me.

"How's that going, by the way?"

When Dani nodded toward the man in question, I tried to come up with the best response. Soren and I had agreed to keep our arrangement quiet, but we weren't necessarily hiding it from Dani or the team. Still, I didn't want to fuel the rumor mill. Feigning ignorance might be the better option.

"I'm sure I don't know what you're talking—"

"Cut the shit, Clarke Gable. I saw a certain third baseman sneaking out of your room the other night, looking like the cat who ate the canary." She arched a brow. "Or maybe the canary ate your cat?"

So much for pretending. At least this time, I could blame my flushed cheeks on the Arizona heat.

"Don't worry, I won't say anything."

When she uncapped her water bottle to take a sip, I couldn't help but notice the stickers on the side.

"Are those different states?"

"Yup," she said after she had sealed it again. "One sticker for every state I've been to and blank spaces for the ones I haven't."

"Which ones do you still need?"

From my vantage point, there wasn't a free space in sight. There was, however, a series of scratches over what had once been Maryland.

"Technically, Oklahoma, Kentucky, and Florida." She braced both hands on the metal arms of the chair and leaned back, tucking her knees up to her chest. "But I have zero interest in visiting states that treat queer people like second-class citizens and women like incubators."

"I can't argue with that." I pointed toward the sticker formerly known as Maryland. "What about that?"

"That's a story for another day." She smiled sadly. "And a pitcher of spicy margaritas."

"Speaking of, the guys are talking about doing their margarita movie night thing tomorrow."

"Diaz told me." She adjusted her tiny blue pigtails. Dani had the gift of effortlessly pulling off any look, including messy braids. "I put in a couple of calls to local movie theaters. We should be able to rent out one of the screens."

That sounded like fun. I'd heard all about the guys' Monday night tradition during our bus ride from Oregon. Right after the most blinding orgasm of my life. In a public restroom.

Good lord, who am I?

I turned back toward the field just as Soren bent over, rocking forward on the balls of his feet. Today was Dani's day for game coverage, but that didn't mean I couldn't create a little something for myself, right? Without second-guessing it, I lifted my phone and pressed record.

I took it all in from behind the camera, like a naughty voyeur.

"My dirty fucking girl."

My nipples pebbled as I recalled Soren's words.

I watched him as he fielded a ground ball with catlike reflexes. His crisp, white jersey with "Sinclair" written across the back was tucked into a matching pair of baseball pants that did wonders for his backside. A backside I had spent a lot of up-close-and-personal time with as of late. I might have accidentally zoomed in on that particular feature.

Panning up and over the stitched number four, I caught the overgrown brown-black hair creeping out the sides of his red baseball hat. Now that I thought about it, his five o' clock shadow was coming in closer to eleven o'clock these days. He hadn't shaved since before we got to Arizona, probably some weird superstition, something baseball was known for. I wasn't complaining though. Not when he looked like a Viking, pirate fantasy come to life.

It was well worth the beard burn on my thighs.

And just when I thought the man couldn't get any hotter, he straightened to full height, adjusted his cap, and turned ever-so-slightly over his shoulder. He searched the crowd, almost as if he could feel the weight of my penetrating gaze. It didn't take him long to find me—we were seated just beyond the team's dugout—and when he did, he tipped his hat like an eighteenth-century gentleman and smiled as if to say, "I know exactly what you taste like."

Because that was Soren Sinclair: the perfect amalgamation of politeness and pussy eating prowess.

"Oh my god, we're so posting that."

I jumped. "Hm?"

"That thirst trap video you just made."

"I didn't— That's not what—"

I trailed off as I reviewed the video I'd captured. The one that I'd meant just for me . . . and my vibrator.

Hells bells.

Dani was right. I'd thirst trapped Soren, and I hadn't even known it. My stomach suddenly knotted, and not because of the hot dogs.

"Seriously, you have to post that."

"I don't know." I chewed my lip, searching for the right words. "Isn't that kind of, objectifying him?"

"Have you heard of the female gaze, Clarke?" I nodded. I'd taken a course on female filmmakers in college, so I was vaguely familiar with the concept of the female gaze. "The female gaze is all about empathizing, showing intimacy while also showing respect."

I had never heard it explained so eloquently, not even by my professor.

"This is a different side of Soren Sinclair, one that the fans will eat up. What person hasn't dreamed about somebody looking at them like that?"

She had a point. Soren was well known by the press, but not for reasons he might have liked. Maybe this is what he needed to rehab his image.

Besides, our arrangement was temporary. I had no claim on his smiles. There had been women in his life before me, and there would, undoubtedly, be plenty more after our fling had run its course. I had a job to do, and like Dani said, fans would love to see this side of him. The one that said, "You're the one person in the world that can make me smile like this."

That. That was what every person dreamed about.

Rather than overthink it any further, I added a sexy, popular pop song, edited down the butt content to a minimum—because there were some parts of Soren that I didn't feel comfortable sharing with the world and I doubted he would, too—and uploaded the video to the Roasters' Tiktok.

"Done," I said around a heavy sigh.

"Good." She must have sensed my hesitation because she quickly added, "I promise it'll be worth it."

A crack of the bat had us both looking up, just in time to see a foul ball heading straight toward us.

People around us squealed with excitement, and Dani jumped to her feet. I, on the other hand, sat frozen, paralyzed with equal parts shock and fear. Before I could even think about getting up, or at the very least protecting my face, a brown leather mitt landed directly in my lap, followed almost immediately by the smack of a ball. The sound rang out through the stands, mingling with the crowd's uproarious cheers.

"Hey, blondie."

My eyes zeroed in on the man with his hand in my lap. The same man who had dominated my thoughts, fantasies, and dreams for weeks.

"Hi." I coughed.

His mouth shifted into an ear-splitting grin, and that was when I realized that I was staring up at him with my mouth open.

He rolled the mitt over, dumping the game ball out in my hands.

"Don't say I never gave you anything."

Soren

Spring Training: Week Two

"Okay, be honest." A collective mix of groans and snickers rang out through the locker room when Roman dropped his towel. "Who drew Winnie the Pooh on my ass last night?"

Yesterday, while I had been balls deep in Clarke's pussy, a few of the guys had gone out to celebrate Bennett's birthday, one that had lasted well into the wee hours of the morning and, apparently, ended with drunken doodling. *Wait a minute . . .*

Upon closer inspection of Roman's caramel-toned behind, I choked back a laugh. "Hate to break it to you, but that shit looks permanent."

"Excuse me?" he hissed, his eyes wide as saucers.

"Dude, the lines are still raised. I know fresh ink when I see it." I held my arms out in front of me. I could practically see the steam rolling off his body. "Don't blame me. I wasn't there."

"You fuckers tattooed a pantsless cartoon bear on my ass?!"

Bennett finished buttoning his slacks. "Dude, you disappeared after the third round of shots with that Australian couple. I'd say you did that to yourself."

"And how is it that you're just noticing now?" Tuck asked.

Roman rolled his eyes and covered back up. "I'm sorry. I don't spend all my free time ogling *my* ass. I'm not Pink."

Our pitcher's head popped out of his locker. "I resent that. It's not my problem you don't have a healthy relationship with your body."

I shook my head and slid my arms into my blazer. Even though it was only Spring Training, management still expected us to wear our finest before and after the game. That meant no jeans, no T-shirts, no breathable fabrics. Didn't matter. The ride back to the hotel was air-conditioned, so I only had to survive the walk to and from the bus.

"By the way," Diaz said loud enough to make heads swivel in his direction. "We're on for M&M night at seven."

"What's playing?" Wes asked, surprising me.

Of all my teammates, Wes was probably the biggest mystery to me. He didn't go out with the rest of us, and he sat in the back during team meetings. Hell, I didn't even know where he lived. It was clear that he preferred to keep his personal life separate from his work life. I, of all people, couldn't fault him for that.

"*Dazed and Confused*. I'll text everybody the address."

Fuck, that meant my plans with Clarke would have to wait. Too bad, too. We'd been making steady progress on her list this week. I guessed I could bend her over a couch—item number five—another time.

Bennett sat down beside me to tie his shoes, an exceptionally shiny pair of loafers that looked like they had never been worn. Maybe they hadn't. Until this week's games, I'd never seen Bennett in anything but Nikes.

"So, how was your night?" I asked him. "Happy birthday, by the way."

"It was alright." He hesitated before adding, "I'm not big on birthdays."

I nodded. Maybe I was reading too much into it, but it seemed like something else was going on, something more than just blowing out one more candle. Bennett had been a little off lately, nowhere near his usual, personable self. Not that he was the loudest of the group by any means. Like me, he tended to hang back and observe. Although, I thought that had more to do with his disability than anything else.

"Everything else okay?"

He sighed. "Dating sucks."

"You don't have to tell me."

"I've been texting with somebody for a while, and we were supposed to meet up last night, but they completely ghosted me."

"I'm sorry, man."

There wasn't much more to say. Bennett was right. It didn't matter if you were fifteen or fifty, dating sucked. Like a bad game of UNO, where your options were limited to skip, pick another, or reverse.

True, it got marginally easier over time, but that didn't make it any less heart-wrenching. Especially when you worked in an industry that already made relationships next to impossible to manage. There was a common misconception that it was easier for athletes and stars to date. That couldn't have been further from the truth. It wasn't difficult to find some companionship for the night, but love and relationships were a different story.

Take it from me, fame did not breed love.

"Their loss."

His lips kicked up on one side. "Thanks."

"Did y'all see that Sinclair's thirst trap is up to three million views?"

Matty's question gave me pause. "My what?"

"Your thirst trap. From Saturday's game."

My eyes nearly bugged out of my skull when he held up his phone. Someone had shared a video of me from yesterday's game, and it didn't take a genius to know who. I remembered the moment vividly, from feeling the weight of Clarke's eyes on me as I adjusted my hat to searching her out in the crowd and finally, the smile we shared. I could see it all, clear as day, even forty-eight hours later.

The video itself didn't bother me . . . much. It came with the territory of being a public figure—and wearing incredibly tight pants. What bothered me more was my reaction, to knowing that over three million strangers had watched a moment that was supposed to be ours and ours alone. *That* had me grinding my teeth.

"Dude, you should see the comments," Diaz added. "They love you."

"Yeah, Booktok is obsessed," Pink added.

"What the fuck is Booktok?"

"The book obsessed side of Tiktok." Pink slipped on a trench coat that was way too heavy for spring and slung his bag over his shoulder. "You're trending on the romance novel side of Booktok."

He left it at that, walking out before any of us could muster a response. Matty's look of confusion matched my own. Pink didn't exactly strike me as an avid romance reader. A laundry list of follow-up questions was already forming in my head, but it would have to wait.

There was a buxom blonde to punish.

Clarke

I had just settled into bed with a romance novel when the onslaught of text messages began. My laugh echoed through the empty hotel room when I noticed that somebody—probably June—had changed the name of our group chat to "Bitchcraft."

June

When do you get back? It's been too quiet around here lately.

Nessa

Too rainy, too. Bring the sun back with you, k?

June

PLEASE.

Clarke

Two weeks down, two to go.

Nessa

And how goes the bucket list?

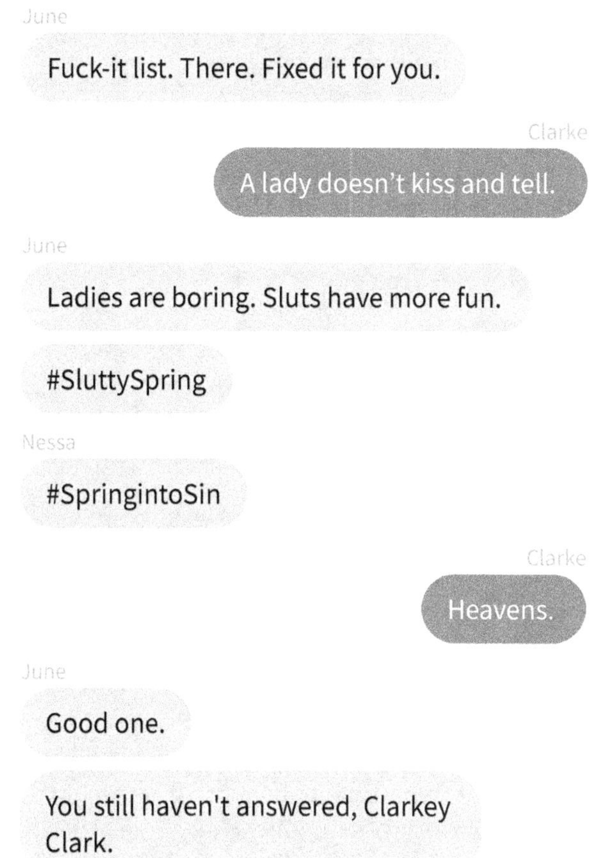

A knock at the door was my saving grace. I wasn't sure how much I wanted to say about my and Soren's exploits. Not yet, at least.

I tossed my phone on the bed, sidestepping my discarded sneakers on the way to the door. When it swung open, I almost melted on the spot. Soren Sinclair looked damn good leaning against my doorframe, blazer slung over one shoulder.

It was exactly the sort of thing that I would pick out for him. Modern, relaxed but still well-fitted to his broad shoulders. The charcoal gray color matched his eyes, and when he smiled, it was, dare I say, a little bit magical.

"Hi, blondie."

"Hi," I somehow mustered. Before Soren, I had prided myself on my public speaking abilities. I'd entertained some of the nation's oldest families, dazzled foreign dignitaries with my knowledge of French cuisine, and yet, with Soren Sinclair, I stumbled over basic greetings.

"You going to invite me in?"

"You're wearing a suit."

He looked down at himself, amused.

"I am."

"I've never seen you in a suit before."

"And?"

And it was a sight to behold. The man could model for Brooks Brothers.

What was funny was that on paper, Soren was everything my parents disapproved of. Never married, raised by (gasp) a single mother in a blue state. No college degree, no family money to speak of, only what he had made for himself. He dated pop stars and actresses but didn't give a hoot about brand names. And yet, the man filled out a suit like no other. They wouldn't even balk if I arrived at some big-wig function with Soren on my arm.

Because with them, appearances were everything. Mama had hammered that into Viv and me before we were old enough to walk.

"What are you thinking about so hard over there?"

I chewed on my lip, deciding between propriety and honesty. Soren liked it when I was honest, when I told him what I wanted. Even when it was indecent. No, *especially* when it was indecent.

So, I told him.

"I'm thinking about whether you look hotter in a suit or your uniform."

His lips kicked up. That cocky smile would be my undoing.

He came off the doorframe, towering over me. There weren't a lot of people who made me feel so . . . delicate, but Soren was one of them. Even after a couple weeks of whatever this was between us, I still hadn't gotten used to it.

He wrapped his arms around my waist, pulling me onto my tiptoes. With shaky fingers, I laced my hands around his neck. The twinkle in his eyes told me I had done good.

I licked my lips when his hands coasted down my back, past my ass, until they slipped beneath the hem of my sundress. It was about three inches shorter than what I usually wore, which was exactly why I'd known I needed it as soon as I'd tried it on. My mother would hate it, but Soren would love it. And that was a thrilling combination.

His heady gaze intensified when his fingers skimmed along the seam of my lacy thong, another new purchase.

"This is new," he said, sliding a finger inside my panties. "I like it."

And just when I thought he might kiss me, his tone changed completely.

"You know what I *don't* like? Finding videos of me on Tik-tok." I swallowed. He walked us farther into the room, shutting the door behind us, all without taking his eyes—or hands—off mine. He backed me toward the bed, until the back of my knees met the mattress and I had no choice but to sit down, bringing my face front and center with the erection tenting his slacks.

"Especially ones I don't know about. Or agree to."

"About that—"

"However," he interrupted. "You've got a job to do. I get it."

He ran his fingers through my hair—I was suddenly thank-ful today had been a hair wash day—before curling his hand around the back of my neck.

My eyes widened when his hand tightened. "But that doesn't mean you shouldn't be punished."

That had my shoulders tensing and pussy clenching.

"Do you like the sound of that, naughty girl?"

"Yes."

He smiled. "Good."

I wasn't sure what to expect next. Maybe for him to order me to unzip his pants, pull his cock out, and take him down my throat. We hadn't done that yet. Truthfully, I wasn't sure I was ready for it either.

What I did not expect was for Soren to reach under my dress and drag my panties down. The look he gave me from between my thighs was downright carnal.

"Roll over, blondie. Knees and elbows.

I blinked, but did as he said. *This* was my punishment?

He climbed onto the bed behind me, still fully clothed. When he bunched my dress up, exposing me completely from the waist down, I looked back over my shoulder. There wasn't much to see from this position, not when my ass was thrust so high in the air. But I felt him.

I felt his warm breath tickle my pussy lips.

"I've been dying for a taste of this cunt all day."

I shuddered when he slipped one blunt finger inside me. Then another. Stretching me, filling me, memorizing me from the inside out. My unsteady breaths mingled with the hotel air-conditioning. I dug my fingers into the duvet, searching for something to anchor me closer to his fingers, to his mouth.

He withdrew, leaving me empty, wanting. But only for a second before he replaced his fingers with his tongue, dragging it painstakingly slowly through my pussy, all the way up to my ass. I almost lurched off the bed.

He gripped my hips, holding me against his mouth while his tongue speared my pussy over and over again. I writhed and bucked against his hold. Even now, I could feel myself dripping onto the bed. Later, I'd worry about what housekeeping would think, but not now. Not while he was lapping at my cream like a man who hadn't eaten in weeks. Like I was his last meal, his favorite meal.

Dang, maybe I should make thirst traps of him more often.

If this was a punishment, I hesitated to think what he might consider a reward. But there was no point trying to think at all when Soren Sinclair was licking me from behind, sucking my clit like a Creamsicle. The man had fried every synapse in my body, reducing me to a bundle of nerves that experienced nothing but pleasure.

So much pleasure.

The assault on my pussy continued. On an especially deep thrust of his tongue, I screamed.

"Fuck, Soren!"

I could practically feel his devilish grin between my thighs. "That's right, Clarke. Say my name." His words pushed me closer toward the edge. When he thrust two fingers back inside me, I screamed again. "Whose pussy is this?"

He wanted me to talk? I could barely breathe.

He curled those fingers deep inside of me and growled, "Whose?"

"Yours," I moaned. "God, it's all yours, Soren."

My hips moved as if by their own accord, fucking back against his mouth. He dragged his tongue over my clit once again, rewarding me. Any second now, I'd reach oblivion, and I feared there wouldn't be any coming back. I was rocketing toward the astral plane at lightyear speed, fire and ice simultaneously licking at my vision.

But just as I reached the edge of atmosphere, Soren ruthlessly tugged me back to Earth.

"We better get going."

"What?!" I came up on my hands, turning over my shoulder.

He grinned, placing one final kiss to my clit before coming to his feet.

"M&M night." He said it as if it were a reasonable explanation for abandoning me on the brink of explosion. "We better grab a car now if we don't want to be late."

Before I could wrap my brain around what was happening, or even bother to catch my breath, he pulled me to my feet, arranging my dress back into place.

"What did you—" I stammered. "Why did you stop?"

"Blondie, you didn't think I was going to make this easy, did you?" He grinned wickedly. "That wouldn't be a punishment."

I blinked up at him, mouth agape. When he set me away from him, my eyes wandered aimlessly around the room. I fingered the material of my dress. Where did we go from here? *M&M night apparently.*

A sudden breeze beneath my dress had me reaching for my discarded thong.

"I'll take those," he said, holding his hand out in front of him. "You won't need them."

"Soren, I'm not going out in a dress with no underwear."

He pulled my hips flush against his. It didn't escape me that I wasn't the only one who had been left wanting. Throbbing.

"Then you don't get to come." The pounding in my pussy intensified. "To M&M night."

We both knew that wasn't what he meant. I handed over my underwear and narrowed my eyes when he tucked them into the pocket of his slacks. Something told me the night was just getting started. And that tonight's showing was about to be the longest movie of my life.

"Are you okay?" Dani did a quick head-to-toe perusal of my body. "You seem, I don't know . . . a little tense."

That was putting it mildly. I was burning from the inside out.

I was going to kill Soren Sinclair. Or fuck his brains out. I hadn't decided just yet.

Here I was, squeezing my legs together, trying to ease my throbbing pussy while I waited for a popcorn refill, and where was he? In a pitch-black theater, laughing his ass off to *Dazed and Confused* with his teammates. Calm as a cucumber, like nothing had happened. Like he hadn't his tongue buried in my pussy an hour ago.

"I'm fine," I lied. "I didn't get to . . . finish everything I had planned for today."

She nodded. "How's everything going with Roasted and Toasted?"

"Good." I was thankful for the topic change. "Roman and Tuck have both committed. Pink, of course, is in. Matty's a maybe, and that's probably perfect for this first go."

"What about your Mr. Sinclair?"

I rolled my eyes, pausing to grab my refilled popcorn bucket from the movie theater attendant.

"First of all, Soren isn't *my* anything." I punctuated each word with another pump of butter into the bucket. "Secondly, I think he's made it pretty clear that he's not interested in any press-related events."

Roasted and Toasted was the amalgamation of the event I had suggested on my very first day. It was a private, ticketed meet and greet for fans and a great opportunity for Roasters staff and players to schmooze with charitable donors. The Roasters' charity, Swing for the Fences, aimed to provide opportunities and resources for youth baseball and softball teams in the Pacific Northwest.

Dani had entrusted me with bringing the event to fruition, and part of that entailed enlisting the help of some Roasters to play baristas for the night. The idea had been well-received by most of the team, but there were more than a few who were hesitant. Some had straight-up declined. I hadn't asked Soren directly, but he also hadn't responded to any of my emails that had been shared with the entire team, nor signed up on the Google form.

I wasn't going to press the issue. Especially not now that he was withholding sex. All because of a stupid Tiktok.

My phone buzzed.

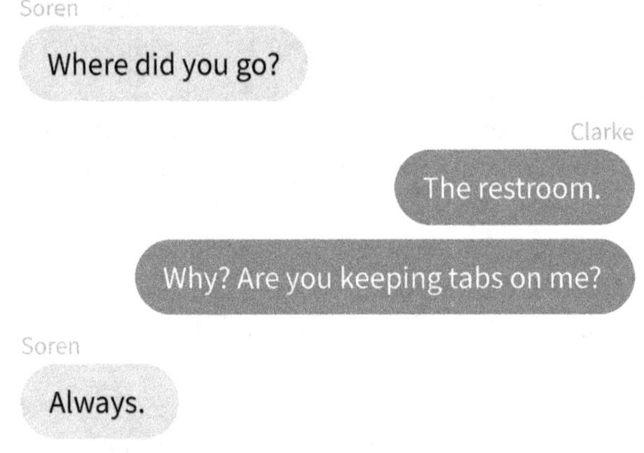

I couldn't contain my groan.

"You good?"

"Yup." I handed Dani the bucket of butter-drenched corn. "I'm going to use the restroom. Would you mind taking this in?"

"Of course."

When I was safely locked away in the bathroom a few minutes later, I checked my phone. He had messaged me again.

I gritted my teeth, trying to ignore the way my heart felt like it was going to thump out of my chest. I was supposed to be pissed at him. *Bastard.* I wasn't going to let his charm get to me.

Soren

Seriously though, where are you?

Clarke

The bathroom.

And then, because I knew it would drive him crazy and because he deserved a little taste of his own medicine, I added:

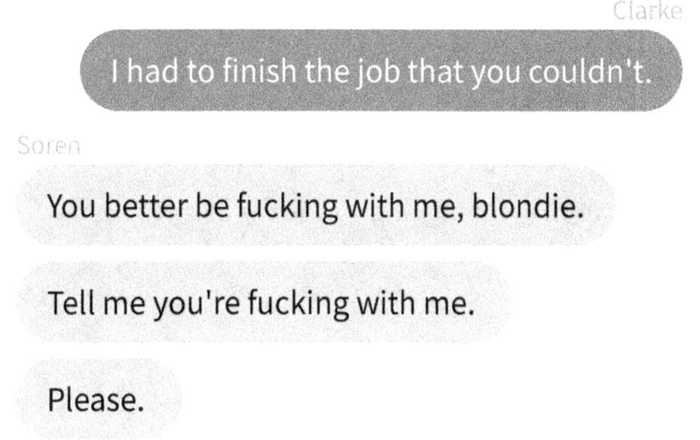

I took pity on him. There was something about the way he pleaded, the way he begged.

Damn this man for making me blush like a teenager. His next words, however, were anything but childish.

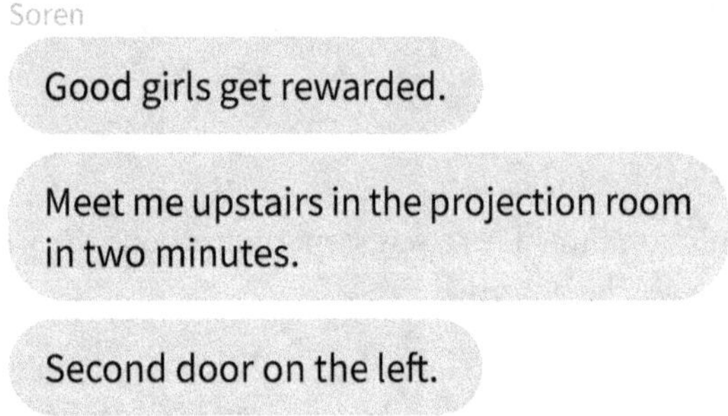

I didn't respond. There was no point. It wasn't a request.

I did however take my time finding the door. Soren had had me squirming in my seat all night, so he could damn well wait. I took a deep breath when I reached the projection room door. Was I supposed to knock? Should I text him aga—

A hand snaked out, pulling me inside. It took a moment for my eyes to adjust to the dark, but once they did, I saw red. Soren was grinning like an idiot. To borrow a line from tonight's film, I wanted to "wipe that face off his head."

"We've got to stop meeting like this."

I swiped at the air. "I can't believe you did that to me. Left me like that." I fumbled my words when those hooded, grayish-green eyes locked on mine. He stalked toward me, crowding me against the wall like a predator hunting its prey. I would be all too happy to let him have a taste. Or bite.

"Are you hurting, blondie?"

"You could have just—" I sighed, running a hand through my hair in frustration. "I wanted you to—"

"What?" He lowered his voice an octave before adding, "What do you want?"

He laced his fingers through mine, pushing my hands against the wall on either side of my face. My breath hitched when his hips pressed forward. I tilted my pelvis, arching into his burgeoning cock.

"Tell me, Clarke." The pressure building between us was reaching a fever pitch—pun intended. "What do you want?"

"I want you to make me come."

And then, as if a dam had been broken, the words poured out of me. The words I had spent years suppressing and, quite literally, paying for.

"*God*, Soren," I moaned. "I want you to fuck me so bad. Please, *please* fuck me. So hard I feel you for fucking days."

His eyes darkened, just before he covered my mouth with his and gave me everything I had asked for.

And then some.

Soren

Spring Training: Week Three

We were down by five runs.

It wasn't looking good. Nothing was looking good.

The clouds had rolled in over an hour ago, and with them, came the wind. And the rain. Just enough to throw us all off our game—and send our opponents' balls soaring out of the park—but not enough to warrant a rainout.

We were already on our third pitcher, Diaz had been pulled out of left field after the fifth with a pulled hamstring, and I hadn't had a hit all game. It was naive to think that every game would go our way. Like every team, we'd seen our fair share of losses during the first half of Spring Training. Losses were inevitable, and there was nothing wrong with losing to a better team.

What I took issue with was playing like shit and losing to a mediocre team.

The Roasters might be new to the MLB, but none of us were new to baseball. You wouldn't know it, though, after watching today's disaster of a game. One that still wasn't over.

Knight was up to bat again. The asshole already had two doubles and a triple today. I groaned when I crouched forward into position. My knees were already barking at me—both of them—and we still had two innings to go. Fuck, thirty-four suddenly felt like sixty.

The crack of a bat had me springing forward. Straight into a brutal line drive that knocked my feet out from under me and had me landing on my knees. *Mother. Fucker.*

At least my shin had stopped the ball. Silver lining? More like a purple and green lining because there wasn't a doubt in mind that that was going to leave one hell of a nasty bruise.

I felt for the ball, firing off a throw from all fours—bad idea—just in time to beat the runner at second. What a way to end the inning. Now I just had to find the strength to limp back to the dugout. If only I could get my leg to withstand my weight.

"Shit, shit, shit," I grumbled under my breath. Suddenly, my bruised shin wasn't the only problem. My knee wasn't cooperating—stubborn fucker had popped out of place.

"Sinclair. You alright, man?"

I looked up. Matty and Tuck wore twin expressions of concern.

"Been better," I said, answering Matty.

"Your ankle?" Tuck asked.

"My knee."

When I tried to stand again, the pressure alone had me seeing stars. For fuck's sake, I was not about to pass out on this field because of a bum knee.

Matty dropped down beside me. "I don't want to add insult to injury, but your girl looks like she's about to rush the field and give you mouth-to-mouth."

"Might be worth the pain, bro," Tuck added.

I chuckled and then groaned. Even laughing hurt like hell.

I didn't dare look over my shoulder to find Clarke. Even though I loved to tease her, I never wanted to hurt her. I'd rather pass out right here on the field than see her in pain.

That's a wild take.

Apparently, at some point during the last few weeks, I'd started prioritizing her emotional wellbeing over my physical health.

I wasn't sure how I felt about that, but now wasn't the time to think about it.

"Do you need a hand?"

"Maybe two?" Tuck added.

I closed my eyes and sucked a calming breath in through my nostrils before blowing it out my mouth. Maybe this was my penance for loafing on my yoga poses for the last few weeks. When the pain finally subsided to a dull throb, I opened my eyes, only to find my two teammates watching me in curious fascination.

"Dude." Amusement colored Tuck's words. "Do you do yoga?"

"Yeah. Got a problem with that?"

"Not at all. Can you teach me?"

He waited in earnest. On the other side of me, Matty arched his brow.

I shrugged. "Sure."

"Dope."

He extended his hand, which I took. At the same time, Matty tucked an arm under mine, helping to my feet. My shin might be bruised, but my ego wasn't. I knew better than that. It was going to take a helping hand (or two) to get me off this field.

They took the bulk of my weight as we walked off. I couldn't stop myself from scoping the seats behind the dugout or zeroing in on the golden-haired goddess clutching her hands to her chest. The question behind her eyes was clear. Hopefully, my forced smile would be answer enough.

"Uh oh," Tuck teased. "She cares about you, Sinclair."

"Shut up," I said through gritted teeth.

Matty sighed. "Told you to be careful, man."

I pretended not to hear him. My feelings for Clarke were growing deeper and deeper by the day, but that didn't mean I was ready to talk about them. Especially not when I could barely admit them to myself. Doing so would mean having to face some hard truths about myself, and that was one of my least favorite pastimes.

"You got one more inning in you, Sinclair?" Coach Ward asked once I cleared the steps of the dugout.

I grimaced, torn between trying to save face—and my spot in the lineup—and bursting into tears. I could already feel both my ankle and knee beginning to swell.

"Eh, give it to Kleiner," I said, feigning benevolence. "I'm sure he'd love a shot."

Our backup infielder, a twenty-two-year-old rookie fresh off the tractor from Kansas, hadn't seen the dirt once this season. I caught a glimpse of him on the other end of the bench practically bursting with excitement at the prospect of playing time.

Ward nodded. He knew better. He knew I wasn't bowing out of the game out of the goodness of my heart.

"Grab some ice from the trainer and have him look you over. I know it hurts now, but that knee's going to feel like shit tomorrow."

That was exactly what I was afraid of. I gave him a half-hearted salute from the bench before resting my head back against the wall.

Nothing was broken. I doubted it was even a sprain or bone bruise. I knew my body better than anybody, and because I was a lucky bastard, I had experienced just about every injury in the book.

That didn't make it hurt any less.

To nobody's surprise, we lost the game. Afterward, I opted to skip a shower and head back to the hotel. I could already feel myself sinking deeper into a post-game funk. Surrounding myself with backslaps and banter wouldn't make my leg hurt any less, but an ice bath might. Which was why I was determined to beat Matty back, so I could claim our bathtub for the next couple of hours.

Getting out of the Lyft and up to my room was a challenge unto itself. One that was made very slowly and with the aid of a hotel luggage cart.

It was a good thing I dragged my sweat-drenched, aching body into my room when I did. My knee had already ballooned to the size of a ripe cantaloupe and my shin had turned an ugly shade of purplish-green. Thankfully, we didn't play again until Friday, which gave me exactly forty-eight hours to moan, groan, and numb the pain.

And it all started with an ice bath.

The phone buzzing across the dresser would have to wait. Clarke had already texted me twice since the game ended, and like the royal asshole I was, I'd left them on read. I'd seen them, she knew I'd seen them, and yet I couldn't bring myself to respond.

Matty was right. Clarke and I were approaching dangerous territory, one that was well outside the boundaries we had set for ourselves. We weren't dating. There were no sleepovers or mornings after, though that probably had more to do with the room share setup. She was bunking with Dani, and I had Matty.

We didn't even really hang out, save for team gatherings. And bus rides. And a breakfast here and there. And yesterday's hot air balloon ride.

That didn't mean anything, though. Friends took hot air balloon rides to see the sunrise after an all-night sexathon, right?

When my phone buzzed again, I put it on airplane mode.

I knew I was being selfish, and Clarke didn't deserve that. But I also knew that if I did message her back—and she jumped into her default sweet, caregiving mode—I would turn into an even bigger, resentful asshole. And she didn't deserve that either.

No, I chose numbness. Literally.

It took ten minutes and three full bags of ice, courtesy of room service, to pack our soaker tub. I filled it the rest of the way with cold water before setting an alarm for fifteen minutes. Anything beyond that was asking for trouble.

I left my boxer briefs on and gently submerged my lower body in the tub, welcoming the immediate shock to my system. Showers were my cure-all, my go-to for sore muscles and stress, but ice baths were something else entirely. A punishment and reward, all wrapped into one.

My fists reflexively clenched as I sunk into the pain, like sharpened needles piercing my skin. Fuck that. I had tattoos, I knew the reality of needles on skin, and it wasn't this. This was much worse. Anybody who said differently was lying.

I took a deep breath in through my nose and counted to three before exhaling. The intense pain had just begun to subside when the door to our room opened.

"I'm in the bath," I forced out, my chest constricting from the cold. I'd left the bathroom door ajar just in case Matty needed to take a piss while I was still in here. "Ten more minutes, man."

There was no response. When a shapely ankle in a neon pink sneaker nudged the door open wide, I cursed under my breath.

"What are you doing here?" I snapped.

"Oh good, you *are* alive," she said, her words dripping with sarcasm. "Matty gave me his key."

She crossed the room until she was toe to tub, planting her hands on her hips like a stern teacher. At any other time, in any other place, I might have been turned on.

I sighed. "I'm sorry, okay? You can yell at me later for not answering your texts."

"And calls."

"And calls." A quick glance at my phone told me I still had nine more minutes. I was, quite literally, a sitting duck. "But, you shouldn't be here now."

"Why don't you let me be the judge of that?"

Stupid, sexy, obstinate woman.

I groaned in frustration. "Clarke," I said through gritted teeth, "I can't be nice to you right now. I'm a grumpy asshole when I fuck up or get hurt. Don't let me make you hate me, baby. Please."

My heart soared when she crouched down beside the tub. I'd spent weeks dreaming of Clarke on her knees for me, but never like this. Not when my dick was practically frozen against my thigh.

She swirled a finger through the frigid water, barely flinching from the temperature.

"Let me be here for you, Soren."

My eyes narrowed. "Trust me, you don't want to be here for me."

"You of all people should know not to tell me what I want."

Well, fuck. She had me there. I couldn't mask my surprise when she thrust a hand into the tub and laced one of her hands through mine.

"And frankly," she said, squeezing my hand. "If you think I'm going to leave you here to wallow in the tub, then you don't know shit from honey butter."

This time, when I laughed, there was no pain. Just unexplainable, unimaginable warmth.

"There's that dirty mouth I love."

I pulled our connected hands out of the water, resting them on the side of the tub.

"Okay," I told her. "But I'm a shit patient, just so you know."

Her pink lips curved. Clarke carried her smile around like a weapon, one that killed on sight and left behind a bright red hue.

"I can work with that."

For the next seven minutes, we stayed just like that. With her kneeling on the bathroom floor, fingers laced through mine, sitting in comfortable silence. When the alarm went off on my phone, she helped me out the tub, bundling me up in a towel like a hug. A warm, fluffy, lavender-scented hug.

She didn't baby me or wait on me hand and foot. I didn't expect her to. I was a grown fucking man, and she was the woman I was sleeping with, not my parent or housekeeper. No, she let me have my space, which was exactly what I wanted. What I *needed*.

While I took my time drying off and throwing on a fresh pair of sweats, she ordered us room service. It was all so natural, so routine. Like we had done this day after day for years. She didn't judge me when I turned on *RuPaul's Drag Race,* my go-to comfort show. She didn't balk when I folded my pizza in half, stuffed it full of Caesar salad, and ate the whole thing like one giant taco. And later, when we crawled under the bedsheets and she nuzzled into the crook of my arm because I kept the room almost as arctic as my ice baths, I couldn't help but think that that felt natural, too.

And for the first time in a long time, that didn't scare me.

Clarke

S oren was on fire today. I didn't even bother trying to contain my ear-splitting smile as I watched him round the bases for the second time. Two home runs, one double, and one single.

I'm sleeping with him! my inner slut screamed. And as of a few days ago, that was true.

Soren and I were actually *sleeping* together. We'd spent every night together since his injury, alternating between his room and mine. Matty and Dani didn't mind. Soren, on the other hand, had almost lost his mind when Matty accidentally walked in on me getting out of the shower. Needless to say, we'd been staying in my and Dani's room ever since.

We were six innings into our afternoon matchup against Austin, and things weren't looking good . . . for them. At this rate, it wouldn't surprise me if they called the game an inning or two early—which, apparently, was a thing at Spring Training. And an early night wouldn't be the worst thing ever.

Dani and I, along with Pink, who had practically become our shadow these last few weeks, wanted to take a Scottsdale public art bike tour. It ran daily at eleven a.m. and four p.m., which made things a bit sticky, what with our game schedule. Maybe today would finally be our day.

The guys in the dugout hooted and hollered as Soren coasted around third base. That cheeky grin I'd come to know and love—especially from between my thighs—spread across his face when his eyes met mine.

Maybe he'd be up for another kind of ride tonight. Heat pooled between my legs just thinking about it.

"That's it, Sinclair!" a feminine voice shouted just steps from my left, shocking me out of my fantasy. "Show 'em what you're made of, Uncle-sorus!"

An attractive brunette was bent over the fence, cupping her hands around her mouth. The best way to describe her style was "grandma chic." From her bejeweled headband to the crocheted "granny square" and electric blue cowboy boots, it was safe to say that this woman looked more out of place at a baseball game than I did. And yet, she oozed confidence.

I'd admit it, my first reaction was a twinge of jealousy. Only for a second or two, though. When she removed her cat-eye sunglasses, though, the final piece of the puzzle clicked into place. She was the spitting image of Soren. Same stormy gray eyes. Same sideways smile. They even had the same mole just above their left eyebrow.

"It's okay," she said when she caught me staring at her. "He's used to this by now. Soren's my baby brother."

"You must be Shelby!" I rushed over to her.

Shelby was the oldest of Soren's two sisters, and based on the way he had described her, like *Dolly Parton meets Penny Lane from 'Almost Famous,'* I knew this had to be her. Soren wasn't a man of many words, but one subject he never ran out of steam discussing was his family. He had nothing but wonderful things to say about his mom, his grandma, his sisters, and their children. It didn't surprise me one bit that he'd come from a family of matriarchs. They had raised one hell of a man.

"Soren's told me all about you."

"I wish I could say the same about you."

"Oh." I held my hand out to her. "Clarke Myers. Social Media Coordinator for the Roasters."

She took her time shaking my hand, and with it came a full body once-over. From the top of my Roasters baseball hat to the tips of my tennis shoes. Her eyes widened then shot up to mine when she spotted Soren's jersey number drawn in Sharpie on the sides—his handiwork, not mine.

Wearing his jersey would send the wrong message, but wearing his number on my shoes seemed innocent enough. Until faced with his family, that was.

"Great to meet you, Clarke."

"Your name is Clarke?" A teenager with multi-colored hair sidled up to Shelby. "That's a cool name."

"Thank you."

This had to be Monty, Shelby's kid and Soren's "nibling." Soren talked a lot about his sisters' children, but I could tell he had a soft spot for Monty. I could see why. They were cute as a button.

"Mom, they were out of pretzels so I got popcorn instead."

"Thanks, baby," Shelby said, wrapping an arm around them. "This is my kiddo, Monty."

"Good to meet you, Monty. Your uncle talks about you all the time."

Their face lit up. It was hard to believe that any day now, Viv and Ellie would welcome a kiddo of their own into the world. I was looking forward to being an aunt—and spoiling the heck out of that kid—but not so long ago, children had been a sore spot in my and Walden's relationship. I had wanted to wait a few years after we got married before trying to have kids. If he had had it his way, I would've been pregnant before the honeymoon was over.

And even though it had bothered me at the time, I'd done exactly as Mama suggested: *"Don't think too much on it, honey. Y'all can figure it out after the wedding."*

Looking back, what she meant was, "You'll change your mind later."

Well, turns out Mama was right about one thing. I had changed my mind. Just not in the way either of us expected.

"I really like your hair," I told Monty. Despite my newfound obsession with color, I didn't think colorful hair was for me. Much like tattoos, vivid hair color was something I could appreciate on other people. Monty pulled off the neon blue and pink balayage—with eye makeup to match—like a cotton candy unicorn.

"Thanks," they said around another crunch of popcorn. "I really love your lipstick. Is it Cherry Tart?"

"Drop Dead Red actually."

The teen really knew their lipstick shades.

"Monty has a YouTube channel reviewing makeup and hair trends." Ah, that explained it. "They just hit two thousand subscribers this week."

Shelby said it like a proud parent. I envied the way she didn't minimize Monty's accomplishments or treat them like a silly hobby. Monty was lucky they had a mom like Shelby, even if they didn't realize it yet.

"Sounds like we've got more than one star in the Sinclair family."

"Well, I could've told you that," a deep voice said from behind us.

I guess they called the game after all.

Monty bent over the short fence separating us from the field, throwing their arms around Soren's neck. I was sure he was sweaty. I was sure he was dirty and rubbed raw from that double play in the third inning. But you would have never known it by the way he embraced his nibling, by the way they loved him back.

"Why didn't you tell me you guys were coming?" he asked his sister.

"We wanted to surprise you. It's this one's spring break, and I had some vacation days to use. Besides, you might not have played as well if you knew."

He laughed. "You little shit."

Shelby stuck her tongue out in response. Yup, they were definitely siblings.

"Okay, well, I'm going to leave y'all to catch up." I spun toward Soren. "I'll see you . . . later."

"You should come!" Monty interjected.

"Yeah, please don't leave on our account." Shelby wrapped one arm around her kid and the other around her brother. "We were just going to check out the river walk, let the big guy buy us dinner. You should join us."

"Are you sure? You really don't have to—"

"Blondie," Soren interrupted. He tucked my hair over my shoulder without a care for who was watching. "Join us."

"Please," Monty added around a fake cough, making us all laugh.

"Please."

I twisted my lips, feigning contemplation. As if it were a difficult choice to make. "Oh, alright," I said, finally giving in. "But I do have a question for you both."

Shelby smiled, amused. Monty waited with bated breath.

"How do you feel about bike riding?"

Later that night—after Soren kicked Matty out of their room yet again and he stripped me down to my favorite lacy, peach boy shorts (which he promptly tore off my body)—I got my answer.

"That was so fucking sexy today," he said around a mouthful of my tits.

Soren was obsessed with my tits.

We were testing his theory of making me come solely by sucking on my nipples. At first, I'd had my doubts, but after fifteen minutes of his nipple-sucking experiment, I was, dare I say, starting to *come* around.

"What was?"

"You. Hanging out with my family." He switched to my other breast. "Giving Monty makeup tips." His teeth tightened around my nipple, jolting me farther up the bed. "God, I wanted to bend you over that bicycle and take you right in front of everybody."

I licked my well-kissed lips. After the game had ended early, we did indeed take our bike tour of Scottsdale . . . with Monty, Shelby, and most of the Roasters' roster. If I hadn't been having so much fun getting to know Soren's family, I might have realized what an incredible publicity moment the entire thing made. But that wasn't what it had been about.

The bike tour had turned into dinner, and dinner had turned into ice cream by the river walk. Through it all, Soren had eyed me like some mythological creature, a mystery waiting to be solved. Or fucked, I guessed.

While he laved the spot he just nipped, I tightened my grip on his shirt. Why he was still fully dressed was beyond me.

"You should have asked. I might have let you."

He growled. The vibration against my already overly sensitized nipples, coupled with his calloused palms cupping me roughly, was the final push I needed to send me over the edge.

I didn't know what kind of magic spell Soren had cast on me—maybe that was a question for my Bitchcraft group chat—but I hoped it would never end. The man made me come without even touching my pussy. If that wasn't witchcraft, I didn't know what was.

He gentled his touch, bathing my breasts and neck with light kisses while I came down from the high. Not that I ever *really* came down from the high that was Soren Sinclair.

As soon as I caught my breath, I tugged his face down toward mine. Our night together was nowhere near through. His lips met mine with fervor. Regardless of where our relationship went, I would forever be grateful for the passion Soren had shown me these past few weeks. Before him, sex had felt like a chore, an obligation to show my partner how much I cared about them. I hadn't understood the appeal. Walden hadn't exactly prioritized my pleasure on the few occasions we'd had sex.

But Soren . . . Soren's pleasure came from making his partner feel good. And while I couldn't speak for any of his previous partners, he made me feel good *every single time* we were together. Whether we had sex or not.

I rolled him to his back, reversing our positions. His eyes twinkled with amusement. He wasn't used to me taking the lead in our bedroom exploits, though he never shied away from encouraging me to do so. We both knew that he had more experience than I did, but it wasn't just that. Generally, I preferred being a pillow princess. It went against every people-pleasing bone in my body, but I kind of liked letting him please me, worship me.

And occasionally throw me around like a rag doll. That was fun, too.

He gripped my hips, groaning when I sat back on his lap, rolling my hips against his cock.

"Fuck, Clarke." His hands slid forward still, smacking the fleshy globes of my ass once, twice, a third time. "You're soaking my lap, baby."

We'd been here before. Just yesterday, we'd crossed the sixth item off my list while half-heartedly watching *Golden Girls* in my room. What had started as a coffee and donut date had turned into a dry-humping session against the hotel room door.

But tonight, I wanted more. There was an ache inside of me, an emptiness. One that could only be quenched by Soren filling me to the brim.

I reached between us, unzipping his pants and pulling his cock out.

"Wait, wait," he said, holding me off of him. "Condom."

"I have an IUD." His eyes darkened when I dragged my dripping sex back and forth over his cock. "I've only ever been with my ex-fiancé, and I got an STD test after we broke up. All clear."

He swallowed. "I get tested regularly for the team, and I haven't been with anybody in almost a year."

That gave me pause. "But what about—"

"Monica and I didn't have sex."

"I thought—"

"Put me inside you, baby." I tucked his cock against my opening, coating him with my wetness. "*Please.* Ride me."

Pleasure spiked when he entered me, stretching me more thoroughly than any man or any toy I'd had before. I pressed my palms flat against his chest, lifting myself up and off his cock, only to fall back down again. All the way, until he was fully sheathed inside of me and my ass slapped his thighs.

"*Fuck,* Clarke. My naughty girl." He fucked me back, meeting me thrust for thrust. "You ride my cock so well."

"You're so deep like this. It's like you're splitting me in two."

"Too much baby?" He rocked up into me.

"No. No, not enough."

"I don't ever want to remember the feeling of not knowing your tight, bare pussy wrapped around me."

That makes two of us.

For the next few minutes—or maybe hours—I rode him furiously. Only stopping when we exploded together, when he held me against his chest and pumped me full of cum. *That* was a new feeling, too. Just one more first I'd saved for Soren. Walden and I had always used condoms, for the convenience of cleanup more than anything else. But maybe it had been more than that. Maybe, subconsciously, I had kept that barrier up between us as a way to . . . well, protect myself. In more ways than one.

I didn't feel that need with Soren.

"It wasn't real," he told me later, when we were both tucked under the covers. "Me and Monica."

"What do you mean?" I whispered against his chest hair. I'd wrapped my limbs around him like a koala bear after he'd cleaned us both up.

"I knew Monica in high school. Back when she was still Monica Jakinsky, not Monica J." I tried to concentrate on what he was saying, but the fingers trailing up and down my back made it next to impossible. I struggled to think of a time I'd ever felt more relaxed. "We reconnected last year while I was home for a wedding and at first, it was great. Like no time had passed. She'd helped me get through twelfth grade English, so when she asked me for a favor, I didn't think anything of it. I figured it was the least I could do."

Uh oh. My stomach clenched. I had a bad—and familiar—feeling about where this was going.

"She was just starting to get her music career off the ground, and she thought that my 'star power'—her words, not mine—might lend a helping hand. My agent was a fan of the idea, so . . ."

An image of one of the books Nessa had lent me flashed across my mind.

"You fake dated?"

"That's one way of putting it, I guess. I hadn't planned for it to last as long as it did." He took a moment before adding, "Or end the way it did, smeared across *Page Six.*"

"And you guys never—"

"No," he answered quickly. "It wasn't like that. We were friends. At least, I thought we were."

I tilted my head back until my eyes met his. They were full of hurt and dejection, nothing like the Soren I was used to.

"Have you spoken to her?"

His lips thinned into a grim expression. "I tried calling her a few times since we ended it. She blocked my number."

"I'm sorry."

He kissed my forehead before tucking me back into his chest.

"You know," he said, "I used to think it was a cool nickname. *Sin.* Maybe not the cleverest, but still, not every player gets one. I thought it meant I was different. Or, I don't know, special."

I pressed my lips against his pec. "You are special."

His hand tightened in my hair, pulling my head back. "You are, too, Clarke." When he slipped a finger inside me, I gasped into his mouth. "And don't let any motherfucker ever tell you differently."

There was no talking after that. Or sleeping.

Soren

Spring Training: Week Four

"**A**dmit it, you missed this."

Shelby looked up from where she lay sprawled out like a starfish on her yoga mat, her eyes full of venom. "Not even a little, you bastard."

She and Monty couldn't have picked a better time to visit. Their trip to Scottsdale coincided perfectly with our only three-day weekend of the entire preseason. For three days, we had seen just about everything Scottsdale had to offer, from Odysea Aquarium to horseback riding along the Bajada Nature Trail. Monty had taken a million selfies amongst the wildflowers, Shelby had taken a Zyrtec when her allergies acted up. I'd even splurged for the three of us—plus Clarke—to take a private tour of an amethyst mine in the Mazatzal Mountains. One that could only be accessed by helicopter.

That was fucking cool.

Clarke had thought I was nuts, dropping a couple grand on an experience that lasted a few hours. But this was what I had worked my entire career for, to give back to the people I loved. The people who had helped get me here.

Today was Shelby and Monty's last day in town, and while the Mont-star slept in, I'd talked my sister into taking a yoga class with me. I might have accidentally left out the fact that it was a *hot* yoga class, but still. She was the one who had gotten me into yoga in the first place. I thought she could hang.

"I'm going to get you back for this."

"You'd have to be able to stand up first," I teased before helping her to her wobbly feet. That class had been no joke, but unlike Shelby, I was feeling fan-fucking-tastic. "You want to grab a smoothie from the place across the street?"

She raised her brow. "After that? You owe me more than a smoothie."

"How about a donut? There's a great place nearby that Clarke found."

Shelby snickered, and it didn't take a genius to guess why. There was no point in trying to hide my relationship with Clarke, especially not from Shelby, the human lie detector. Clarke had spent most of the last three days with us—and every night with me. Hell, she didn't even need me around to charm my sister and nibling. Just yesterday, she and Monty had given each other makeovers for Monty's YouTube channel. And I was pretty sure Shelby had already added her to a group chat with our sister, Sadie.

"You're in deep, baby brother."

"It's not like that," I told her. It was a lie I had been telling myself since we got to Arizona, so at least I was consistent. "We're just having fun."

"Uh-huh."

"Don't be like that."

"Like what?" she goaded me.

"All big-sisterly. Like you . . . know things."

She threw her head back and laughed. "Oh, brother of mine, when are you going to learn that I know *everything?* And one thing I know for sure is this thing between the two of you is so much more than just fun."

I sighed. "That's what we agreed on. No feelings, no commitment, just—"

"Fun," she finished for me. "You should know by now that shit like that never works. The last time I 'just had fun' was . . . well, count how old my kid is, then add nine months."

Shelby, of all people, knew that a casual fling wasn't my usual MO—and it definitely wasn't Clarke's. But just because we were both relationship people didn't mean we were ready for a relationship. Or capable of one.

Together, we walked side by side across the plaza to Holy Smokes, the nearby donut shop. It wasn't until after we left the shop with a boxed dozen donuts—plus an upside-down caramel macchiato for Clarke—that Shelby mentioned Clarke again.

"You like her."

I rolled my eyes. "Are we back on this?"

"Did we ever leave?" She sipped her latte. "Just admit it. You never would have let her spend so much time with us, especially Monty, if she didn't mean *something* to you. She makes you happy."

"Yeah," I agreed begrudgingly. If only it were that simple. "She does."

She clapped a hand on my shoulder. "Jeez, Sore, that's a *good* thing."

"But you know what else makes me happy? Playing ball. Making a name for myself. Providing my family with everything they deserve and more."

Confusion colored her face. "Do you think that's what we expect from you?"

"That's the least you *should* expect from me."

"Oh, sweetie." Her face softened. "I don't know what happened between you and the pop star, but forget about it. Clarke is not her. Clarke doesn't give two shits about your name or your money or where you come from. And neither do we. Win or lose, we're all so proud of you."

My jaw clenched. This conversation would be better suited for a bottle of bourbon than a box of fritters.

"Okay, enough of this," she said, lightening the mood. "We've got a flight to catch, and you've got a girl to wake up."

Shelby threaded her arm through mine. Apparently, all it took to revive her was some fresh air and a vanilla latte.

"By the way, since when do you drink upside-down caramel macchiatos?"

"Oh, that's not for me. That's for—"

"Let me guess. For 'fun'?" I cleared my throat. "Mm-hmm, thought so."

By the time I reached Clarke's hotel room, I had officially made up my mind. I was going to show her just how great we could be together. As in, together for real.

No expiration date, no sex list. Not that there was much left on her sex list at this point anyway.

Maybe it's time to create another list together.

I still had my reservations about being in a relationship during baseball season, but I also knew that I wasn't ready to let Clarke go. I couldn't. Now, I just had to show her that I was boyfriend material. And what did good boyfriends do? They surprised their girlfriends with spontaneous dates.

"Wait, where are we going?" Clarke asked after she'd polished off her second donut. I'd put away four, but after this morning's hot yoga session, I figured I deserved it.

I laced my hands through hers, and because I was a masochist, I held them against the small of her back so her unbound breasts pressed against me. Finding her in bed—exactly where I left her this morning—wearing nothing but an oversized T-shirt that barely covered her ass was something I could get used to.

"Wear comfortable shoes, pack a change of clothes, and bring sunscreen." I ran a hand over her ample cheeks before smacking one hard enough to make it jiggle.

She jumped out of my arms, rubbing a hand over her ass. "Okay, Mr. Bossy Pants."

While she spent the next thirty minutes getting ready for the day, I cleared the crumbs off the table and made her bed. *Our bed.* I pretended to be lost in my phone when she pranced out of the bathroom wearing nothing but a pink bralette and matching panties held together by a bow on each side. I was going to be thinking about those bows all day. More specifically, about how easy it would be to untie them.

"Okay," she said, twirling to show off her floral print romper and sneakers. "Right as rain, and I packed a bag."

"You look beautiful."

"Oh, stop. This isn't anything fancy. I just—"

"Don't," I told her, coming to my feet. "Don't do that. I don't ever want to hear you minimizing yourself, your looks, your accomplishments. You're never 'just' anything."

Her eyes grew wide with surprise and then drunk with desire. She fisted my shirt in her clutches, pulling my mouth to hers. "You're something else, Soren Sinclair," she whispered against my lips.

"Don't ever forget it, baby."

When we got downstairs, we piled into the car I had rented for the day. Nothing fancy, no bells and whistles—Clarke didn't care about those—save for the moonroof. Clarke squealed in surprise when the glass panel retracted, letting in the warm desert breeze.

"Hang on to your hat, blondie."

"I didn't bring one," she said, wind whipping through her bouncy curls.

"Let's change that, shall we?"

One hour and about a dozen feathers later, we were now the proud owners of two custom hats. Our first stop of the day had been the Rancher Hat Bar. Dani had actually given me the idea when she said that Clarke had been on the hunt for a cowgirl hat during our stay in Arizona. Who would have guessed that there was an entire business built for DIY-ing your very own hat—while also enjoying a drink or two—right here in Scottsdale?

Clarke had chosen a white, rancher hat, adorning it with an orange ribbon, a mixture of bird feathers, and a vintage button. She'd even used a blow torch to darken the brim's edges. I had opted for an army green trucker hat, covering it with patches featuring vintage cartoon characters and cereal mascots.

"Do a twirl, Sinclair."

Clarke's beaming smile beat any motivational speech I had ever heard. She wanted a twirl? I could do that. I'd happily drop to my knees and eat her pussy until she came all over my trucker hat if she asked.

"I don't think I've ever been more attracted to you," she teased.

"Don't be jealous," I argued playfully. "I can't help it if I pull off hats better than you."

She gasped and clutched a hand to her chest. "Who licked the red off your candy?"

"Oh, blondie." I tapped her brim. "If you want something to lick, all you have to do is ask."

Her eyes darkened. My cock twitched when she ran her tongue over her lower lip. Sometime in the last few weeks, I had created a monster.

"Hold that thought," I told her. Not that I didn't want to fulfill every one of the naughty fantasies that were no doubt circling around her brain, but we had a schedule to keep.

We spent the next few hours checking off *my* list of things to do to make Clarke Myers fall in love with me. We shopped Old Town Scottsdale, popping into small boutiques and souvenir shops, before stopping for a bite to eat at a hole-in-the-wall pizza spot built in an old train car. When we got our fill—of both pizza and knick-knacks—we got back in the car and headed for Tucson.

The next two hours were spent counting cows, sharing silly stories, and belting out showtunes. Miguel, the catcher from my last team in New Jersey, and I had shared many bus rides and hotel rooms during my two-year stint with the team. He taught me what little Spanish I knew and how to make *arepas*. I'd taken him to every show on Broadway since he had a thing for musicals. Thanks to him, I now knew every word to "Defying Gravity" (or "*En Contra de la Gravedad*") in two different languages. Clarke held her own, though, impressing me with her rendition of "So Much Better" from *Legally Blonde.*

Her brows shot up when we pulled through the gates of the ranch, then again when she spotted the long, elegant table dressed for dinner.

"Is this where we're eating?" she asked excitedly. I loved that all it took to win her over was a craft project or dinner on a dude ranch.

"Yup."

"This is so cool!"

Her excitement never subsided throughout our farm-to-table meal—all six courses of it. She asked our chef thoughtful questions about each dish and cocktail pairing, from the mesquite-smoked prosciutto and homemade sourdough to the miso, blackberry duck, and baby squash. I was going to be burning off today's carb fest for weeks to come, but it was worth it if it meant watching Clarke moan around her fork for a second more. Pleasure bloomed deep in my chest as I watched her savor every bite, every sip.

I knew that years from now, I wouldn't remember the meal—despite how delicious it was. I wouldn't remember the high-pitched neighs from the nearby horses or the name of the Michelin star chef that prepared our meal—and hugged the pants off Clarke at the end of it. What would forever be embossed in my memory was the image of Clarke's smile, illuminated by the setting sun and twinkle lights. I added it to the mental scrapbook I'd already begun building. The one labeled "Our beginning."

Much to her surprise, the night didn't end there. We still had one more stop to make.

When we pulled up in front of the performance venue in downtown Tucson, she turned to me, a silent question in her eyes. "Lawrence," the name of tonight's performer, was written across the marquee in big block letters. I didn't know much about them, other than the few songs Matty had played for me on Spotify. I had liked their sound immediately, and I had a feeling Clarke would, too.

"Time for another first," I told her. Her eyes glistened with unshed tears. "Hey, what's with the tears? Baby, if you want to save your first concert for another time, we can just go back to the hotel."

"No, no!" she protested. "I was just . . . I was just thinking that I'm glad I get to experience so many firsts with you. I know I already said it, but you really are something else, Soren Sinclair."

Oh, blondie. What am I going to do with you?

I smiled and kissed her hand. The real question was what was *she* going to do with me? Date me, trust me? *Love me?* I'd never been a betting man before, but I was starting to realize that for Clarke, I might just be willing to risk it all.

Especially because, when she called me "something else," what I really wanted to tell her was, *I'm nothing without you.*

Clarke

"**H**as the heat turned you into a raisin yet?"

"You'll be happy to know that I survived," I said, smiling into my phone. "And got a free tan out of it."

Scottsdale temperatures were no joke, but at least it was a dry heat. Nothing compared to the sweltering humidity of the South. But after a month in Arizona, I was actually looking forward to the doom and gloom of the Pacific Northwest.

I kicked off my shoes and settled back against the mountain of pillows. I was going to miss having such a big bed to sprawl across. The double bed in my trailer was nothing compared to this. I was seriously going to have to start looking into a more permanent rental when we got back to Oregon the day after tomorrow.

"How's my niece or nephew cooking?"

Viv sighed, exasperated.

"Wow, that good?"

Viv was closing in on her thirty-sixth week of pregnancy, and she looked utterly exhausted. A sheen of sweat covered her face, her hair looked like it hadn't been washed in days, and I was pretty sure she was using her belly to prop up her phone. I made a mental note to search for prenatal massages in her area first thing tomorrow.

"I swear to Sarah MacLachlan." She pulled the phone close enough for me to count her freckles. "I'm *this* close to buying a trampoline and jumping 'til I shake this meatloaf out of me."

I rolled to my side, giggling. That was something I'd been doing a lot more often lately—laughing. Not soft, polite laughter either. I was talking deep, aching belly laughs. I laughed with the guys over drinks by the pool. I laughed with Dani when we decked out the team bus with pastels for Easter. More often than not, I laughed with Soren.

In bed late at night, on the bus in the morning. After sex. Sometimes, during sex.

He'd shown me so much this month, given me so much. Beyond sex, although that was still top-notch. I'd already changed my ringtone to Lawrence's "Don't Lose Sight" after this weekend's concert. For as long as I lived, I would never forget that night.

My stomach lurched when I remembered that tonight was supposed to be our final night together. Tomorrow morning, we boarded the bus back to Rose City.

"And are you being a good patient and letting Ellie take care of you?"

"What do you think?" she said, rolling her eyes. "When are you coming to visit? I miss you."

"We're in Atlanta next month. Maybe I could drive up to see y'all."

"Forget that." She held the phone away from her face as she shouted into the other room. "Babe, we're going to see my sister at a baseball game next month."

"But honey . . ." My sister-in-law trailed off, her protest falling on deaf ears. It was no use. When Viv made her mind up about something, that was that. Typical Aries behavior.

"No buts. We're going."

"I'll grab us tickets," I told her. "I can't wait to see both of you. Well, all three of you, I guess!"

On the one hand, I was excited by the prospect of seeing Viv and Ellie in person. It had been far too long—well before Viv's second trimester—and that was my fault. On the other hand, I was a bit nervous about venturing so close to home. Atlanta might not be Charleston, but I still couldn't help but feel a twinge of anxiety.

"By the way," she said. Her tone of voice ratcheted my anxiety up another level. "I heard from Mama today." And another.

"Do I want to know what she said?"

"Oh, you know, the usual." She rubbed her belly. "She asked about me and Ellie, the baby. And you."

My eyes welled with moisture. When I first told my parents about calling off the engagement, I'd expected some kind of reaction. Tears, yelling, bargaining maybe—Daddy had never been able to resist a deal. Instead, I had been met with indifference and disappointment. Silence.

I hadn't heard a peep from either of my parents in over two months. No phone calls, no text messages. Nothing.

"Funny," I said around a sniffle. "Because she hasn't called me. Not once."

Her eyes filled with pity. "Clarke—"

"It's okay." I looked up, trying—and failing—to will the tears away. "I don't know why I was expecting something different."

"Probably because they've spent the better part of your life controlling your every move."

"And I let them."

"No, honey," she choked out. "You survived them. We both did."

Maybe if we were lucky, our generational trauma would be enough to send her into labor.

"They dictated the first twenty-seven years of your life, Clarke. That shit ends now. No matter what, you've got me." She rubbed a hand over her swollen belly. "You've got us."

My lips quivered. "Thanks, sissy."

We talked for a few more minutes before I cut our call short. There wasn't much to talk about, not when we were both blubbering messes. At least Viv could blame it on pregnancy hormones.

I wasn't sure how long I lay there like that, curled up, bawling like a baby. It could have been ten minutes or two hours. But that was how Soren found me.

"Ugh, this is awful."

"Do you want me to heat it up again?" Soren reached for my bowl of Tom Kha soup.

"No." I gestured to the flat screen across from us. "I mean Phi Phi O'Hara. She already has it out for Willam, but Sharon Needles, too?"

He smiled weakly. It was safe to say this wasn't how either of us had imagined our final night together, and yet, somehow it was perfect. *RuPaul's Drag Race* marathon, takeout Thai food, and all.

Viv and Ellie had taken me to my first drag show in Asheville a few years ago, and like a tween at a Billie Eilish concert, it was love at first sight. What wasn't to love? The gowns, the pageantry, the performances. Plus, as far as I could tell, the queens were a lot less bitchy than the girls I'd grown up with on the pageant circuit.

Soren hadn't given me much of a choice after I'd all but cried myself to sleep in his arms. It wasn't exactly the sex fest either of us had envisioned, but romantic nonetheless. I hadn't expected him to be as attentive as he'd turned out to be.

He'd held me for over an hour, stroking my back silently while I soaked his shirt with my tears. He didn't press me for details about what set off my crying jag. I offered a bare bones explanation, and he accepted it. I could have told him more. Maybe I should have. When I finally pulled myself together enough to blow my nose, he carried me to the soaker tub in the en suite. I promptly burst into tears once again after seeing that he had already drawn me a bath, complete with bubbles and lavender bath salts. The lengths this man was willing to go to, all to make sure I felt comfortable and safe. Even though he knew it wasn't going to lead to sex.

Our relationship might have been unconventional, but one thing it wasn't, was transactional.

When Soren helped me undress and get settled in the tub, he wasn't doing it to seduce me. When he left me alone to wallow in my bubbles and feelings while he ordered us takeout, he wasn't trying to talk me into sex. There wasn't anything sexual about this.

This was care. This was respect. This was the side of Soren Sinclair that hardly anybody else had taken the time to see. And that was their loss because Soren Sinclair was a teddy bear.

A soft and squishy, kind-hearted, rubs your feet while you slurp your noodles teddy bear.

After my bath, he bundled me up into a fresh set of pajamas, tucked me into his outrageously large king-sized bed, and proceeded to force feed me Thai food while we watched old episodes of his favorite show. He'd even gone as far as spooning carrots out of my soup, since he knew I didn't like the texture. What kind of person did that?

Someone who loves you, that's who.

I nudged that thought out of my head and straight over a cliff. I'd been telling myself for weeks not to fall for Soren, a feat that was proving more difficult by the day.

I turned away from our show just as Phi Phi shouted something about likening Sharon to Party City and peeked over at the man in question. He'd kicked off his shoes hours ago and was now cozied up on the opposite end of the bed, stroking my feet with one hand and nursing a mug of tea with the other.

I guess he just can't get enough of piping hot tea.

Just because there was a lot to love about Soren, didn't mean that I was *in love* with Soren. Sure, I loved how engrossed he was with the outrageous lives of celebrity drag queens. I loved the way he cared—about his family, his teammates. Me. I loved the way he was honest with me about his past.

After he opened up about Monica, the sharing didn't stop there. He told me about the bar fight in Detroit. The one that had started after he defended his batting coach from some jerks one night after a game. He told me about the teammate who made his life hell when he found out Soren had hooked up with his wife . . . years before they were married. Mostly, we talked about his first stint in the major league. The one that had gone terribly wrong.

"I just choked," he had said me while we waited for our takeout to arrive. *"Two errors in my first game, three in my second. Two strikeouts, one ground out. I never even made it on base."*

"You just weren't ready."

"I just wasn't focused."

And that was why I had to walk away. Even though I didn't want to. Even though I loved this sensual, confident side of myself that he had brought out of me. Even though I loved—

"What's that look?" he asked, startling me out of my stupor.

I knew that all I had to do was say the word and he'd be on his feet, bound to deliver on whatever request I had. But it wouldn't be fair to make *this* request. Not now, not on what was supposed to be our last night together.

"Nothing." The lie tasted bitter, like the darkest roast of black coffee. There was a reason I only drank lattes drenched in caramel. I curled onto my side and closed my eyes. "It's nothing."

The next time I awoke, it was to find myself cuddled against Soren's chest, warmth radiating throughout my body. The TV was still on, though the volume had been lowered exponentially, and he'd traded *RuPaul's Drag Race* for *The Great British Baking Show.*

I rolled to my back and blinked my eyes fully open. I found myself staring up at a very chiseled chin.

"What time is it?"

"Almost midnight," he said softly. At the same time, he drew his hand through my hair, curling a lock around his fingers.

"Mm, that feels good." I burrowed my face into his neck. His pulse beat wildly against my nose. "I'm sorry about tonight."

"I'm not."

"This was not how our last night together was supposed to go."

He stiffened and fell silent. I could tell that he wanted to say something, but I wasn't sure I wanted to hear it. Not if it meant saying goodbye.

"Clarke, I—"

"Wait. Please let me say something first." It wasn't a question, and I didn't wait for an answer. "The last few weeks have been so incredible. Truly. You've shown me a side of myself I pretended wasn't there for a long time. And I just want you to know that I will forever be grateful for that, for you, and our time together."

I knew it was cowardly not to look him in the eye while I said my piece. But I also knew that if I looked into his big, beautiful eyes while I said it, I might do something really dumb, like burst into tears or tell him I loved him.

When he didn't respond right away, the doubts kicked in. Should I not have said something at all? Should I have told him I wanted more? Had he fallen asleep? Only when I started to detangle my limbs from his did he tighten his arms around me and speak.

"Thank you."

My heart sunk. I didn't want this to end. A part of me had hoped he might feel the same way, but I guessed this was it. I'd known it was coming all along, and yet, now that it was here, I felt lower than the last rung on the ladder.

I choked back a sob. "You don't have to stay if you don't want to."

"Do you want me to go?"

Did I?

"No," I answered honestly. I didn't want to ruin our last night together, but I also couldn't imagine spending it anywhere other than in his arms. "But I know I put a lot on you tonight and we've got a long bus ride ahead of us tomorrow, so I would understand—"

He tipped my chin up with his fingers. "There's nothing more important than being with you. Right here and right now."

Well dang, good answer.

I rolled back into him, this time laying my head upon his chest. As I closed my eyes once more, I came to a startling realization. I had never felt like this before. Not with Walden, not with anyone. Maybe it was just because it was our last night, maybe it was a PMS-induced haze, but I didn't think so.

Maybe, just maybe, I loved Soren Sinclair.

Soren

Roasters 1-0

"Alright, you handsome fuckers." Roman stood up, lifting his vodka soda toward the sky. "One down, one-hundred and sixty-one to go."

"Plus the playoffs," Pink amended. "And the World Series."

Roman's piercing look had Pink slinking back behind Bennett, like that Homer Simpson in the hedges GIF. Whereas Pink captured attention with his antics, Roman demanded it with his stare, no words necessary. When he was finally satisfied that we were all paying attention, Roman finished his toast.

"Here's to us, to the season, and to the people we love who give us a reason."

Cheers rang out around the table. Glasses and bottles clinked together. As far as first games went, we couldn't have asked for a better start to the season. Personally, I was riding an all-time high. It had been four years since my disastrous debut in the majors, and yet, I was playing better than ever. I was healthier, happier. Hell, I might have been the second oldest player on the team, but I was running circles around these guys. I was also more at ease, and that was perhaps the most surprising of all.

It was hard to believe that just a couple of months ago, I'd been wound tighter than my grandmother's pocket watch. This was my make-or-break season, my big comeback. That came with a lot of pressure and expectations—from me, more than anyone else.

But here I was, celebrating my first official win in the major league with a group of guys who—whether they meant to or not—had ingratiated themselves into my heart. I kind of loved these fuckers, and I didn't mind admitting that. Except to Pink. He didn't need my love; he loved himself plenty already.

"Real talk," Tuck said, drawing our attention. "Is it too early to start planning our victory vacay? Because I'm just going to say it: Caribbean cruise."

Wesley beat his fists on the table, bursting with excitement. "*Aye!* We can visit my *abuelita*."

Like me, Wesley had been raised by his mother and grandmother. He had already booked their flights and bought them tickets for this summer's Puerto Rican Pride Night at the ballpark.

"Disneyworld, bro," Roman argued. "Disneyworld." I tried to picture our six-foot-seven, two-hundred-and-eighty-pound first baseman in Mickey ears.

"*Or* maybe, we should win the dang thing first?" Matty said before finishing his drink. Unlike most of us, Matty had actually seen a World Series. "Isn't it bad luck to start planning an end-of-season trip after the first game?"

"Let 'em have their fun." I pointed to the empty glass in his hand. "You want another one?"

He nodded. "Thanks, man."

While the rest of them argued over our hypothetical future trip to the Bahamas and Yosemite, I went to refill my and Matty's drinks.

Thorn Tavern was a dope spot, the perfect blend of a neighborhood sports bar and low-key British pub. Nothing fussy, not a kale leaf in sight. Usually, when the team got together outside of work, we did it at somebody's house or apartment, but tonight, we wanted to celebrate in Rose City. With Rose City. And as it turned out, our fans were the shit.

"Another round?" the tattooed bartender asked.

"Please. For me and the Southern ginger." While he poured us two fresh beers, I admired the ink swirling around his forearm. That shit was immaculate. I was going to have to ask where he got it done. "Thanks for making space for all of us, by the way."

"No problem. You guys killed it tonight."

"Thanks."

I rested a hip against the bar. Despite my ease and contentment, I couldn't help but feel like something—or someone—was missing. A thick-thighed, honey-haired beauty to be exact. I was going on day five of PC (aka "Post Clarke") and I wasn't loving it. We had seen each other in passing at practice, and again around Bed of Roses, though I'd avoided the communal showers like the plague.

No surprise, I'd fucked that up. She'd given me the perfect opener during our last night together and what had I done? Let it slip right through my fingers like a fumbling virgin. Maybe it was better this way.

Or, maybe you need to fight for her.

A glass crashed from the other end of the bar. I twisted to see Pink shoving two guys away from him. The first, a bulky guy in a Roasters jersey, cocked his fist back, ready to coldcock Pink. The second held his buddy's arm, tugging him away from our pitcher with murder in his eyes.

In the periphery, I saw a few of the guys jump out of their seats, but I was already on my feet. It only took a second or two to reach Pink and wrap my arms around him from behind like a bear hug.

"Walk away."

"Fuck that." He fought my hold, and I let him. It might mean an elbow to the gut or balls, but I was willing to risk it. "Get out of my way, Sinclair."

"Not a chance, asshole."

I stood my ground, tightening my hold on him, while the rest of the team formed a protective circle around us. This could only go one of two ways—with me buying the kid another round or the kid buying us all first-class tickets to the emergency room. I was ready for either.

He fought me for a minute, his original targets long gone. Finally, he settled. "You didn't hear the kind of shit they were saying," he said between angry huffs.

"It doesn't matter." I relinquished my hold, turning him to face me. "I've been here. I've been you. I know where this leads, and it's not fucking worth it."

His eyes were full of fury—and maybe hurt—something I'd never seen from him before, even in game mode. This wasn't the loveable, albeit slightly annoying, golden retriever we were all used to. No, this was a darker side of Jared Pink.

"Jared," I said, drawing his full attention. "Do yourself a favor and walk away."

He clenched his jaw. I couldn't blame him for wanting to fuck those guys up, even if they were fans. They had douchebag written all over them. But I could prevent him from blaming himself. For years to come.

"Let's take a walk."

This time, when I clapped a hand on his shoulder, he didn't shrug it off or fight me. I gave the guys a nod, letting them know I had this covered.

He followed me outside to the front of the bar. Thankfully, the rain had let up.

"Where are we going?" he asked, matching my pace. "Everything in this stupid town closes at nine."

"I told you, we're taking a walk. What, they don't walk in Portland?"

He shrugged. "I usually scooter."

I belted out a laugh. It echoed down the empty street.

"Fuck, now I really feel old."

We walked side by side for the next ten minutes, taking up the entire sidewalk. Pink was right. With the exception of the tavern, the town had shut down hours ago following the game. Most of the fans had long since headed home to the metro area.

When we rounded the corner to Bed of Roses, Pink stopped. "What are we—" Realization dawned across his face. "Is this where you live, Sinclair?"

"Temporarily."

"All this time, you've been living in Rose City?"

I tucked my hands into my pockets, thrilled to be back where it was chilly enough to wear a hoodie. A few of the guys knew I had been staying somewhere in Rose City, but I had never had them over. There wasn't exactly room for entertaining. Plus, I preferred my privacy, for obvious reasons.

"C'mon," I said, gesturing toward the outdoor shower. "I'm about to give you a gift."

His eyes widened. "Seriously, Sinclair? I know I fuck with you a lot, but you really aren't my type."

"Look," I said, leveling with him as I removed my hoodie. "I don't know what those guys said to set you off, and I'm not going to make you tell me. But I've been at this a lot longer than you, so I can tell you that that shit isn't going away." Next, came my shirt. "Assholes are always going to asshole. That's out of your control." I toed off my shoes and removed my socks. "What you *can* control is your sanctum, the place or thing that brings you peace. This is mine."

When I pulled my joggers down, he averted his eyes.

"Damn, Sinclair. Warn a guy, would you?"

"Think about it." I gathered my discarded clothes and took off down the path, calling back over my shoulder, "You can grab a towel from Moira. Key is under the mat."

I wasn't his parent. I wasn't going to hold his hand or lie just to make him feel better. I had given him the keys to the Bat Cave; the rest was up to him.

I'd just finished rinsing the shampoo from my hair when I heard the shower across from me turn on. I smiled into the stream.

"They were making jokes about an autistic girl." I slicked my hair out of my face and met his gaze. "The assholes at the bar.

Asshole A was telling Asshole B about the girl he's been seeing, and Asshole B said some nasty shit about it. I didn't like that. My sister's autistic."

I nodded.

"Still think it's good you pulled me off them?"

"I'm not saying they didn't deserve it," I told him. "They usually do. But believe me, beating the shit out of them wouldn't have done much good. You can't beat the bigotry out of somebody."

He stared blankly into the dark. "Yeah."

We soaked up the silence after that, along with the hot water. I didn't push him for more. I had a feeling he didn't have more to give just yet. I'd been there before, multiple times. I wasn't lying when I told him that. He had some reflecting to do, and I was happy to leave him to it. Besides, this wasn't the first time Pink and I had shared a shower, but it was certainly the quietest. I might as well enjoy it while I could.

Any thought of Pink melted away though when I caught a glimpse of blonde hair peeking out of the neighboring trailer's window.

Clarke

"**N**ext up behind the pull, hailing all the way from Scratch Ankle, Alabama, is your shortstop, Matty Miller."

Patrons clapped and hollered when Matty took his place behind the counter, trading places with Roman. Of all the Roasters, Matty was by far one of the fans' favorites, and I could see why. The drawl, the freckles, the effortlessly bouncy curls that most of us had to spend money at a salon to achieve. I could practically hear the sound of panties dropping when he ran a hand through his unruly, strawberry-blonde hair.

"Mm, what is it about redheads?" Nessa asked from my left.

"I don't know," June answered. "It's the curls for me."

They clinked their espresso martinis together. In lieu of tonight's Dungeons and Dragons get-together, I had invited them both to our inaugural Roasted and Toasted event. Jo had opted to stay in with his husband.

"How's the martini?"

"De-freaking-licious." June licked her lips. "Your first baseman is a generous pourer. Just the way I like it."

"I second that," Nessa croaked after another sip. "He might give my brother a run for his money."

Roman was, apparently, preparing vodkas with a side of espresso, rather than espresso martinis. No wonder his line was so long.

Roasted and Toasted was shaping up to be a major success. The event had sold out within an hour, we already had a waiting list for the next three events, and all of our VIP sponsors seemed to be having the time of their lives. Between the silent auction and ticket sales, we'd already raised well over our goal. And thanks to the guys' unofficial side wager to see which of them could earn the most tips throughout the night, we were on track to double that.

Dani stepped away from Banks Coppola—yes, *those* Coppolas—and moseyed over to us, and Banks's eyes stuck to her ass the entire way.

"What a creep," she said through gritted teeth. I knew a pageant smile when I saw one. "Keep an eye on him, will you?"

"Sure thing."

"And please, let me know if he says or does anything out of line. I'd love any excuse to kick his misogynistic ass out of here."

June's eyes glowed with admiration—who could blame her? She gestured toward Dani with her glass.

"Have I told you how much I love your boss yet?"

Dani flipped her hair over her shoulder.

"And thank you so much for including us," Nessa told her.

"Of course." This time, Dani's smile reached her eyes. "It was important to us to include local business owners and Rose City residents in addition to the bigwigs with deep pockets."

"That means a lot."

I listened half-heartedly while scanning the room for any out-of-place chair or empty drink, but alas, there were none. Our event team had knocked this one out of the park.

"Ladies," Roman said, shouldering his way into our circle. "How are those espresso martinis treating you?"

June lifted her glass. "Well done, sir."

"Roman, would you mind escorting Nessa and June to the swag bags?" Dani asked. "I need a minute with Clarke."

"It would be my pleasure."

"Believe me," Nessa murmured into my ear. "The pleasure is *all* mine."

My chest shook with laughter when she winked. Dani waited until all three of them were well out of listening range before turning back to me. "Is it true you caught Pink showering with Soren the other night?"

I smiled. It was a little embarrassing how quickly I had leapt out of bed when I heard the outdoor shower kick on the other night. There weren't many folks staying at Bed of Roses that showered after midnight, so I'd known—I'd hoped—it was Soren. What I hadn't expected to find when I looked out my window was Jared Pink, naked as the day he was born.

I should have known that he'd tell Dani. From what I had seen, Jared Pink had no shame, especially about his body. Frankly, he didn't have anything to be ashamed of.

"Yes and no," I told her. "They were showering, but not in the same stall."

"Oh." Her face fell. "How disappointing."

"Soren has a thing about showers," I told her. "They're kind of his cure-all." I didn't offer more than that. It wasn't my place to spill all his secrets.

"I got that. Pink, apparently, had . . . a night."

"Is he okay?"

She pursed her lips. "I'd say he's about as okay as the rest of us. Don't let that goofy smile fool you. He's still a person, flaws, feelings, and all."

Flaws, feelings, and all.

Like usual, Dani was right. She had a knack for actualizing ideas I had never been able to find the words for. It didn't matter where we came from or how we were raised. In one way or another, we were all hurting. Some of us just had a more convincing pageant smile.

For the next thirty minutes, we made the rounds, making small-talk and snapping photos with attendees, players, and our mascot, River. River had also taken a turn behind the counter earlier in the evening. As a mustached hipster barista, how could he not? We were quickly broaching the final hour of the event, which meant it was time to switch up our baseballer barista once again.

"Have you seen Tuck?" I asked Dani after double-checking my list. "I know he's here, but I haven't seen him in over an hour."

"Oh, he left a while ago."

My head snapped up from the clipboard. "What?"

"He wasn't feeling well, so I told him he could go home."

That was news to me. Tuck was slotted to be our last barista of the evening. There wasn't any time to call up any of the other guys. Most of them lived in Portland anyway.

"Okay." I racked my brain for a solution. "Well, maybe one of the guys won't mind giving it another go. Roman, maybe? Although we might run out of vodka—"

"No worries. Your boy-toy already has it covered."

I stopped cold. "What?"

"Sinclair. He's already aproned up and ready to go."

My stomach dropped when she pointed across the room.

Well, damn. Soren in an apron instantly zipped up the chart of sexiest Soren moments, landing somewhere between buck-naked Soren and game-day-suit Soren. They all paled in comparison to backwards-hat Soren. That was top-tier masturbatory material.

"And can I just say?" She leaned into me. "It should be a crime for somebody to look that good in an apron."

She breezed away from me, presumably to relieve Matty—whose line had finally started to die down—and introduce Soren. My head was still trying to catch up with my heart. He hadn't RSVP'd. He hadn't so much as mentioned the event, even while sharing my bed. And yet, here he was, freshly shaved and (gulp) sporting a backwards Roasters hat.

I carved a path through the partygoers, my feet moving as if of their own accord like a wind-up toy.

"Alright, Roasters fans." Heads swung toward Dani as she stepped up to the small stage beside the coffee counter. "We've got a special surprise for you. His illustrious career began twelve years ago, and now, he's *our* top hitting third baseman. Give it up for Soren Sinclair."

The room erupted in applause. Phones clicked and flashed, almost as if everybody in attendance knew this was a rare, unexpected treat. They couldn't believe he was here, and hell, neither could I. This was so out of his wheelhouse. And yet, if he was uncomfortable, he didn't let it show.

He waved to the crowd as he took his place behind the espresso machine. Only then—in a move that surely burst every ovary in attendance—did he roll his sleeves up to his elbows, exposing his arm tats for all to see.

I waited in line like everybody else, my eyes glued to Soren the entire time. His smooth pull of the espresso machine was nothing compared to the genuine, toothy smile on his face. He split his attention between the baristas at his side—the *real* ones who actually knew what they were doing—and the fans surrounding the pickup counter. I studied him, admired him for the next ten minutes, until, finally, it was my turn to order.

"Hi, Jeanette," I told the twenty-something, bright-eyed barista with a nose ring. "I'll have—"

"I've got this one, Jeanette."

I just about swallowed my tongue when Soren swapped places with her.

"Hi," he said around a smile.

"Hi."

"Busy night?"

"You could say that." I narrowed my gaze. "You're here."

"I am."

"You didn't sign up or answer any of the emails or—"

He leaned across the counter. "Not to be a huge dick, but you're holding up my line."

I arched my brow. Evidently, Mr. Bossy Pants had stayed in for the evening; he'd sent Mr. Sassy Pants in his place.

"Fine, I'll have a—"

"Upside-down caramel macchiato," he finished, already writing out the ticket. "Are you sure I can't interest you in something slutty?"

My cheeks flamed. Was he really insinuating—

"One of our boozy options, I mean."

I swallowed. His eyes flicked down my throat before jumping back up to meet mine, this time full of amusement.

"No." I spoke slowly, overemphasizing every syllable. "Just the latte, please."

"And the name for your order?"

What was he playing at? The two of us had barely spoken since the season started and even then, all of our interactions had been nothing short of professional. But this—the longing glances, the obvious flirtation—was anything but.

If he wanted to torture me—torture us both—like that, well then . . . two could play at that game.

"Blondie," I told him. His eyes widened. I licked my lips for added measure. "The name is Blondie."

Checkmate, Sinclair.

Soren

Roasters 5-1

Today was our second game in Atlanta and I, for one, was not looking forward to it. These guys were good. How did I know they were good? Because I'd played with three of them, lived with two of them, and, for a brief time, reluctantly watched as my sister, Sadie, dated one of them. Thankfully, she wised up and married a sociology professor instead of my dumbass teammate.

The guy could barely lace his own cleats.

We'd barely pulled out a win yesterday, so I knew the other team was hungry. Nobody liked to lose on their own turf. Especially not to their ex-roommate.

On top of that, I had a lot to prove in Atlanta. This was where my pro career had began, and promptly ended three days later. The hackles on the back of my neck told me that every reporter, blogger, and analyst would be scrutinizing my every move. More so than usual.

"Sinclair."

"Coach?"

He waved me across the visitors' locker room, a grim expression on his lips. Never before in the history of men in glasses had there ever been a more imposing man. You never knew what to expect from Coach Ward, and I thought he preferred it that way.

"I heard about the other night," he said as soon as we were away from the others. He didn't have to clarify which night. We both knew what he was talking about. "Is there anything I need to know?"

"No, coach. It's all taken care of."

"Pink?"

"He's okay," I assured him. "Just needed some guidance. Nothing I couldn't handle."

He nodded.

"Thought you should know I'm naming you as team captain." He must have recognized the surprise on my face because he quickly added, "I know it's a little antiquated and not many teams still do it, but fuck it. I'm a little old school."

"We have that in common."

His lips kicked up.

Well, I'll be damned . . . I made Brooks Bailey-Ward III smile.

Team captains weren't common these days. At least not to the degree that were in other sports, like hockey or football. Though I had played on a couple of teams with captains in the past, nobody had ever offered *me* the role.

"Keep in mind this title comes with zero perks," he told me. "No bonus, no badge. If anything, I've just dumped more work on you, because it's your responsibility to keep an eye on your teammates."

"Yes, coach."

"I don't want to hear about a repeat of the other night. That could have ended a lot differently."

"Yes, coach."

When he extended his hand, I took it. I had the feeling that Coach Ward didn't give out handshakes on a whim. What I didn't expect was for him to hold my hand hostage.

"This team looks up to you. With good reason." I forced myself not to recoil from his penetrating gaze. I might have had a couple of inches on him, but when it came to the intimidation factor, I was severely outmatched. "Don't forget it."

I bobbed my head, acknowledging the responsibility he was bestowing on me.

"Good. Now let's go. We've got a game to win." His hand tightened around mine. "And I know you're hungry for this one."

That was putting it mildly. Every game was important to me, but this series against Atlanta was my chance to break the curse, to prove to everyone—every coach that gave up on me, every news rag that slandered my name—that I was more than the caricature they had created. I was more than *Sin.*

The breath whooshed out of me when he finally released my palm.

I walked back to my designated locker with a newfound sense of purpose. The weight of this honor wasn't an easy load, but it was one I was more than willing to shoulder.

"All good, man?" Tuck asked.

My response was immediate. "Yeah," I told him. "Great actually. Let's fucking do this."

I had just finished taping both of my wrists per my pregame ritual when coach bellowed for us to gather around. All chatter evaporated. Coach Ward wasn't a man you kept waiting, and he never asked something twice.

"I don't want to hear anything about the fact that we beat these guys yesterday," he told us. "That was then, this is now, and a lot can change in a day. We are not going out there to make them lose. We are going out there to win. Got it?" A series of affirmations echoed through the room. "Good. I'm gonna turn it over to your captain."

My attention roved the room, interested to see my teammates' reactions. There was no need. Almost every set of eyes turned toward me, full of respect and reverence.

"Coach told you all before he told me?"

Matty grinned sheepishly. "He didn't need to tell us."

"We know who our captain is," Pink said.

We annihilated the other team—their words, not mine.

"That was embarrassing," my former teammate and roommate, Miguel, told me after the game. "When did you get so good, Sinclair?"

Miguel and I had played together in New Jersey, but he had since been traded to Atlanta. He and Kevin, another former teammate, had approached me after the game to congratulate us on the win.

"That first baseman of yours is scary shit, by the way," Kevin said. I smirked, knowing that Roman would consider that to be high praise. "He nearly mowed me down during that pickle in the fourth."

"I saw that," I told him. "You got lucky."

Kevin crossed his arms over his chest. He had definitely filled out since we played together in the minors. That might have had more to do with what his husband was feeding him though. The guy was a professional chef.

"Seriously, though," he said. "You killed us."

"Don't be too down about it. Your team is great."

He shrugged. "Yours is better. I'm happy for you, dude."

"You want to join us for a drink?" Miguel offered. "There's a great spot up in Marietta. Best empanadas you'll ever have."

That was high praise coming from Miguel, whose mom shipped him homemade empanadas by the dozen. "Does your *mamita* know you're dissing her cooking like that?"

"What *Mamita* doesn't know won't kill her."

We laughed. It was like no time had passed, like just yesterday the two of us had been sitting on the floor of a shitty hotel room, eating microwaveable ramen and stale empanadas.

"Yeah, just let me check with the guys—"

I turned over my shoulder toward the dugout, expecting to find a teammate or two. What I hadn't prepared for was the sheer panic that set in when I found Clarke pacing on the sideline, crying into her phone.

"Hold that thought," I told my friends, already rushing to her side.

I leaped over the short wall separating the stands from the field just as she disconnected her call.

"Clarke, hey." She spun toward me, shaking. "Baby, what's wrong?"

"My sister . . ."

"Vivian?" I pressed when she trailed off. She nodded. "Is she okay? Is the baby okay?"

From what I knew, Vivian was eight or so months along, so I hoped she wasn't having any complications.

"She's in labor!" she blurted out. "She and Ellie were supposed to come down for today's game, but they never showed. My phone died halfway through the third inning, so I just now got their messages, and I don't know what to do. I don't know—"

She choked back another sob. I pulled her into my chest and rubbed my hands up and down her back.

"Breathe, baby. Breathe."

I took a deep breath in through my nose and held it for a beat before exhaling. I did this over and over until her breathing matched my own and her pulse settled back to a near-resting rate.

I kissed her forehead. "What do you need?"

She pulled her head away from my neck. I wiped a stray tear from her cheek.

"I need to get to Asheville. I need to be there for her and Ellie."

"Okay," I said, nodding vigorously. "Stay put for a second."

I wanted to tell her that she could have it all. That anything she wanted, needed, I would make it happen. Even if it meant piloting the team's bus myself or arranging for the world's most expensive Lyft ride. There was a third option . . .

I raced back over to Kevin and Miguel.

"Kev, do you still drive the Mustang?"

"You've got to be kidding," he said, rolling his eyes. "Ty made me trade it in after we adopted Nina. You're looking at the proud owner of a Honda Odyssey now."

Imagine that. "Cocky Kevin" drives a minivan.

"I need a favor," I told him.

"Is that your girl?"

He nodded toward Clarke, a shit-eating grin on his face.

"Yes."

"You sound serious about this one."

"Kev," I warned.

He laughed under his breath. "Alright, alright. What do you need, man?"

Twenty minutes later, Clarke and I piled into Kev's minivan. I hadn't even changed out of my uniform.

"Soren, who's van is this?"

"Don't worry about it, blondie." I helped her buckle her seatbelt when her hands faltered. I'd never seen her this nervous, not even the first night we hooked up. "It's three-and-a-half hours to Asheville. If I drive fast, we can do it in three."

She twisted in her seat, laying her hand on top of mine. "You're not missing tomorrow's game. Absolutely not."

I rolled her hand over in mine, lacing our fingers together. "You let me worry about that." I brought our entwined hands to my lips. "We've got twenty-four hours, plenty of time."

She looked up at me with a sense of reverence or admiration, like I was some prize waiting to be won. Little did she know that her love would be the ultimate prize.

It wasn't an expectation, though. I didn't have any for what Clarke could give to me, only for what I could give to her. What I wanted to give her.

And that was everything.

Clarke

B y the time we made it to Asheville, it was almost midnight. Soren had driven like a madman, shaving nearly an hour off our trip from Atlanta. We hadn't even stopped to eat or relieve our bladders.

He dropped me off in front of the hospital, leaving me to race inside while he found a parking spot. Not that there was a lot happening at Asheville General this late on a Wednesday, but still. This was a big moment for my older sister, and I wasn't going to miss it. I'd already missed too much over the years.

A nurse in superhero print scrubs led me to the waiting room in the maternity ward, where I tapped out a quick text to Ellie. After that, there was nothing to do but wait.

I couldn't sit, couldn't relax. Instead, I paced the room, distracting myself by counting floor tiles and admiring the wall full of baby photos.

It was quiet, so I spun toward the end of the hallway the second I heard feet squeaking across the linoleum. But it wasn't a doctor or nurse or my sister-in-law. It was my knight in shining armor.

Er, make that my knight in dusty pinstripes.

"Any word?"

I threw my hands up. "Not really. A nurse led me here, but nobody's told me anything else. Ellie's not answering her texts." I crouched down until I was almost sitting on the floor, hugging my knees to my chest. "I don't know what else to do."

Next thing I knew, there was a six-foot-something baseball star sitting on the hospital floor beside me, tugging me until my back rested against his front.

"She's gonna be okay," he said against my neck. "They both are."

We sat like that for nearly an hour. He pulled my hair loose from the ponytail, combing his fingers through every strand and massaging my scalp until I relaxed fully into him. I knew he had to be starving—I know I was—but I couldn't even stomach the idea of eating anything until I knew Viv and the baby were okay. Soren didn't complain.

By the time Viv's doctor found us, I was half-asleep, cuddled against his chest.

"Are you Vivian Myers-Lim's family?"

"Yes, that's me," I told the doctor, leaping to my feet. "I'm her sister, Clarke."

"I'm Dr. Potts. Vivian and Ellie wanted me to tell you that everything went smoothly." The doctor smiled when I heaved a sigh of relief. "Oh, and I quote, 'to get your ass in here to meet your niece, already.'"

My heart stopped.

"What do you say, Auntie Clarke?"

Nodding my head, I told her, "Yes, please."

I had only taken a few steps, Soren hot on my heels, when the doctor spoke again. "Family only, please."

"Oh!" I clung to his shirtsleeve like a lifeline. "He's my fiancé."

Dr. Potts smiled and gestured for us to follow her. I snuck a peek at Soren's face, relieved to see that he wasn't put off by my lie. In fact, judging by the arrogant smirk on his face, he was pleased.

We came to a stop outside the door marked "Baby Myers-Lim." Dr. Potts nudged the door open, holding it wide for Soren and me. My legs were like putty. The only thing holding me up at this point was Soren's hand on the small of my back. That and the tiny human bundled in my sister's arms.

"Well, look who finally showed," Viv taunted, her eyes half-closed. "Ready to meet your niece?"

I nodded, willing myself to cross the room. Viv pulled the edge of the blanket back to show off the sleeping baby in her arms. She looked just like Viv. Same nose, same mouth, same furrowed brow. Lord, my niece had resting bitch face.

She was practically perfect in every way.

Viv carefully passed the baby off to Ellie, who then placed her in my arms. *Wow.* I'd held babies before, but never one fresh from the oven, so to speak.

"She's beautiful," Soren said from over my shoulder. "What's her name?"

"Amelia Clarke Myers-Lim."

My watery eyes met Viv's. She smiled warmly and nodded. There was no choking back the tears after that.

We visited with Viv and Ellie for the next twenty minutes. Most of that time was spent with me hogging baby Amelia to myself while Viv ruthlessly grilled Soren. I was too tired, too distracted to defend him. Hell, it was kind of fun watching him defend himself.

"Are you sleeping with my sister?"

"No."

"But you *were* sleeping with my sister?"

"Yes."

"Are you sleeping with anybody else?"

"No."

"What's your credit score?"

I came to my feet, baby Amelia still fast asleep in my arms. "Okay, that's enough of that."

"Yeah, honey," Ellie said from Viv's bedside. "How about we *thank* the man who drove your sister here in the dead of night, rather than interrogate him about his finances?"

"That's no fun," Viv said around a yawn.

The fatigue was finally starting to set in. It was going on two a.m. I hadn't eaten in almost fourteen hours and even with baby

Amelia in my arms, I was struggling to keep my eyes open. My head was heavier than a pile of bricks.

"We better be going." I handed the baby back to Ellie. "But we'll stop by in the morning, if that's alright?"

"Of course it is." Viv reached out, taking my hand in hers. "Thank you so much for coming, babe."

"I wouldn't have missed it for the world."

I ambled toward the hall. Soren looped an arm around my shoulder, guiding me through the doorway.

"You're dead on your feet."

"I'm fine," I grumbled.

"Is that why you almost just walked into a wall?"

I snorted under my breath but didn't argue with him. I leaned into his hold, trusting him to guide me. When he jolted to a sudden stop, I opened my eyes.

"What's wrong?" I asked, looking up at him.

He nodded toward the other end of the hallway. I wasn't sure what—or who—I was expecting to find when I looked over, but it certainly hadn't been my parents.

Pat and Melanie Lynn Myers in the flesh. Dressed to the nines, as per usual. Because, to quote my mama, *"You never knew who might be watching."*

"Mama."

"Clarke," Mama said coldly, clutching her purse tight. "You look well."

"I am, thank you." I swallowed. "Hi, Daddy."

"Clarke."

They spoke as if I were a thorn in their sides—an inconvenience—rather than their daughter. I'd seen them make better pleasantries with busboys at the annual holiday party.

Soren nudged my back. I knew he meant it more as a comforting gesture, but it would've been rude not to introduce them.

"Oh! This is my . . . Soren."

"Soren Sinclair," he said, stepping forward to offer his hand. "Pleased to meet you both. You've got one hell of a daughter here."

My eyes bounced between Mama and Daddy, silently pleading with them to do the right thing. *For once.* She turned her nose up at Soren's grass-stained uniform. Daddy's eyes lingered on the tattoos creeping out of his jersey. Neither of them made a move to shake his hand.

After a moment, Soren withdrew, resting his arm awkwardly at his side. The old Clarke would have left it at that. She would have kept her mouth shut—like she had been taught—and avoided rocking the boat. But a lot had changed in the last few months. I had friends now, family, a community that loved me. Unconditionally. Even when the people who were supposed to didn't.

Mama's eyes narrowed with disdain when I laced my fingers through Soren's.

"You've got a beautiful granddaughter," I told them. When neither of them responded, I kept talking. "Seven pounds, eight ounces. She's got curly blonde hair, and—"

"Enough."

I blinked, taken aback by Mama's icy tone.

"When are you going to end this farce and come back home? Back to your family, to Walden?"

"Mama, Walden cheated on me." Soren squeezed my hand, anchoring me down. Not back, down. "He's dating some nineteen-year-old sorority girl. I saw it on Instagram."

"He's just sowing his oats. Having fun." She lifted a brow at my and Soren's clasped hands. "It seems like he isn't the only one."

"Melanie," my father's baritone voice boomed. "We have to get going if we're going to make our flight to Texas."

"Texas?" I asked. "Does that mean the Dallas deal went through?"

"Yes, the grand opening is next week."

The Myers Hotel Group was the fastest growing hotel and spa chain in the Mid-Atlantic. For the last few years, they had been desperately trying to expand west, and from the sound of it, things were working out exactly as they wanted. As per usual.

"I wish you would have told me."

"Where was I supposed to send the invitation?" Mama snapped. "It seems I misplaced your address."

"Did you misplace my phone number, too?" She blinked, trying to conceal her surprise. Never in my life had I spoken to my mother this way. "You didn't call. You didn't text. You didn't respond to any of my messages."

"What did you expect, Clarke?"

"I expected you to love me!" I yelled. "I expected you to support me. To trust me to make my own decisions. To try, and fail, and learn from my mistakes. To treat me like a human being, not a living, breathing doll."

"I don't have time for this," Daddy said, tearing down the hallway. "I told you this was a waste of time."

"Daddy, please—"

"I'll be in the car."

His patent-leather footsteps echoed down the hall, growing quieter and quieter until, finally, all that remained was bitter silence.

"You're asking for too much," Mama finally said. Much as I loathed to admit it, as a woman, I had a lot of empathy for my mother. As a daughter, however, I had a lot of anger.

"No, Mama," I said sadly, mourning the fact that this would most likely be the last time we spoke. "I'm asking for the bare minimum."

I clung to Soren's hand, willing back the tears, the pain, until all that was left was numbness. Only when she spun and began to walk away in her three inch heels—Mama never wore anything less than three inches— did the weight of it all finally come crashing back down on me.

The past few months had been packed with firsts, each more memorable than the last, and yet, this . . . This was a last. The last time I let them make me feel this way. Less than. Unworthy. The last time I watched them walk away from me, from our family. This was it. I was done. The purse strings had been cut months ago, but now went the final emotional tie.

I only hoped I didn't float away.

There was only one bed.

I thought that kind of thing only happened in romance novels. Nessa was going to have a field day with this one. As soon as I found the will to text her. As soon as I found the will to breathe again.

Maybe everybody's sister was having a baby tonight in Asheville. Even then, everybody didn't have a hot, bulky baseball player sharing their bed.

When we got to the hotel, I showered first while Soren scavenged for something to eat. There wasn't much open this late, just a twenty-four-hour gas station. I'd come out to find a mountain of snack foods and sports drinks stacked in the center of our bed.

"Just leave me a Ding Dong, would you?" he asked before closing himself in the bathroom to shower.

After everything he'd given me in the last six hours, I'd say a pack of chocolate snack cakes was the least I could offer him.

By the time he finished, I had already climbed into bed. He clicked off the light and slid under the sheets, tucking his body close to mine but hesitating. We'd shared a bed. Many times. We'd also slept together without having sex. Not as many times, but still.

This was uncharted territory, one without a map or rules.

One of us needed to make a choice, make a move, and I could tell by Soren's stiffness and the space between us that he was leaving it entirely up to me. And frankly, it was a no-brainer.

For the first twenty-seven years of my life, I'd chosen my family.

For the last few months, I'd chosen me.

But tonight, I chose us. Even if it was just for tonight.

I sat up, stripping off my T-shirt until I was bare from the waist up.

"Be sure, blondie."

I slid my panties off and climbed onto his lap, rubbing myself against his protruding erection.

"It doesn't have to mean anything," I told him, breaking off into a gasp when one of his fingers entered me, followed quickly by another. He swirled them around inside of me, coating my pussy from the inside out.

"Oh, Clarke." I shivered when he said my name. I liked it when he called me blondie, but I *loved* it when he growled my name. "Of course, it means something. It's *always* fucking meant something."

He slammed his mouth onto mine. There was no talking after that, save for a few passionate words exchanged between staccato breaths. Later, long after he made me come twice—once on his cock and then again with his tongue and fingers—did he speak again.

"So . . ."

"So . . ." I echoed.

"So, where do we go from here, blondie?" he whispered into my hair.

I chewed my lip, strumming my fingers through the thin layer of hair that blanketed his chest. "Back to Atlanta, I suppose. We have a car to return."

"You know that's not what I meant."

The colorful hues of sunlight were already starting to creep in through the motel room's blinds. We were both going to feel like leftover garbage tomorrow. Even orgasms couldn't make up for a sleepless night.

I tilted my head back, my stomach doing somersaults when I met his steady gaze. "We said we would cut things off when the season started."

He chuckled. "And look how that turned out."

I stroked the stubble on his chin. "Tonight was amazing, and I really appreciate you being here with me, but—"

"No buts." He squeezed my ass. "Unless we're talking about me fucking yours."

My fingers stopped. My heart might have, too.

"Do you like that idea, blondie?" Soren purred. "Me fucking your ass?"

"I don't know," I told him, surprising us both. "Maybe."

"We should add it to the list."

It unnerved me that he could be so cool and cavalier about this. Not the anal sex stuff, though I hadn't given that much thought until now, but our relationship. Maybe "situationship" was a more appropriate term.

"Soren . . ."

"I get it," he said. "Tonight can just be a one-time thing, if that's what you want."

Curse this man for always having the decency to ask what I want.

He was so good about attending to my wants and needs. For the first time, I didn't have the heart to tell him what I actually wanted. Instead, I lied.

"It is," I told him, my mouth suddenly dry.

If he didn't believe me, it didn't show. Not in his dark, stormy eyes nor the line of his lips. Instead, he cradled my hand in his, kissing each of my fingers one by one. Slowly, preciously.

"I understand."

I was caught between a rock and a hard place, aka my head and my heart, respectively. On the one hand, there was no denying the connection between Soren and me. On the other, I had already had a lifetime of being known as someone's daughter or fiancée. Just once, I wanted to be my own person, without having somebody else's name attached to me.

"I think it's best if we walk away before things get messy." He pressed his lips together and raised his brows. "Okay, messier than they already are. I owe you one, by the way. Facing my parents is no easy feat."

"I thought you handled them perfectly."

"Really?"

"Better than I would have." He fixed me with heady stare. "Better than they deserve."

I believed him with every fiber of my being. That was more than I could say about my ex-fiancé. In the four years that I dated Walden, he had never spoken with such confidence or conviction. He certainly had never said anything that went against my parents or their wishes.

"Thank you," I told him. "For everything."

"That's what friends are for, right?"

"I can do friends." My cheeks warmed when amusement colored his face. "Not *do* friends, but we can be friends—"

"I know what you meant, blondie."

He smiled widely. God, I was going to miss that goofy grin in my bed. At least this way I could keep him around.

The truth was I didn't want to *just* be Soren's friend, but I also didn't want to lose him. I couldn't. Maybe it was time to stop thinking about what I wanted and focus on what I needed. What we both needed.

I needed to be on my own, to be my own person. Soren needed the Roasters. They were his shot—his big one—and I'd never forgive myself if I got in the way of that. At least this way we could still be in each other's lives.

Plus having another friend couldn't hurt, right?

Soren

Roasters 10-3

"Guys, check it out," Roman whispered, loud enough for the rest of us to hear, but not so loud that it woke the sleeping puppy cradled between his thighs. "Eenie fell asleep on me."

Pink tilted his head to the side. "I think that might be Meenie."

"Who do I have?" Matty asked.

I released my ankles, transitioning out of butterfly hold and into a relaxed sit. When I turned to my left, I bit back a laugh. The tiniest of the basset hound litter had nestled herself into Matty's neck.

"That's Mo," I told him. "She's the runt."

"She's not a runt," he said defensively. "She's just petite."

"That must make you Miney," Pink whispered to the puppy snoring soundly between the two of us. "Don't tell the rest of them, but you're the cutest one of them all. Yes, you are."

Pink plied Miney with baby talk and belly scratches, both of which she seemed to enjoy. Though I could only feel his warmth, I knew it was Eenie resting against the base of my spine.

When some of the team had shown an interest in taking up yoga, this wasn't exactly what I had had in mind. Dani and Clarke had seized the opportunity to organize an entire team-bonding shindig, one that included puppies, pictures, and a livestream on YouTube.

Apparently, two-thousand people were interested in watching us stretch and cuddle puppies.

"Stretch and Fetch" was a new collaboration between Rose City Dog Rescue and Now & Zen, a nearby yoga studio. Tuck, Matty, and I had already made plans to check out a class or two at the studio, but the dogs had been an added bonus. Not to mention, the push needed to get the rest of the guys on board.

While Roman had spent the bulk of our class vying for the instructor's attention, Pink had done the same with the puppies. Tuck and I seemed to be the only ones actually interested in the yoga part of the yoga class.

Well, except for Clarke.

I thought bare and breathless Clarke was a work of art, but Clarke in yoga pants was a goddamn masterpiece. Especially since I was fairly sure she wasn't wearing anything underneath them. I'd nearly fallen flat on my face—and crushed poor Meanie—when she transitioned into downward dog.

"Damn, I miss having a dog." Pink sat up, resting Miney's back against his raised knees. He toyed with her long, droopy ears, flapping them back and forth. "We had a German shepherd named Rex growing up. He slept in my bed every night."

"My mom has two Cavapoos," Tuck said.

"What the hell is that?" I asked him.

"Cavalier King Charles spaniel mixed with toy poodle. They're small, loud, and cute as hell."

I flexed my legs out in front of me, mirroring our instructor's movements. My knee had been holding up well since the season started, mostly because I was actually taking care of it. Coach Ward had set me up with one of the league's physical therapists, I'd developed a healthy workout routine that wasn't too strenuous, and I hadn't engaged in any . . . extracurricular activities since Asheville.

There would be no extracurricular activities moving forward. Not now that Clarke and I were *friends*.

"How about you, Sinclair?" Roman stared at me expectantly.

"What about me?"

"Any pets growing up?"

Pink chimed in before I could answer. "I feel like you're a cat person. I can just picture it—you sitting in a plaid arm chair, smoking a pipe, surrounded by five or six cats."

"What am I, eighty?"

Tuck and Roman snickered while Matty mustered a smile. That's practically all he could do. Any other sound or movement might wake the dog stretched across his neck like a wool scarf.

"And no," I told Pink. "My grandmother was allergic. By the time she passed, we were all out of the house anyway. My sister, Sadie, has a couple of dachshunds."

I liked dogs as much as the next person, but I had never considered getting a pet of my own. Not with my lifestyle. Then again, there were several things I'd been thinking about lately that, until meeting a certain blonde, had always felt like a pipedream.

Starting with buying a house. *A home.* Planting roots in one place with one woman—and maybe one dog?—hadn't seemed like a feasible possibility six months ago. Yet here I was, cuddling a basset hound and browsing Zillow listings before bed. I had even made an appointment to meet with a local realtor next week.

Rose City was beginning to feel like home.

There was only one thing missing . . .

"Alright, friends," our instructor said, her dulcet tone barely louder than a whisper. "Thank you for sharing your love, light, and energy with me today. I hope to see you again next week. Namaste."

"Namaste," we echoed, bowing our heads. Well, those of us who could. Matty was still trapped under Mo.

I slowly extracted myself from the floor so as not to disturb Eenie. When I climbed to my feet, relishing in the looseness of my muscles, I was pleased to see that Eenie was still fast asleep.

He'd toppled onto his side which meant I wouldn't be going anywhere anytime soon. If Eenie needed to rest his little head and oversized ears on my yoga mat, then I guess I'd move into the studio.

"God, I feel amazing!" Dani announced to the room, stretching her arms toward the sky. "And taller. Do I look taller?"

I bit my lip, fighting back a smile. Our sprite like social media director was barely scraping the five foot mark. She was a tiny little thing, especially next to her so called BFF, Pink, who could undoubtedly wear her like a backpack if he wanted.

"Sooo much taller," he said, goading her. "At least an inch or two."

"How about you, Clarke? Do you feel taller?"

My attention shifted to the woman beside Dani. I tried to focus on her fresh, makeup-free face rather than the hint of cleavage peeking out of the top of her tank top. Or the sweat pooling between her breasts. Or the small strip of exposed skin between her tank and yoga pants.

Just friends, just friends.

I'd been repeating the mantra to myself over and over for a week now. Hopefully, someday soon, I would start to believe it.

"I don't know about taller," Clarke said. "Definitely more flexible."

Fuck, is she trying to kill me?

Pink and Tuck shared a not-so-covert smile. If we were anywhere else—and there wasn't a phone livestreaming our every move—I would have smacked them. Instead, I crossed my hands in front of my crotch, just in case something . . . came up.

"Here, Sinclair." I turned just in time for Roman to deposit a puppy—Eenie, again—into my arms. "You dropped this."

"Er, thanks."

Eenie wiggled into the crook of my arms before rolling over to expose his belly.

"Aw, he's so cute." Clarke exclaimed. She stepped forward—close enough for the familiar fragrance of peaches to invade my senses—and reached out to scratch Eenie.

Lucky bastard.

"Have you ever had a dog, Clarke?" Tuck asked.

"No," she said, smiling sadly. "We were never allowed. My parents aren't exactly pet people."

When her eyes met mine, I nodded with understanding. I wanted nothing more than to take her into my arms and hug away the hurt. Some emotional scars never went away, but with time—and maybe the right person—Clarke would start to see them differently, as a sign of strength and not pain.

Then again, maybe it would be better, smarter if we didn't touch. Touching led to kissing and kissing led to, well . . . stuff that *friends* didn't do.

"You look good with a puppy," Clarke said.

"We should go grab a drink," I blurted out. Clarke's eyes widened with confusion. "All of us, I mean. Drink?"

I was trying to be her friend—really I was—but until I trusted myself not to maul her, group settings in public were the safest bet.

"Sure," she replied brightly. "A drink sounds good."

"I'm in," Dani added.

The rest of the guys echoed the same sentiments.

Thankfully, the rain had let up by the time we left to grab a *friendly* beer. All of us, except Roman who had opted to go home with our instructor for some afternoon delight. He wasn't the only one who picked somebody up from yoga . . .

Matty adopted Mo two days later.

Clarke

Roasters 11-4

June and I had graciously volunteered to help Nessa set up for tonight's book club at Smutty Buddies . . . in exchange for free snacks and hard seltzer. Readers were set to arrive in the next thirty minutes, so I should have been stacking books. Instead, my eyes were glued to my phone screen, taking in Soren's post-game interview.

"Soren, your major league career is off to an incredible start. What are you doing different this time around, and how has it affected your game play?"

"First of all, I appreciate you saying that."

I had never seen him look so relaxed in an interview before. Soren hated the press, and frankly, I couldn't blame him. Based on the negative things they had written about him over the years and how some of those things had directly impacted his career, I wasn't a fan of them either.

"Secondly, the biggest change is time. I'm a little bit older, a little more vigilante when it comes to my diet and . . . extracurricular activities. Yoga has also played a major role in strengthening my mind and body."

"And in regards to your extracurricular activities . . ."

"Why don't you just ask the question you want to ask, Brock?"

Brock Heller, *Portlandia Press*. Part of my job meant mingling with the press and influencers, and Brock Heller was a dangerous combination. In addition to writing the sports column for the *Press*, Brock also hosted one of the most downloaded sports talk podcasts on the web. He was a nice enough guy, but he also asked some hard-hitting questions.

"It's safe to say that your personal relationships have interfered in your professional life over the years. What are you doing to avoid making similar mistakes with the Roasters?"

"As I said, I'm staying healthy, I'm staying focused."

"And are you seeing anybody now?"

I swallowed. Just the possibility of Soren seeing somebody else made my heart sink. That was my own dang fault, though. I was the one who had decided we should "just be friends."

"Respectfully, moving forward, I will not be discussing my personal life. And I hope you and everybody else can respect that."

Dang, great answer.

"This doesn't look like book stacking."

I jumped, dropping my phone to the ground. I was going to have to start calling her Ninja Nessa. Last I checked, she had been on the phone with Nero discussing the catering for tonight's event. I hadn't even heard her come back inside the shop.

She handed me my fallen device, her eyes catching on the paused video. ""Rumor has it you and the bad boy of baseball broke up."

"Let me guess. Dani." Nessa's smile was a dead giveaway. I shrugged. "Well, fine. Gossip all you like. It's not like we were ever really together anyway."

"You just haven't reached the final act yet," she said, holding up a copy of tonight's a book pick. Maybe I was crazy, maybe it was an optical illusion, but I couldn't help but feel like silver fox's eyes on the cover tracked my every move.

"Huh?"

"Your story. There's still one more act to go." Nessa pointed at me. "When are you going to realize that you, my dearest friend, are living a romance novel dream?"

"Pfft! In what world is my life a romance novel dream?"

"I don't know," June chimed in before crunching down on another chip. She was doing a lot less helping and a lot more snacking. "I might be with Ness on this one. You two are like the most romance novel-ish of romance novels."

"Oh, please."

"Opposites attract?" June suggested.

"Work colleagues," Nessa added.

"Fling-to-lovers."

Dang it, June knew romance novels as well as Nessa. My eyes ping-ponged between the two of them while they listed off my and Soren's relationship tropes.

"Don't forget the sex list." Nessa bit her lip, but it was too late.

June's eyes lit up like a sparkler on the Fourth of July. "Sex list?! Oh, Clarke, please." She placed her palms together and continued to beg. "Please tell me about the sex list."

"Okay, that's enough." I held my hands out in front of me, backing away from them. "I might not know romance novels like the two of you, but I've read enough to know that this thing with Soren certainly isn't the stuff of romance novel dreams. It was fun while it lasted, but now it's run it's course, so that's that."

"And?"

"And we both agreed that it was best to walk away before things get too . . . intense."

"*And*?!" June probed again.

"And what more do you want?" I hadn't said anything about our night in Asheville. There was no way they could possibly know about that. Right?

"The sex list, Clarke," June practically shouted. "Obviously."

"I'm not giving you that!"

"Come on, we're your best friends. Both of whom are having a dry spell right now." She flicked her finger between her and Nessa. "The least you can do is regale us with your sexploits."

I stopped. "Is that true?"

"The dry spell?" June asked. "Sadly, yes. My vagina has sealed itself tighter than a tomb in the desert."

"Ew." Nessa crossed her arms in front of her body. "But yes. Ditto."

"No, I mean about you being my best friends," I clarified, relaying their words back to them. "Is that true?"

For a minute, they both stared at me. Then at each other, almost as if there was another conversation happening that I wasn't privy to. When they finally came around the display table, they each wrapped an arm around either side of me.

"Of course, it's true," Nessa said around a smile.

"You should know by now that we're pretty blunt with our words," June added. "We love you, Clarke."

My heart skipped a beat. To think, just a few months ago, I was sharing a sterile townhouse with a man who didn't respect me—both of which my parents had handpicked—without a clue of what I wanted. In life, in the bedroom, in a partner. And here I was living in an vintage camper named after one of my favorite film icons, surrounded by people I admired and loved. Nessa, June, Dani. *Soren.*

Don't go there, Clarke.

And they loved me back. Well, most of them anyhow. What more could a girl ask for?

"I love you both, too."

They squeezed my sides.

"Okay, enough lovey-dovey crap," June said. "Now, can we talk about the sex list?"

Nessa and I both rolled our eyes, choosing to go back to arranging books and snacks over dignifying June with a response. I had already given her my answer. Maybe someday soon, I would feel comfortable dishing out the details of my sex life, but someday wasn't today.

A little later, after I finished fanning out the cocktail napkins, a bell chimed over the door. My eyebrows nearly shot up to my ponytail when I saw who walked in.

"Jared?"

"Clarke Kent." He removed his designer sunglasses and base-ball cap. "What are you doing here?"

"What are *you* doing here?"

"Oh, you know." He tucked his hands into his pants pockets, rocking forward on his toes. "Just doing a little shopping. Some light reading, maybe."

I eyed him wearily. Pink had pleasantly surprised me on more than one occasion, but I never would have guessed that he was a romance reader. Or a reader in general.

"What's going on with you and Sin?"

"Nothing you need to worry about. We're just friends." I felt the need to add, "And please, don't call him that."

Soren hated that stupid nickname. A slow smile spread across Pink's baby face.

"Pretty defensive of your *friends,* huh, Clarke?"

"What is *he* doing here?" Nessa hissed, interrupting my internal battle. She and June had left me to man the front for any early arrivals while they grabbed more ice from the market. I didn't think we would need it, though. Nessa's icy demeanor toward Pink would be cold enough to chill the drinks.

"Well," he fumbled, eyes searching the tables. "I heard there were tartlets. And I'm a ho for tartlets, so here I am."

Her eyes narrowed, shooting daggers back at him until he wavered under her gaze.

"So, there's a book club tonight? What are we reading?"

June and I exchanged a look. Poor Pink. Here was a guy who probably never had to work for women's attention, faced with the one woman who couldn't be bothered to give him the time of day.

"*Selene,*" June answered. "It's an age gap romance."

"What, like he's older than her?" Pink asked, confusion written all over his face. Nessa stared him down like he was a bug in need of exterminating.

"Actually, she's older than him," I said. "She's in her mid-thirties and he's in his late-twenties."

Pink scratched his chin. "Do you . . . like that? Younger men, I mean?"

His question wasn't directed at any of one of us in particular, or so he wanted us to believe. From my vantage point, he only had eyes for Nessa.

June shrugged. "Sure, they can be fun, but—"

"Excuse me," Nessa finally said through gritted teeth. "We've got over two dozen people arriving any second, so unless you plan on making a purchase, I'm going to have to ask you to leave."

"What if I wanted to join—"

"Ticketed event. Sold out, I'm afraid."

Pink's jaw clenched. An undecipherable expression fell over his face. This was a guy who was used to charming the pants off every woman—and probably man—he met. It looked like he had finally met his match. Maybe I was getting ahead of myself, but I had a feeling that I wasn't the only person in Rose City living a romance novel fantasy come to life.

"Okay, then," he said, slapping a smile on his face. "Well, ladies, it's been a pleasure. As always." He bowed in that overly-exaggerated way a peasant—or in this case jester—might do before royalty in a Shakespearean comedy. He put his hat and sunglasses back on before adding, "Until next time."

I had a feeling that the last part was just for Nessa.

When she stormed into the back room, he carried himself out the door with the air of man who hadn't been shot down, yet again, by the woman he was all-too-obviously interested in. *Bottle of confidence, aisle two?*

"I can tell you one thing," June said cryptically, nodding toward the front windows. Just outside, a small crowd of passersby had begun to swarm around Pink. So much for his disguise.

"What?" I asked.

"One way or another, that boy's gonna be trouble."

"Agreed."

What I didn't tell her was that I had firsthand—and as of recently, mouth—experience with trouble, and from what I had seen, touched, and tasted so far, it was worth it.

Soren

Roasters 11-8

So much for our winning streak. Our trip to Vancouver had been a major bust.

To say the Tridents had cleaned our clocks would be putting it mildly. Our clocks had been cleaned, polished, buffed, and shined. Four games, four losses, which meant I was looking forward to four hours of nursing my wounds—both mental and physical—under the shower spray. After I iced my knees. Both of them.

Much to my disappointment, Clarke hadn't made the trip to Vancouver with us. Which sucked because I had gotten used to seeing her everyday. I missed her beaming smiles, her doe-like eyes, those pouty red lips that made me picture things I shouldn't.

Friends don't think about other friends' lips wrapped around their cock.

I just missed her. More than anything, I missed the way I felt when I was with her.

At first, I thought just being her friend might be enough. Hell, any sad sap would be lucky to have Clarke in their life. But I was a greedy fuck. I wanted to be the last person she saw before she fell asleep at night, and the one who woke her up with a sickly sweet latte every morning.

I wanted all of her. I needed all of her.

Starting now.

When I pulled up to Bed of Roses, I dumped my bags off at my trailer, swapped out my game day suit for some gym shorts and a hoodie, and headed next door. I didn't even bother putting on my shoes.

Clarke must have seen me coming because the door to her trailer flew open before I even reached the first step.

"You're back."

"Hey, blondie."

We stood there, just staring at each other for going on a minute. She was already dressed for bed, her legs naked save for a tiny pair of shorts that barely covered all my favorite parts and some knee-high socks with coffee beans on them.

"New socks?"

Her eyes flicked down her legs. "They just came into the Roasters shop this weekend. Like them?"

"I do."

She must have noticed the edge to my voice—or maybe it was the dark circles beneath my eyes—because the next words out of her mouth were, "Rough weekend?"

"You could say that."

"I'm sorry. You played well, though. Two homeruns."

My lips kicked up. Knowing that she had been watching me play, even from four-hundred miles away, gave me a certain level of satisfaction.

I kept my hands at my sides, resisting every instinct to race forward and take her into my arms. That was until she stepped forward and wrapped her arms around my shoulders, drawing me into her.

I wasn't used to her being the taller one of the two of us, but with her on the top steps of the trailer's front stoop, I barely reached her breasts.

I leaned into her hold. These were some of my favorite moments with Clarke, the ones where she just let me hold her—or in this case, where she held me. I had figured out pretty quickly, that Clarke did not sit still. On the rare occasions when she did, her brain was usually running Olympic hurdles. Which made moments like this even more special.

When we finally pulled away, she ran a hand through my overgrown beard. I hadn't shaved since we left for Vancouver, opting to let my beard grow out a little. At least until it got too hot to manage.

My focus was locked on her face when I asked, "Shower with me?"

There was no hiding from my feelings any longer. I was in love with Clarke—I had been for a while—and I was done pretending that my feelings for her were anything less than. I just hoped she felt the same way.

When her eyes connected with mine, the last remaining bits of tension drained from my body. *She wants this, too. She wants me.* Her nod was all the answer I needed.

Together, we walked hand-in-hand to the showers. As soon as we were safely tucked away inside the stall, I stripped off her pajamas before taking care of my own.

There was no talking. There were no sounds at all, aside from the water cascading over us.

We stood under the water until it ran cold. I shampooed her hair, and she did the same for my beard—mostly because she couldn't reach higher. When I bent down for her to scrub my head, I couldn't resist taking a nipple in my mouth, sucking until she dropped the shampoo bottle.

After that, any thoughts of getting clean were long forgotten. For the next few minutes, I bent her over the stall—low enough so that anybody passing by would only see one head instead of two—and fucked her from behind. This wasn't our usual frenzy, though. No, this was a slow, deep, passionate fucking. One that ended with her choking back a scream and me spraying her back with cum.

And then, using it to draw my jersey number. *Mine.*

Later, after we dried off and piled into her bed, I nuzzled into her neck and just breathed in the smell of her. *Mm, peaches.* I didn't tell her, but I had started taking a bottle of her shampoo with me when I traveled without her. One way or another, I was going to bed at night on a pillow that smelled like her. Even if it meant smelling like peaches the next day.

"I'm sorry you had a bad weekend," she whispered into the dark.

"It happens," I told her. "Besides, the welcome home more than made up for it."

And then I felt it—she stiffened in my arms. I had noticed it a couple of times before I left for Vancouver, too. One second, we would be talking with Dani or messing around with the team, and then the next, she would freeze. Almost as if she was guarding a piece of herself, one she refused to give away.

I knew that feeling well.

"You want to tell me what's going on over there?"

"Hm?"

"You're thinking too hard. Are you regretting tonight?" *Please say no. Please say—*

"Definitely not."

I smiled against her neck. My fingers wound a path down her side, memorizing every freckle and stretchmark. Each dot, each line was more beautiful than the next.

She rolled over to face me. "Just realizing that we suck at being friends."

A laugh bubbled from my lips. "You got that right."

Despite the warm, fuzzy feelings racing through my body—the ones I'd only heard about in romcom movies and Clarke's romance novels—I couldn't help but feel like that was only part of whatever was on her mind.

We had covered a lot of territory over the last few weeks, but was she ready to make this thing between us official? She had had no problem confiding in me about her ex and shitbag parents, so the fact that there was still something holding her back baffled me. *What am I missing?*

"Fess up, blondie. There's something else on your mind."

Rather than formulate an answer, she shoved at my shoulders, climbing on top of me when I settled back against the pillows. "It sounds like you're the one thinking too hard, sugar."

"Clarke—" My words trailed off into a groan when she slid a hand between us, cupping my balls. Damn, but I loved it when she played dirty.

"No more talking, Sinclair."

Whatever she was holding back would have to wait. Tonight, I'd let Clarke suck me and fuck me to her heart's content, but tomorrow? Tomorrow, I would get the answers I so desperately craved.

Starting with whether or not the love of my life loved me back.

I was already dressed and waiting, latte in hand, when she woke up the next morning. She looked up at me with a sated, sleepy smile. Like a woman who had spent the half the night getting fucked sideways. Because she had.

"Good morning."

"Coffee?" I asked, passing her her signature drink.

"Thank you." She sat up, straightening the T-shirt she had put on sometime in the night. "You didn't have to do that."

"Baby, you should know by now that I only do what I want. Whether I have to is irrelevant. Besides, I want you fully awake for this." She stared back at me, puzzled. While she sipped her latte, I swallowed my nerves. "Here's the thing . . . I've been doing some thinking about this whole 'just friends' thing, and I don't think it's going to work out."

"Oh." An adorable crease blossomed between her brows. "Okay."

"And that's because I'm in love with you."

There was no hiding from it now. Not when I had laid my cards out, front and center, and bet it all. From here on out, it was all up to her. *Dealer's choice.*

"Soren," she croaked, her eyes filling with moisture.

"You don't have to say it back. I just thought you should know that *this*," I said, gesturing between the two of us, "is more than friendship to me. And I'm not talking about sex, I'm talking about you and me together. For real. Because I can't imagine my life without you in it."

Tears spilled down her cheeks as she buried her face behind her hands. For a second, I thought I might have overstepped, pushed her too far, too quickly. Were grown women supposed to cry hysterically when you poured your heart out? I'd only said those words to my high school sweetheart, and even then, my eighteen-year-old heart had barely understood what that meant at the time.

Clarke had made me feel things I'd never felt before, things I'd never thought I deserved to feel.

I peeled her hands away from her face. "You okay?"

"Fine," she said around a sniffle. "That's the sweetest thing anybody's every said to me."

"Well, give me some time, blondie. I can make things even sweeter."

I wrapped a hand around her freckled neck and ran a thumb over her thrumming pulse. When I leaned in to connect our lips, she met me halfway. It would have been so easy to fall back into bed and make love to her again, if she hadn't pulled away prematurely.

"I can't do this."

My shoulders tensed. All of me tensed. "Do what?"

She wrestled with the bedsheets, drawing her bare legs up to her chest. I didn't like seeing her like this—withdrawn and vulnerable—and I definitely didn't want to be the person who made her feel that way. But I also knew that there was a very good chance of me spending the rest of my life with this woman, so we needed to be on the same page.

"Soren." For the rest of my life, I would never forget the way she said my name just then. Full of painful longing and false hope. "You are a formidable human being, an incredible leader for your teammates, and the best uncle any kid could hope for. You're also the best man that I've ever known."

Why did it feel like she was saying goodbye?

"But—"

"We've been here before, blondie. You know there's only one butt I'm interested in."

She barely cracked a smile.

"Here's the thing. I don't know if I'm ready to be . . . somebody else's girlfriend."

My brows pulled together. "I don't want you to be somebody else's girlfriend. I want you to be my girlfriend."

Wasn't that obvious?

"That's not what I mean." She heaved a sigh. "Give me a second."

A part of me was relieved to know that I wasn't the only one lost in this conversation. What the fuck was she talking about?

"I've always been somebody's something," she said. "Pat Myers's daughter. Walden Winters's fiancée."

She placed her hand over mine when I growled. *Fuck that guy and his stupid fucking face.*

"And as much as I love you—"

She said it. Holy fuck she said it.

"—and *please* Soren, believe me when I say I'm in love with you, too—I can't just be Soren Sinclair's girlfriend." She looked up at me with watery eyes. "I can't be *Mrs. Sin.*"

I pulled my hand back reflexively. Damn, Clarke didn't pull any punches. This wasn't how things were supposed to go. One second, she was saying, "I love you," and then the next she was saying she didn't want to be my girlfriend. How was I supposed to respond to that?

"Huh. I don't remember putting a ring on your finger."

"Soren, that's not— I hope you don't think I'm expecting—"

"You could've said something. I wouldn't have . . ."

Opened my heart.

Introduced you to my family.

Discussed my deepest, darkest insecurities.

I silently filled in the blank.

"It's not that, I promise. It's not you—"

"It's not you, it's me? Really?"

"Please don't go." She scrambled to her feet when I stepped back toward the door. "This is coming out all wrong, and I promise it'll all make sense once I find a better way to put it—"

"I think you were pretty clear. You don't want to be my girlfriend."

She sniffled again. That was all the confirmation I needed.

My chest tightened, swelling like a balloon ready to burst at any moment. The familiar feeling of rejection burrowed its way beneath my skin before going deeper and deeper, all the way to my heart. The one I had all but wrapped in a bow and delivered to Clarke.

And look where that had gotten me.

"I'm gonna be honest, blondie. I'm not really sure what to do with that."

"I'm so sorry, Soren."

It would be one thing if she didn't love me, but that wasn't the case. She did love me, and I loved her. Wasn't that enough? Fuck Diaz's stupid romantic comedy movies starring Captain America. Fuck Clarke's romance novels that she had taken to reading before bed where the couple always ended up together, no matter what. It was all a lie.

Here I was, pouring my heart out to the woman I loved, who, despite all odds, loved me back, and she still didn't want to be with me.

"Please," she begged. My stomach dropped when tears began to fall again from her big beautiful eyes. "Please don't give up on me, Soren."

"Why not?" I said callously, even though I knew I'd regret it later. "It seems like you already gave up on us."

Clarke

Roasters 14-9

Five days, twelve hours, and thirty-six minutes. That was about how long it had been since my heart had been ripped out and stomped on by the man I loved. It was safe to say, the hurt wouldn't be subsiding anytime soon. No matter how much I tried to distract myself.

In fact, as it turned out, playing Dungeons and Dragons with a broken heart wasn't the distraction I had hoped it might be. It was a full-blown disaster.

"Clarke, you've taken too much damage from last night's demon attack," Nessa reminded me. My fate seemed appropriate considering I had let my personal demons get the better of me and my relationship. "Your health is too poorly to cast a spell."

Of course it is.

"So, what? I'm just shit out of luck?" Here my character was on the edge of death, just when I was starting to get the hang of this dang game. "How am I supposed to protect myself from getting hurt?"

"You can't."

"For fuck's sake!" I threw my hands up in the air to signal that I was rapidly approaching my breaking point. "Am I just supposed to trust that it's all going to be okay? Or that one of y'all will protect me? That's not fair. It's not fair to you, to me, and it definitely isn't fair to the residents of East Salem."

Three sets of eyes blinked back at me, each of them full of horror and pity I didn't deserve. Not after my awful behavior this past week.

I was late for work. Twice. I had been avoiding calls all week from Nessa, Dani, and even my sister. My little house on wheels was a mess, as was my hair. I hadn't washed it in days, mostly because I couldn't stomach the idea of running into Soren while one (or both of us) was naked.

I might have done something real crazy then like drop to my knees and beg—for his dick or forgiveness, I wasn't sure.

It wasn't like I hadn't been through a breakup before. I had—twice. For heaven's sake, it had only been a few months since I had called off my engagement. And yet, neither of those had left me feeling broken, empty, like a shell of my former self.

Breakup Barbie: potato chips and mascara-stained cheeks not included.

"Clarke, honey." Nessa reached a hand across the table to cover mine. "Are you okay?"

"Yeah, I feel like we've segued away from Bitchcraft and into breakup?"

The lilt of June's question told me she was hoping she was wrong. That made two of us.

"I'm sorry," I told them, rolling Nessa's hand over in mine. "I'm not really myself right now. Something happened between Soren and I."

"Who do we need to hurt?"

"Do we need to cast a spell?"

"*Mi titi* is a *bruja*. I can have her put a curse on him if you'd like?"

A smile touched my cheeks, the first I'd had in days. Though I was interested in hearing more about Jo's *titi*—and what kinds of curses she could cast—I shook my head.

"No, I'm pretty sure this was my fault. I kind of scared him off."

June's brows furrowed. "*You* scared *him* off?"

I had replayed our conversation that morning in my trailer over and over again, wondering where it had gone wrong. A different person might have dumped the blame entirely in his lap because let's face it, his response could have been better. I, on the other hand, had a tendency of putting the blame on myself, even when it wasn't warranted. So I had to believe there was some place to meet in the middle.

An unhappy medium, if you will.

It didn't take long to realize my error. I'd called him *Sin.* The stupid, degrading nickname I knew he hated, and even still, I'd used against him. He had every right to be mad at me.

But did he still love me?

"I didn't mean to," I told them. "Or, I don't know, maybe a part of me did. Subconsciously. I just— I don't want to lose myself again. I'm just starting to get to know me, and I kind of like her."

June and Nessa both nodded.

"I like her, too," Jo added, tilting his beer to me.

"And you know how we feel," Nessa said.

It was refreshing to know that however my relationship with Soren panned out, I would still have June, Nessa, and even Jo to count on.

"Can I offer you some advice?" Nessa asked. "Only if you want it, though."

That was what I liked most about Nessa. She was fiercely protective of her friends and family, but also respected their boundaries. Maybe if I had had better boundaries with my parents, they would still be in my life.

"Please."

"I know I'm not the bastion of romantic relationships, but I've had my fair share—and not just fictional ones, at that." She winked. "So, I can tell you with my full chest that life is hard. Relationships are complicated at best. Loving somebody though? That's the easy part. People are made to be loved, so if you find somebody that makes life a little bit easier and that you don't mind waking up next to every morning, they might be worth the fight."

She was right. My relationship with Walden had always felt more like a business arrangement, one with a strict timeline and measurable goals. With Soren, it was about the things we wanted and supporting each other to make them happen. It was about listening just to listen, not to respond. There wasn't any kind of competition or envy or image to maintain.

It was just him and me. Just us. And if that wasn't worth fighting for, I didn't know what was.

"Are you a fighter, Clarke?" Nessa asked. "Because I'm going to be honest, I don't think Brogan and his army of demons are going to give up anytime soon."

I snorted, grateful for the sudden tone shift. It was the gentle nudge I needed to remind myself that while I appreciated my friends' love and support, I owed them the same. Friendship was a two-way street. Until I repaired things with Soren—and even after that—they deserved my time and attention, too.

"Good thing I have a shield, then." I lifted my drink toward the ceiling. "And one hell of a coven by my side."

There wasn't a patron at the tavern that missed the, "Huzzah!" that rang out.

The next day, I beat Dani to the office with an oat milk, chai latte in tow.

"I owe you an apology," I said in lieu of our usual greeting. I handed her the drink.

"What for?"

"For acting like a zombie all week."

Understanding dawned across her bronze complexion. "You don't have to apologize for that. I kind of figured something might be going on when you showed up on Monday wearing no makeup and were fifty shades of gray."

A small smile tugged at my lips. She was right. I had been dressing on the drabber side as of late.

"Soren and I hit a road bump."

"Okay." She kicked back in her chair, resting her boots on the top of her desk. "And?"

"And I'm hoping that we can get past it because I think he might be the love of my life."

Her eyes widened. "Well, that's good to hear." She took another gulp of her latte before adding, "Even if it means I owe Pink twenty bucks."

"Sorry?"

She sat up and set her drink aside. Whereas I kept my desktop relatively bare, save for some brightly colored stationary and sticky notes, Dani's desk was littered with knick-knacks, empty cups, and framed photos of her and her loved ones.

"Don't be mad," she pleaded, "but Pink and I had a bet going on whether you and Sinclair were just a fling or something more."

"And you bet against us?" *Ouch.*

"No, I bet against love," she said, very matter-of-fact. "And believe me, that has more to do with my insecurities than anything else."

It was hard to imagine Dani Bernal having insecurities of any kind. Then again, you never knew what was going on inside of somebody.

"Actually, I've come to realize that you and Sinclair might be perfect for each other."

"Thanks, boss."

"Knock knock," a chipper voice cooed from the office door, almost in singsong.

It wasn't unusual for Pink to visit our office. He and Dani often met for lunch when their schedules aligned. In fact, they had decided to move in together—as roommates and room-mates only—so lately, their lunch dates had involved pouring over long-term rental listings in the area. Apparently, Pink was coming around to the idea of living in Rose City.

I wonder what—or who—changed his mind.

"Come on in," Dani called back to him. "I assume you've already heard the news."

"What's that?" Rather than rehash my relationship woes, she slapped a crisp twenty-dollar bill in his palm. He stared at it, amused. "Normally, I have to dance for that kind of cash."

When his eyes met mine, a lightbulb went off. He looked down at the money and then back at me.

"You've got to be shitting me," he said, venom behind his words. "What did he do?"

"Jared—"

"Seriously, how did he mess this up? Because I'll—"

"Jared, stop."

He looked down at me, a fierce protective streak in his baby blue eyes. It was sweet to know he cared, that he had taken on some sort of protective little brother role in my life. I had told Soren not to write him off as just another arrogant wannabe, and I was glad I had.

"Believe it or not, I think this one's on me. I miscommuni-cated something about me, and unfortunately, that hurt Soren in the process. But I want to fix it." He still didn't look like he believed me. "I promise, I don't need you to avenge my honor or anything like that. Okay?"

"Fine," he mumbled.

"Good. By the way, I'm excited to meet your mother this weekend."

As if a switch had been flipped, he morphed back into his usual bright and bubbly self. "She's excited, too. This will be her first trip to Oregon. Kayla, too."

"That's your sister?" He nodded.

For Mother's Day this weekend, many of the players and staff had invited their moms, grandmothers, sisters, and aunts. Dani and I had been coordinating with the event staff all week to create content featuring the players' female family members, even those that couldn't make it.

We talked with Pink for a few more minutes before he had to leave for batting practice. Just as I turned back to my desk to plan my day—and how I might apologize to Soren—his words stopped me.

"You know, when I made that bet, I didn't think it would end this way."

The corner of my lips kicked up. "I know."

"You're good for him," he said without a trace of humor.

"We're good for each other."

Soren

Roasters 18-10

Tomorrow was Mother's Day, and frankly, I had never been more excited to hug my mom. And sisters. My entire family was coming for tomorrow's game, which meant I had twenty-four hours to get my shit together and fix this mess between Clarke and me.

I'd felt like shit for going on a week now, from the second I'd walked out of Clarke's trailer after dropping the love bomb on her.

All my life, I had excelled at helping to solve other people's problems. When Shelby and Monty needed a place to stay, they moved in with me. When Mom needed the money for a new roof, I picked up a part-time job. When Pink wanted to beat the crap out of some ableist assholes, I stepped in. How was it that I could help them see through their issues, but when it came to my own, I went running every time? You would have thought that I might figure it out by thirty-four, though thinking about it now, I had my doubts that we ever truly figured it all out.

Here was what I *did* know: I loved Clarke Myers, I had fucked up royally with her, and I was prepared to grovel for however long it took to win her back.

I just needed to figure out the right way to do it.

"Did you pull your head out of your ass yet?"

I turned over my shoulder to see Pink staring expectantly back at me, fresh from the shower.

"Sorry?"

"I'm not the one you should be apologizing to." He dropped his towel before slipping on a bright blue pair of boxer briefs. "You know, I used to look up to you, man. Ever since I was a kid. You were who I wanted to be when I grew up."

"Way to make a guy feel old," I grumbled. Was there a point to this story?

"All this time, I thought they were wrong about you. The media rags, the shit on social media." He slammed the locker shut despite his state of undress. "But then you go and throw away a woman like that."

That had me seeing red and balling my fists. The locker room probably wasn't the place to be having this conversation, but I didn't care if he was my teammate or not. Nobody was allowed to talk about Clarke like that.

"You don't know anything about it, kid."

"I know that you don't deserve her," he said, puffing his chest.

"That we can agree on."

A clump of half-dressed guys gathered around us, close enough to stop a fight if it came to that, although I hoped it didn't. I had just started to like our loudmouth pitcher.

"I also know that the second she, what, got a little scared, you went running. Is that it?"

"That's enough," I said through gritted teeth. I wasn't about to air my and Clarke's dirty laundry in front of the entire team. "You don't know anything about me, or her, or—"

"For fuck's sake, dude. I've known exactly who she is since the minute we met."

And then, in an especially daring move which made me think he might have been looking for a fight, Pink took two steps forward, bringing us nearly nose to nose.

"I grew up in the same rich bitch circles that she did. She's not the only one who made it out."

That stopped me cold. For as much talking as Pink did, he hardly ever spoke about his family history. He'd mentioned his sister a couple of times, usually when somebody ribbed him about the stuffed bear he kept in his locker, but that was it. I might've guessed he came from money, due to his luxurious spending habits, but that could've also been chalked up to him being a young, hot baseball player. Rookies tended to spend their signing bonuses like Monopoly money.

"I didn't know."

"You never asked."

He had me there. Some team captain I was.

There was a lot more to Pink than the smooth-talking goof-ball. I'd realized that the night I brought him back to Bed of Roses. I had expected some story about an ex-girlfriend or boyfriend, but not this.

I wasn't the only one hurting, that much was clear. Pink just did a better job of hiding his hurt.

"You're right," I told him, admitting my wrongdoings, something I would have shied away from a few months ago. "As your captain, and your *friend,* I should have asked."

He blinked, clearly taken aback by my words. And he wasn't the only one.

"Fuck, guys," Diaz said, cutting the tension faster than my mom's garden shears. "Can you kiss and make up already? We're going to be late for movie—"

Bennett smacked Diaz's stomach with his catcher's mitt, hard enough to knock the wind—and the words—out of him. He nodded for me to continue.

I turned back to Pink. "I'm sorry, man. I've been so caught up in my own shit that I didn't—"

"It's fine," he said, cutting me off.

"I'll do better."

Matty stepped forward. "We all will."

Fuck, I loved these guys. I still kept in touch with a few of my previous teammates. I attended their weddings and called them on their birthdays, but this was something else. Something special.

"I appreciate that," Pink said. "But back to your girl—"

"She's not my girl. She doesn't want to be with me."

"She said that?" Diaz asked.

Matty answered for me. "I don't believe it. That girl loves you more than cornbread on Sunday."

I stuffed hands into my pockets. "She told me she loves me. That's not the problem. She said she didn't want to be 'somebody else's girlfriend.'"

"Dude, you don't get it." Pink shook his head, eyeing me like I was the village idiot. "Put yourself in her shoes. Imagine every person you meet, date, fuck, knows you *only* by your father's name. Or your fiancé's."

I swallowed. I could already see where this was going and I didn't like the view.

"She's probably never had anything of her own. Her entire identity has always been tied to some other fucker. Can you blame her for being a little scared that it would happen again?"

Five minutes ago, if someone were to ask me about my lowest point, I would have told them my second at bat in the majors. I'd fucked up a bunt, and in the process, broken two of my fingers. To make matters worse, my mom and grandmother had been there just behind home plate, first-row witnesses to my poor performance—and the pity party that followed.

That was the only time my grandmother got to see me play in the big leagues before she passed.

All of that was still miles above how I felt now, fifty feet below six-feet-under. Literally lower than worm food.

"Fuck." I scrubbed a hand down my face. "Fuck!"

It all made sense now. Clarke's hesitation to discuss our relationship label, her adversity to being known as my girlfriend. It wasn't me—or us—she had the issue with. It was the label, the way people might perceive us together. The fear that she might lose her own identity and take on mine. Because it had happened to her before . . . more than once.

I'm a fucking asshole.

Her words ran through my brain, like a record stuck on a loop. *"I can't just be Soren Sinclair's girlfriend."* For fuck's sake, she couldn't have said it any plainer, and still, it hadn't clicked for me until now.

Clarke wasn't *just* anything. To use the two in a sentence was blasphemy.

I needed to show her that she was so much more than any label, with or without me. So she didn't want to be my girlfriend? Fine. Then I'd be her boyfriend. I would shout it from every rooftop between Portland and Manhattan if that was what it took to get her back. For her to take me back.

"You're realizing how badly you fucked up, aren't you?" Pink's question wasn't so much a question, as it was stating the obvious.

I nodded from behind my hands.

"Are you going to fight for her, asshole?"

I nodded again.

"What are you gonna do?" Matty asked.

When I removed my hands, I was both embarrassed and honored to see the entire team staring back at me, eager smiles on their faces. They might not be smiling after they heard my plan.

"I have an idea," I told them. "But I'm going to need your help."

They voiced their agreement. All but one. The young man who had just given me the emotional ass-handing I deserved.

"I'm not going to pretend like I have it all figured out," I told him, "because I don't. But please, let me show you that I'm not that guy."

Pink's jaw clenched while his eyes looked me up and down, from the tips of my bruised toes to the unkempt beard that was in desperate need of a trim. Silence fell over the locker room as the rest of the team waited in earnest.

"What do you have in mind?" he finally asked, eliciting a series of smiles and back pats.

This was going to work. This *had* to work. And even if it it didn't, I was prepared to try again. To grovel at her feet until she forgave me for refusing to see things from her point of view. For letting my past cloud my judgment, so much so that it might affect our future.

No more. For Clarke Myers, I was going all in.

"Well?" Tuck prodded.

"Does anybody know how to sew?"

Clarke

Roasters 19-10

We were minutes away from the first pitch of the game and my stomach was knotted tighter than Little Bo Peep's corset. I hadn't eaten a thing all day. I'd even passed on my usual latte.

There would be plenty of time to eat later. Maybe after we won the game and I won back the man of my dreams, we could celebrate with him eating my pussy for dinner. Or hot dogs?

For today's Mother's Day matchup, the Rose City Roasters were taking on the Denver Bandits, one of the better teams in the league. We all wanted the win today, especially when so many of the staff's and players' families were in attendance.

I had already had the pleasure of meeting Pink's mother, a petite woman who had a quarter of her son's energy. Matty's grandmother had raised him and she was in attendance as well, decked out in every piece of Roasters gear she could get her hands on. Within minutes, she was handing out laminated copies of her peach cobbler recipe to every person in her section.

All of the moms and maternal figures were seated in the section behind the Roasters' dugout, which made it easy for us to grab pictures with them during the game and difficult for me because it meant being so close to Soren.

And he wasn't the only Sinclair I was nervous about seeing.

"Clarke, hey!"

I spun to face Monty, who was quickly barreling down the aisle, headed straight toward me. They raced into my arms, wrapping me up in a warm hug.

"Hiya!!

"Look," they said, peeling away from me to show off their look. "What do you think? I got your Drop Dead Red lipstick."

Even though it was a cloudy day, I felt my cheeks pinken. That lipstick would forever evoke a certain special memory for me. One that was not suitable for discussing with teenagers.

"It looks great on you," I told them. "Where's your mom?"

"She's coming. Grandma has to stop and talk with everyone she sees wearing a Sinclair jersey." They rolled their eyes. "So embarrassing."

I scanned the aisle behind them, quickly recognizing Shelby as the brunette with a soft pretzel in one hand and a red foam finger on the other. The thirty-something woman beside her—the one corralling three children under the age of ten—had to be Sadie, Soren's other sister. Where Shelby was all things boho chic and Americana, Sadie was rocker chick. Black on black on black. In fact, her only pop of color was the toddler in her arms, dressed in a green dinosaur onesie.

And then there was Soren's mom, Mrs. Sinclair. While Shelby and Sadie had dark hair like their brother, Mrs. Sinclair rocked a silver-gray bob. All three of the Sinclair women sported red and white jerseys with Soren's number on them. Just like me.

"I see we've upgraded from the shoes," Shelby said, pulling me in for a hug. "Good to see you again, Clarke."

"You, too. And *you* must be Sadie," I said, turning to the taller woman next to her. Her three-inch, knee-high boots gave her some added height, but even without them, she'd still tower over me.

"I didn't realize I was wearing a name tag today."

"No, your brother's told me all about you." When her brows drew together, I added, "I mean, he's showed me photos of you and your entire family."

And now I sound like a stalker.

Figuring it was better to quit now, I held my hand out to her. "I'm Clarke. I'm with . . . your brother."

"*With* him, with him?"

"That's still to be determined."

"She's the one I told you about," Shelby said under her breath.

Surprise dawned on Sadie's face. "Oh, *you're* the one."

Was I "the one" for Soren? I certainly hoped so. Hopefully, I'd have my answer after today, assuming everything went as planned.

"Oh, another Sinclair fan, I see."

I held my breath when Soren's mother approached me. This wasn't how I had envisioned "meeting the parents," but at least I had my game face on. Drop Dead Red lipstick and all.

"Hi, Mrs. Sinclair." I held a hand out to her. "My name's Clarke Myers, and I'm the social media coordinator for the team. I also—"

"You're Clarke?" She turned to her daughters. "*The* Clarke?"

They nodded. Had Shelby told the whole family about me? I wasn't sure what to expect after that, but it certainly hadn't been a bone-crushing hug from the pint-sized woman.

"Honey, it is so great to meet you." When she pulled back, I couldn't help but see so much of Soren in her, especially in the eyes. "Soren's told us all so much about you."

"He has?"

"For weeks now. In fact, I'd love for you to sit with us today."

My mouth opened, but nothing came out. I could already feel my eyes beginning to well. How could this woman welcome me into her arms, into her family's life, so easily when we'd only exchanged a few words? I couldn't even get my own mother to return my phone calls.

"Mom," Shelby said, nudging her mother's arm. "How about we let Clarke do her job?"

"Oh, that's right! I'm sorry, Clarke."

"No, you're fine." I blinked back the moisture in my eyes, adding, "And thank you for the offer. You'll definitely see me around your section a lot today."

A genuine smile stretched across her cheeks. "Wonderful."

The first half of the inning flew by before we knew it. I was finishing up a video message with Tuck's sister—that would play during the seventh inning stretch—when it was Soren's turn to bat.

That was when I heard it.

The band we had seen in Tucson.

The song that I had made my ringtone weeks ago.

"Did he change his walk-up song?" Shelby asked her mom. Mrs. Sinclair just shrugged.

"Sin City" had been Soren's walk-up song for years, even in the minor league. It was his own subtle way of saying he didn't give a fuck what they wrote or said about him—even though we both knew that he did.

But that wasn't AC/DC playing; that was Lawrence.

"Don't Lose Sight."

That was the name of the song, but it was so much more than that for Soren and me.

As the brother and sister duo sang about not giving in, even when the world gives up on you, I tried to stop the tears from streaming down my cheeks or the smile that split between them. If this was an apology, it was a damn good one.

The blend of emotions washing over me was overwhelming, to say the least. I thought I might be able to dry my eyes and get back to work without too many people noticing my tearful interlude, but then I saw the jersey.

And I absolutely lost it.

Embroidered across the back of his jersey, just above the number four, were two words: Clarke's Boyfriend.

Heavens to Betsy. He still loves me.

There was no stopping the waterworks after that. Not when Mrs. Sinclair—the entire Sinclair brood, in fact—turned around in their seats to find me with something between shock and awe on their faces. Then, there were the guys. The dozen or so familiar faces that popped out of the dugout to see my reaction. The shit-eating grins on all of their faces told me that they probably had something to do with this, too.

But none of that compared to the man staring back at me from the batter's box. The one who held my heart in his hands and had my name on his back.

My name, not his.

He'd given me another first.

If the song had been an apology, the jersey had been a promise.

And much to my pleasure—and the surprise of some forty-thousand fans at the ballpark that day—he wore that promise for the rest of the game.

I was still reeling from Soren's public display of devotion in the sixth when the kiss cam came on. This was probably my least favorite game day event, partly because too many people went overboard with tongue action, but mostly because I would never have the opportunity to kiss the person I wanted to. Not while he was playing the game.

"You don't look happy enough for somebody whose man all but declared his love for her in front of forty-thousand fans," Dani said from beside me.

"Oh, believe me, I'm happy." My mouth was aching from smiling. "Cloud nine."

"So what is it then?"

I pursed my lips. "Don't judge me, okay?"

"I make no promises," she said around another sip of coffee. That had to be her third of the day.

"It's going to sound really petty, but I'm jealous of the couples who get to kiss. I can't even kiss *my man*," I said, parroting her words, "even though he's right over there."

I stared longingly toward the infield as Soren took the field, sighing when I saw my name on the back of his jersey. When I flipped back around toward Dani, she was smiling coyly, like she knew something I didn't.

"What?"

"Nothing. I'm just glad it all worked out for you."

"Thanks."

She leaned back against the small wall separating us from the field. "And you thought you were going to have to work for it."

"I still feel like I should."

"Well." She paused, gesturing toward the big screen. "Now's your chance."

I looked up at the screen in centerfield, only to find my-self staring back, bewildered. When I looked back at Dani, she smiled again. "Don't take too long. We've still got work to do."

My eyes bounced back to the screen, only this time the cam-era was on Soren. Running past the dugout, heading straight for the wall. The crowd roared when he stopped in front of me.

"Hey, blondie."

"Hey, Clarke's boyfriend."

He removed his hat and cracked a smile. *Oh, heavens.* That was the kind of smile that melted my panties clean off my body. The kind that held a certain, *sinful*—pun intended—kind of promise for all the wickedly delicious things he planned to do to me.

"You liked that?"

"I loved that."

"And I love you."

That was all it took to snap my last vestige of self control. I dug my fingers into his messy, sweat-soaked hair and tugged his mouth to mine. A deafening cheer echoed throughout the stadium, drowning out the sound of my desperate moan.

My breath shook when he finally removed his lips. "I love you, too."

"I'm sorry I left like that. I didn't understand what—"

"No, I'm sorry. I shouldn't have thrown that stupid nickname in your face. You're so much more than that."

He wiped a tear from my cheek. "I should have just told you that I don't care if you don't want to be Soren Sinclair's girlfriend, because I'd count myself fucking blessed to be Clarke Myers' boyfriend."

I laughed against his lips before he kissed me again. This was one of the moments, the kind I would never forget. Right up there with the first night we'd spent together without having sex or our trip to Tucson. This was a forever moment.

The kind you couldn't plan for or put on a list.

"You know this is going to be all over the internet, right?" I told him, cradling my hands around his neck. "There's no hiding from it now."

"That's what I'm counting on, blondie," he said against my lips. "The world needs to know that Sin's taken."

Soren

All-Star Break

As it turned out, I was a fucking awesome boyfriend. Growing up in a house full of women had definitely helped prepare me—I was no stranger to late-night milkshakes and tampon runs—but Clarke made the rest of it so fun, so easy.

There wasn't anybody I would rather hold hands with in public—because yes, I was a hand holder—and fuck sideways in private. We were several months into our relationship and still going at it like rabbits.

"Do you really need three bedrooms?" Clarke asked.

"Might be nice if family comes to visit," I told her. "Or if some of the guys want to crash after the game."

"Do y'all have a lot of sleepovers?"

"Jealous?"

She rolled her eyes. I arched a brow in return, the one that said, *You're asking for a punishment, blondie.* It was hard—*very* hard—not to envision her bent over every surface of this house, her luscious ass stained pink from my hand.

We were on our third house tour of the day. I had long since overstayed my welcome at Bed of Roses, and despite the convenience of having Clarke living one trailer over, it was time I found a more permanent situation. While most of the guys chose to live in Portland—for ease, nightlife, and ample late-night takeout options—I had grown fond of Rose City.

And a certain blonde who lived there. Living so close to the stadium also made my commute to work practically nonexistent.

A developer had already drawn up plans for a condo building just outside of town—one that would most likely house some of the team as well as visiting opponents—but I was dead set on a house. I'd grown up in a townhouse, I'd lived in apartments, and I'd spent the better part of a decade sharing hotel rooms with one or two other guys. I wanted a standalone house. One where I didn't have to share a wall with anybody I didn't handpick myself so I could fuck the woman I loved into the wee hours of the morning without having to worry about who heard her scream.

And boy, did she scream.

Thankfully, I was finally in a position—financially and emotionally—to put down roots. To create a home.

"I really like the fireplace," she said, running her hands over the rustic stones. "That would be perfect for rainy days."

"So, everyday then?"

"You could put a big, old chair right here in the corner and read by the fire. Oh, it sounds so cozy!"

I wasn't much of a reader, but I trusted Clarke's judgment implicitly. She hardly ever missed. For instance, she hadn't been exaggerating when she said that the internet would go nuts over our gameday kiss.

For the second time this year, I'd gone viral.

The kiss cam clip had been viewed, posted, shared, and whatever else you could do to a video on social media over ten million times. Fans and media alike had eaten it up and fallen in love with *Cloren,* the stupid fucking nickname something called *The Roast Rag* had given us. *Bennifer* had nothing on *Cloren,* according to them, whatever that meant.

Coach Ward seemed to be the only person that wasn't completely taken with my public stunt during our Mother's Day game, but that had more to do with the team and me going behind his back than anything else. Something told me there was a love-obsessed softie under that gruff, intimidating exterior.

Thankfully, after a lecture (or four) plus a small fine for altering my uniform without permission, the whole thing had blown over. With coach, that was. The news outlets and social media were *still* having a field day with it. Clarke and I had even had late night talk show requests, all of which we declined.

Nonetheless, the Roasters' PR department assigned a media consultant. Some couples went to counseling, Clarke and I went to media training.

Together we decided that the world could speculate about our relationship all they wanted. They could judge us or berate us—as keyboard warriors often did—because at the end of the day, we were the only two people in the world who knew what was real. We might not be able to stop the paparazzi from taking pictures of us or digging up some of Clarke's family business, but we didn't have to dignify any of it with a response.

Our relationship was ours. Nobody else's.

I smiled, watching as she rubbed her hands together as if she were conspiring, even though we both knew that wasn't the case. I leaned back against the kitchen island, which was bigger than the entire trailer I'd been living in for nearly half of a year now. The single-story, 1950s ranch had had significant updates—a renovated kitchen, dark-stained bamboo floors, and a new roof as of last year—but the previous owners had done a fantastic job of preserving the integrity of the home.

"Can you see it?" she probed.

I could see it. I could see myself here. On the couch, watching a game or playing Jackbox games with the guys. In the backyard, hosting a barbecue. I could see a Christmas tree in the front window, surrounded by my sisters and their families.

What surprised me most, but didn't scare me in the least, was that I could see Clarke here, too. Cuddled up to my side, prepping the potato salad, ripping into a stocking with her name on it. She was there.

"Yeah," I told her. "I can."

"So, what do we think?" Jane, the realtor, chirped. Normally, I wasn't one for the hyper cheerleader-like energy, but even I could admit her smile was infectious. No wonder it was plastered on every bus bench in town.

"I'm interested."

"Fantastic! I think the two of you would be really happy here."

My chest warmed at the prospect of living with Clarke . . . someday soon. We weren't quite there yet.

Clarke had decided to move into Nessa and Nero's spare room, and I was doing my best not to act too butt hurt about it.

Besides, she spent most nights in my bed anyway. Even when I was on the road and she stayed back at the Roasters' offices. Two days ago, I had come home from my first ever All-Star game to find her in *my* bed, lying in wait while wearing *my* jersey. The night had ended with me making her pancakes and her making pancakes of my face.

She smiled back at me when she caught me staring. Like she knew exactly what I was thinking about.

"Just so you know, the owners have already vacated, so I think we could get them to drop the price a little bit. And I don't want to get you too excited, but I think we might be able to talk them into covering closing costs, too."

Jane finally took a breath when her phone buzzed across the eat-in dining table. "I'm so sorry, would you mind if I take this? It's my business partner."

"Please," I told her, "go ahead."

I was already thinking about a few ways Clarke and I could pass the time while we waited, and they all involved one of the eight thousand closets in this place.

I waited until she was out of earshot before reaching for Clarke.

"So, do you think you'll buy—"

She didn't have a chance to finish her question. I grabbed her by the front of her hoodie—my hoodie, actually—and pulled her to me, slamming my mouth down on hers. She melted into me, her body going lax as I maneuvered us toward the closest wall. Only when my hands moved down and around her body to cup her luscious ass did she pull her lips away.

"What are you doing?" she asked between gasps of air. "Jane will see."

"Jane will be on the phone for at least ten minutes." I licked at her lips. "And that's more than enough time to make you come."

"Soren," she moaned.

"C'mon, let's check out the closets."

I was already half-dragging, half-carrying her down the hall to the bedroom at the back of the house, and then into the walk-in closet. If I *did* buy the house, this would be my room. And maybe, if I played my cards right, Clarke's, too.

The closet had more than enough space for what I planned to do with her, and as I had told her, it wouldn't take long.

When I skated a hand over her zipper, she swatted it away.

"C'mon, baby," I begged. I wasn't above begging when it came to Clarke. "Let me make you come. Please?"

Her lips curved up as she backed away from me.

Fuck, I know that smile.

That was her plotting smile. The one she reserved for moments like this, where she knew something that I didn't. Why did that make me so hard?

"What?" I asked.

Clarke dropping to her knees was all the answer I needed. She'd gone down on me before, several times in fact. But she hardly ever initiated it like this. Boldly, confidently. It was a fucking turn-on.

After what she had told me about her spineless, tasteless, dick-less ex-fiancé—or the STD, as I called him—the last thing I ever wanted to do was pressure her. I never pushed her to suck me off. Truly, I was just as happy to bury myself in her tight cunt or suck on her clit any day of the week. This was her show, and I was more than willing to pay VIP admission if it meant her mouth wrapped around my cock.

"Fuck, blondie. You look good on your knees."

"Remember, Soren." She tugged my boxer briefs and joggers down in one quick swoop, freeing my cock. "Ten minutes."

I'd be lucky if I lasted half of that. I had a mental library of images featuring Clarke on her knees for me, just like this. In the showers at Bed of Roses, in the locker room after practice, once in the backseat of my car. Although, now that I thought about it, there was *one thing* that would make this moment more magnanimous than the rest.

"Do you have that red lipstick?"

She smiled up at me. "Which red?"

"The *red* red. My favorite red. The one you were wearing that day you met my family."

The memory of my sister and nibling should have been a turnoff, but it had just the opposite effect. Because for the second time today, it had me thinking about Clarke with my family and how she had so seamlessly carved a place into my world. Into my heart.

"Drop Dead Red." The name hit me like a line drive to the nuts.

Fuck. The things this woman does to me.

It wasn't just me either. Mom was absolutely smitten with her—her words, not mine. She and the rest of the family had gotten the picture, loud and clear, during the Mother's Day game. They knew that I wouldn't have made that kind of bold gesture for anybody. No, Clarke was it for me.

End game.

"Actually, you might be in luck." She reached inside her small, crossbody bag. "I still have it in here from when we went out the other night."

"Would you—"

"Would I suck your dick while wearing it?"

I groaned. She blinked up at me innocently when her words were anything but. The sweet and sassy side of Clarke had been enticing from the very beginning, but this confident vixen? That was downright irresistible.

"I'd be happy to."

She applied the lipstick, smacking her pouty red lips together and moistening them with her tongue. Every muscle in my body coiled tightly when she wrapped a fist around around me, dragging it from the base of my cock all the way up to the swollen head and then back down again. She did it over and over, until I was gasping with need.

"*Fuck*," I growled. "Baby, please put me in your mouth."

A pretty pink rushed to her cheek, her eyes darkening with hunger.

"Like this?" she asked, swirling her tongue around the head, but never covering it with her mouth. Was she trying to kill me?

"No," she said, answering the question I hadn't realized I'd posed aloud. She tongued the pearl of precum beading at my tip. "Just loving you."

My fingers tightened in her messy bun. If it wasn't messy before, it would be now. Clarke might have been inexperienced, but judging by the way she looked up at me, her eyes full of hunger and longing, she knew exactly what she was doing to me.

"I love you," I moaned.

"Say it again."

"Fuck, Clarke, you know I love you. You're my heart, my life. I—"

Any coherent thoughts or reasoning were sucked clear out of me. Literally. I fought to stay on my feet when she wrapped her lips around my cock and swallowed me whole. All the way until I tapped her throat.

"Fuck!" I moaned loudly, forgetting where we were. Hell, I could barely remember my own name. Not when saliva was pooling in the corner of her lips, stretched wide around my cock. I tried to pull back. "Baby, that's too much. I don't want to hurt you."

"Number four, Soren," she said looking up at me, licking her swollen lips.

I stared down at her quizzically. *Number four?* A lightbulb went off.

The list.

Damn, I hadn't thought about that list in months. There hadn't been any need to. Clarke knew that if she wanted something, all she had to do was ask.

We had spent the first few weeks of our relationship testing her boundaries, figuring out things she liked—spankings, hair-pulling, and surprisingly, anal—and didn't like—ice cubes and reverse cowgirl, because it made her thighs cramp up—but we hadn't needed a list to make that happen.

I thought back to that piece of paper with her delicate handwriting.

4. Fuck my face.

"Jesus, are you sure?"

"Tick tock, Soren."

This time, when she took me down the back of her throat, I didn't stop her. Instead, I threaded my fingers through her hair, tilted her head back so I could watch her watching me, and gave us both what we wanted.

It only took six minutes to make me come.

We used the last four minutes to get her off.

Two days later, I bought my first house, and eight weeks after that, I had carpet installed in every closet.

Thanks for Reading!

Thank you so much for reading *Hit it and Quit it*.

I'll admit, this one took a little longer than planned . . . mostly because several of the side characters kept interrupting. But don't worry, they'll all get their stories. Eventually.

Stay tuned for Pink and Nessa's book, coming in August 2024.

If you liked this book, please let me know and share with others by leaving a review on **Amazon** or **Goodreads :)**

Acknowledgements

I didn't set out to write a baseball romance. In fact, when hockey romance took Booktok by storm in 2023, I thought I was going to write a hockey romance. And then I remembered that I don't know shit about hockey. Thus, the Rose City Roasters were born.

There are a lot of people to thank for this one. Starting with Mom & Dad. You'll never know how grateful I am to have parents who have always supported my choices—no matter how crazy they might seem—and encouraged me to embrace my independence. Clarke would be lucky to have a family like mine.

Shoutout to the Beta Team—Jared, MK, Becky, & Laura—for putting up with my long-winded voice messages at all hours of the day.

To my amazing editor, Norma, and proofreader, Valerie. Thank you both for reminding me—over and over—that Soren had bad knees every time he ate her out. Much appreciated.

As always, shoutout to the Bridesmaids chat, the Real Housewives of Alameda group, Wednesday & Thursday night writing groups, and my Voxer Pod Squad—you all know who you are and how much you mean to me. Thank you for the hours of input, memes, incessant questions (mine, not yours) and TikTok videos.

To the baristas at Cathedral Coffee in Portland, Oregon, thank you for the writing space. To the Sou'wester Lodge in

Long Beach, WA, aka the inspiration behind Bed of Roses, thanks for making trailers cool again.

Finally, to Romancelandia, and to every person who has supported Boobies & Noobies over the years, thank you for welcoming me into your community. Every day, I am more and more thankful I picked up that copy of *I'm in No Mood for Love* by Rachel Gibson back in 2009. Who knows where I'd be or what I'd be doing today if I hadn't. Above all else, Boobies & Noobies has always been a podcast about exploring readers and writers' unique romance reading journeys. Thank you all for being a part of *my* romance reading (and writing) journey.

About the Author

By day, Kelly Reynolds works primarily as a freelance writer, professor, and author's assistant. By night, she hosts the romance novel review podcast, Boobies & Noobies.

She currently lives in Portland, Oregon. When she isn't writing, you can often find Kelly eating her way through hole-in-the-wall restaurants, sampling cider at the nearest brewery, or bingeing the latest season of "Top Chef".

Keep up with Kelly on social media @authorkellyrey and on her website.

Keep up with Boobies & Noobies on social media @boobiespodcast, and listen wherever you stream your podcasts.